The Haunted Ghost Tour

The Haunted Ones Book 7

Michelle Dorey

About This Book

Like a broken roller coaster, things go from scary fun to terrifying

Ryan Wheeler's new job will launch his acting career. He'll be a tour guide for 'The Haunted Walk Of Villmore'. It's a pretty sweet gig! Performing live for small groups will look great on his resume when he heads to New York for 'real' acting roles.

But from the start, things are strange. His first tour is with a group of eight people—four elderly couples who are sweet as any grandparent.

But weird.

At the very first stop, one of them becomes enraged about the ghost story he's telling. He's trying to tell the tale of a tragic story of unrequited love, but Doris knows the truth!

It wasn't a love story... it was a murder.

How would this woman know? It happened more than a hundred years ago!

When the tour is over, walking back home he's followed by an unseen stranger—a stranger doing their best to terrify him. And it works; he barely makes it back to his place. But the stranger's not finished; it pounds over and over at his apartment door, trying to get in! Mustering his courage, Ryan goes to confront the jerk.

But nobody is there.

On the following night things get even stranger. The old people are back. And once again, they have a problem with him.

Back home after work, someone's waiting for him...

Or is it '*something*'?

Ryan's about to learn a lot of secrets. About life...and death.

This 'easy job' is going to cost him everything.

Bestselling author Michelle Dorey's latest stand alone ghost story is based on a true story. Grab your copy and start reading!

Just don't pay any attention to those noises at your door.

Contents

Chapter One

Get This Show On The Road

Ever since they were children, Ryan and Melanie Walker loved to scare the hell out of each other. It began when Ryan was only five years old. Coming into the living room, he saw his fifteen-year-old sister (who he idolized) poring carefully over a jigsaw puzzle on the coffee table.

With a glint of mirth in his eye and moving as silently as a cat, he crept up behind her.

"BOO!" he shouted, poised at the back of her head.

The reaction was priceless. The memory of Melanie leaping straight up, scattering puzzle pieces hither and yon while letting out a bellowing howl still made Ryan chuckle fifteen years later. So started one of their most beloved traditions: *'Gotcha! Gotcha Good!'*

Throughout his childhood, even when Melanie matured and moved out on her own, through holidays and reunions while he was at college himself, they always, *always* had an episode of scaring the living be-jeezuz out of one another.

He woke in the bedroom of his two-bedroom flat to the sound of clattering in the kitchen area. He had lived there for four years and the lease was going to end on January 1st, a little more than two months down the road. At first, he thought it was a break-in. During the summer, his college roommate had landed a great job in California as a systems engineer for a dot com outfit, so he knew it wasn't Josh. He moved quietly down the short hallway and heard Melanie's voice, singing one of her favorite songs.

He smiled with a grin of delight. He was already dressed; he must have taken a nap.

So, on that Thursday night in October when Ryan got out of bed to start his new job and heard Melanie rooting around in his apartment, it inspired him to add one more 'Gotcha!' to his side of the ledger. They actually began keeping count when he was five years old, and he knew that if he could scare the hell out of her it was going to be number one hundred, seventy-three to her one fifty-seven.

From his vantage point in the hallway, he faced the living room. On the other side, behind a partition wall was the kitchen. To the left was the dining area with the scuffed-up table he and Josh had bought years earlier when they decided to become roomies. To the right was the entranceway to the apartment. He figured he'd have a better chance sneaking up on her by coming around that way. Any noise he'd make had a better chance of being dismissed as just some racket from the hallway. He crept like a ninja.

"BOO!" he shouted as he leapt out, waving his arms and laughing.

Melanie was a sight to behold. She jumped straight up into the air letting out a scream of blue bloody murder. She turned and faced him; her eyes wide in shock. She put her hands over her chest and backed away from him, her legs skittering on the floor until she backed right into the dining table.

"Wha- wha-Ryan!" she gasped.

Whoa...he might have overdone it. She was shaking all over!

"Hey! It's just me you, idiot! What the hell did you expect?"

"Ryan!" Melanie stared at him hard. She bent at the waist catching her breath. Straightening, she cocked her head. "Where the hell did you come from!"

"My freaking bedroom! Thanks for waking me up!"

"Buh-but—"

"But nothing. You told me you'd come with me to my premiere, sure!" His eyebrows knitted. "How'd you get in?"

"Keys..." she managed to get out between gasps.

Shit, he ought to get bonus points for this 'Gotcha'. He caught her completely off guard! "You okay? And where'd you get the keys? Did Josh leave them with you or something?" Why Josh would do that was beyond him. But he didn't remember getting his set when he moved out.

She stared at him again. Her mouth was opening and closing, but she wasn't saying a damn thing.

He crossed the kitchen to her. "Hey...you okay, sis? I'm sorry, Mel; but it was too good a chance to pass up, right? You'd do the same to me, right?" He rubbed her shoulder.

"Oh Ryan!" She threw her arms around him and hugged him so tight he thought she'd break a rib. "Rynie! Rynie! Rynie!" she said over and over again. It didn't hurt, but man oh man she had a hella grip on him. He held her right back, but not with the Wonder Woman bearhug.

He chuckled. "Haven't been called Rynie..." he paused; "For some time, huh?" She was still hugging him, but at least wasn't passing out from fear, so that was good. "So, you coming to my first performance as a tour guide? What time is it anyway?" He glanced at the clock on the microwave. "Holy shit, it's almost ten! We're going to have to get going!"

She continued to hold him. "Uhhh...Mel?"

She let go, and stepped back, still grasping his shoulders. "You're really—"

"Of course, I'm really gonna do it! It's not that big a deal, right? I got the script, and they gave me the top hat and cape, so of course I'm ready!"

Oh shit! He patted his denim jacket. Phew! He pulled out a soft covered manual. Printed on the cover was *'City Of Villmore Haunted Walk Host Script And Guidelines'*. He leafed it open. "Uh-oh...I don't think I studied the lines all that well..." He looked at Melanie. "You think they'll let me use this on my first couple of go-rounds? I really didn't study this as much as I should have, I guess."

Wide eyed, she whispered, "Sure..."

"I guess you're going to walk me the four long blocks to the pickup point, huh? Sorta like when I was little and you'd take me to school?"

"Well, it *is* your first paid acting gig..."

"Damn right. Like I told you—I'll just do this for a couple of months, and then have a professional role in my resume when I head to New York city to start my career."

Melanie's face fell. In a soft voice, quivering and barely above a whisper, she said, "I wish you had just let me pay for you in New York for a year...even two! But no... you had to do it your way..." Her eyes glistened when she looked up at him. "You had to do this job first for a while, right?"

"That's right. Why the hell are you so damn upset? I'll head off to The Big Apple soon enough. You're still going to front me expenses like you said when that happens, right?"

She nodded silently. She raised a hand and placed it against his cheek. "Whatever you need, Rynie. Whatever you need."

He made a frown. "I stopped letting people call me that kiddie name years ago, Mel." Shit, she was still shaken up. He stepped back and looked at her. "You okay Mel? Look—I'm sorry for jumping out at you..."

Her eyes filmed with tears. She patted his chest. "Don't be." She smiled wanly. "We've been doing that since you were a kid!" She blinked a couple of times. "What's that now, one hundred and fifty-six for you?"

"One seventy-three to your one fifty-seven! Don't cheat!"

"Okay then...looks like you win, huh?"

"Win?" Ryan shook his head. "No... this game will *never* be over!"

She let out a light laugh. "I suppose not." She squeezed her eyes and Ryan saw tears running down her cheeks.

"Hey...Mel..."

She snuffled and wiped her eyes with the back of her hand. "It's nothing. I just wish Mom and Dad could see you, that's all... After all, it's your first *paid* acting role, isn't it?"

"Yeah..." he looked at his feet. "I think of them too..." He looked up at her. "That's why I call you every time it snows, you know." Now he felt like *he* was going to start blubbering. Three years...almost four now... a stupid freaking patch of ice on a snowy February night and poof... He clamped his lips tightly together and gave his head a shake. "You know, make sure you get home okay and... stuff..."

Mel patted his shoulder. "Yeah, still gets ya every now and then, huh?"

He nodded, coughed and straightened up. "Yeah." He looked back at the kitchen. "Just what the hell were you doing in here anyway? What's with those boxes?" On the counter in the kitchen were two boxes she must have gotten from a liquor store. His cabinets were open, and the cans of beef stew and Spaghetti-O's were on the counter.

"Uhhh...just dropping off a care package?"

He rolled his eyes. "I'm moving in a couple of weeks, Melanie. This gig's only temporary, you know. More crap for me to pack later on...but hey, thanks."

She nodded.

"Hey!" He held a finger up. "I think I'm gonna kill it in New York!"

"Really."

He nodded. "I was looking. There's tons of work in commercials, they're always looking for fresh faces in that game, right? And this Haunted Walk thing could give me a leg up as a tourist guy down there for a day job, y'know? Then I'll go to auditions on my down time and start hunting for my break." He spread his arms. "Whaddya think? Maybe I can land something on Broadway even!"

"Broadway? From Villmore New York to The Great White Way, huh?"

He did his favorite Bogart imitation. "Look, sweetheart...in The Big Apple it's go big or go home, get me?"

"Oh yeahhhh?" she replied with a smirk.

"Yeah!" They both laughed at their re-enactment of the film star from the Golden Age of Hollywood. "Maybe I'll make my stage name to Humphrey, whaddaya think, doll?"

"Well, it's the 21st century, big boy...I think Ryan Walker's a fine name. Can't wait to see it in lights!"

He put his hands on his waist. "And what the hell...it's only a three-hour drive from here, right?" He gestured at the boxes in the kitchen. "Well, thanks for the care package, Mel. I think I better get going, don't you? Why don't you walk with me down to the place, huh?"

Melanie looked aside for a moment, then back at him. "Okay."

"Hey, I hope I'm not interrupting your plans or something..."

She shook her head. "Not at all." She let out a sigh.

"Then what?"

She jerked her shoulders. "I..." then shook her head. "Never mind. I was on the road for a couple of hours getting here from my place, you know? I'll head down with you to your job, then I think I'm going to get a hotel room."

"You can stay here you know."

Melanie looked around the apartment. "You had a Jacuzzi put in?" She stretched her arms over her head. "I'm all knotted up. The Sheraton has a Jacuzzi and sauna. I think that'll be just the ticket for me. Tell ya what—I'll stop by tomorrow, okay?"

"Fair enough."

She stood as he gathered up the black cape and top hat they had given him when he was hired. She repressed a giggle when she saw his hands tremble just a bit as he gathered his things. Her brother was something else. He had a BA in Dramatic Arts and yet, despite his dreams of making it as an actor, still had stage fright. She had seen it at every one of his school plays. He shook like a leaf before every performance; even puked a couple of times in high school; but once he stepped out on stage it was like he was born there.

"You seen my phone?" he asked. "I don't know what the hell I did with it?"

Melanie started to speak and caught herself before replying, "You don't know what you did with it?"

Ryan shook his head. "No...and I had it yesterday when they hired me." He patted his back pocket. "Nope, no hole there. Damn it..."

"Well...if you need to, we'll go get you another one, okay? My treat."

"Your treat." He eyed her suspiciously. "You're pretty generous throwing your money around, y'know."

Melanie shrugged. "What can I say? I got a great job." She hoped he didn't ask what she did for a living. Keeping her lies straight about where her money came from was tough. And seeing Ryan so unexpectedly rattled the hell out of her. If he asked, she'd just as likely say 'astro-physicist' as 'pharmacy tech', neither of which were within a mile of the truth.

Instead, Ryan smiled. "Well, in that case, the latest iPhone will be just the ticket!"

She put her hands up. "No problem!"

"You ready? I am! Let's get this show on the road!"

Chapter Two

Buster

They went down the three flights of stairs of the converted brownstone home. Once upon a time it had been a stately house for a doctor, or perhaps lawyer. Maybe even a successful merchant in the city had built or purchased it. It sat cheek to jowl with the other homes, a limestone and brick edifice of bygone days.

But starting right after World War 2, the local State University branch expanded its student body, and by the time the 60's rolled around, all of the homes in a five to seven block area around the campus became converted to student apartments. Ryan spent three of his four undergrad years living on the top floor; a two bedroom with his now departed roomie. The rent for the place was paid up until the end of the year; the new tenants would be moving in January first. At any rate, Ryan would be departing the student ghetto this winter, one way or another for New York City!

It was one of those crystal-clear nights; the air as crisp as a new twenty-dollar bill. Ryan gave a huff with his mouth. Nope; not really all that cold yet—he didn't see any fog from his breath. He looked up at the trees; they were forlornly bare of leaves; that rainstorm the other day had taken care of any stragglers. The clouds and stars behind the naked branches accentuated their emptiness.

When they descended the steps from the entranceway to the sidewalk, he fluttered his cape and tilted his top hat at a rakish angle.

"How do I look?" he asked Melanie. "Spooky enough for ya?"

She nodded as she finished zipping up her leather jacket. "I think you'll do great!" With a bow and sweep of her hand she said, "After you, oh omniscient tour guide!"

With a flourish of his cape, Ryan headed down the sidewalk.

They hadn't gone half a block before Ryan stopped. "Did you hear that?" he asked.

Melanie looked around. "Hear what?"

"I... don't know...like a squeaking or something." He looked around. "Almost like a baby..." His head shot upwards. "Oh man..." he pointed up into the branches of a maple tree.

Melanie followed his gaze. "What the hell?"

Fifteen feet above them, perched in the 'V' of the two main branches, was a small kitten; its front paws clasping at the bark of the tree. It saw them below, and let out another faint mew. Its eyes reflected the nearby streetlight; two dark blue mirrors casting down on them below.

"We can't leave it." Ryan said. He untied his cape and folded it, placing it on the ground. He dropped the top hat onto it and stretched his arms up. There was a branch about a foot above his hands. "If I can grab that branch I ought to be able to swing up."

"Wait a second. Aren't you afraid of heights?" Melanie was still staring upwards. "You sure that's a kitten up there? Maybe it's a squirrel?"

He looked at her. "Since when do squirrels have pure white coats?" He jumped up and snagged the branch as near to the trunk as he could. It was as solid as oak; it didn't bend an inch under his weight. Holding onto the branch he scrabbled his feet up the trunk until he wrapped his knees around it. He was hanging by his knees and hands. With a twist of his shoulders, he spun over it until he was resting on top of it. "Pizza cake!" he called down to Melanie. "Easy as pie!" Holding another branch above him, he stood up.

"Don't look down," Melanie called. "You'll get dizzy!"

He gave her a quick dismissive wave. "That was when I was a kid!" Still, she could be right. That summer afternoon he almost snapped his skull tree climbing. He hadn't gotten much higher than this, but when he looked down, he got so dizzy from the height he tumbled off the tree. If Mel hadn't broken his fall, he probably would have hurt more than his seven-year-old pride. He took in the view of the street and sidewalk from his perch. "Been a long time…" he whispered to himself.

"Mewww" the kitten called to him softly.

He looked up. "Don't worry, little guy; I got this."

In no time he picked his way up the tree, branch by branch until he was nose to nose with the kitten.

It stared at him calmly; the only movement was its nose twitching, as if to say *'Took you long enough'*. Ryan stroked it. Its fur was downy soft, and it immediately began purring. He scooped it up; it was remarkable how thin it felt under its coat—his hand wrapped around the poor little thing with no problem.

"Man, how old are you bud?" he said aloud. The tiny cat just looked at him. *'Old enough'.*

He looked down at his sister below. It was as if he was leaning out of a second story window. He looked over to the brownstone on the other side of the sidewalk. Yep, second floor for sure. The lights in a living room were on, and a flat screen was showing an episode of Game Of Thrones.

He looked down again and held the kitten up for Melanie to see. The memory of the tumble from the tree filled his mind and he felt a sense of satisfaction. The height didn't bother him a bit. One-handed this time, he made his way back down. At the lowest branch, he held Buster in one hand (sounded like a good name) and suspended himself from it with the other before dropping to the ground.

He held the kitten out to Melanie. "Cute as a button, isn't it?" He held it up above him, looking at its tummy. "Isn't *he* I mean. Well, Buster works, then."

Melanie stared at him. "You want to hold him?" Ryan asked. He held his prize out to her.

She shook her head. "I... think I'm allergic. No thanks." Tilting her head, she asked, "What are you going to do with him?"

"Maybe I'll keep him." Buster didn't like that. He began squirming in Ryan's hand. "Hey, take it easy buddy!" But despite his firm hold, the kitten leapt out of his hand, landing on its feet on the grass apron around the tree. It looked back up at Ryan and darted away. "Hey!" It shot down the sidewalk and cut into an alleyway between two homes. "Yeah, that's okay!" Ryan called after it. "You're welcome!"

Melanie's mouth twitched. "So that's that, then, huh?"

"I guess so." It was a surprise to him how he felt a sense of loss. He'd only held that stupid kittten for about a minute, but now...he let out a huff of air. "Guess it knows where it's headed, right?"

Melanie nodded. "I'm sure it does."

"Well...onward ho then. Don't want to be late."

Chapter Three

Just The Way You Are

It was just a couple of blocks to the base of downtown. Villmore sat along an enormous lake in central New York state, and the city had begun as a settlement along the lakeshore. The oldest part of the city stretched for about a half mile following the shoreline. Back in the 1800's they built a railroad spur into the downtown for passengers and freight from the inner counties and big cities. The railroad line had been abandoned in the 20th century when the interstate was built. But the St. Regis Hotel was still in business. Built in 1810, it was the grandest edifice of its era. Today, its claim to fame was its antique bar, over two hundred years old. The rooms above had been converted to luxury loft apartments for the professional class. On the corner of St. Regis Avenue and Main Street was the gathering spot for The Haunted Walk. A Victorian era hotel was the perfect backdrop for the spooky tales the guides would tell their clients.

The office for The Haunted Walk was tucked into the side of the building, with a podium out front by the sidewalk. A sandwich board beside it announced The Haunted Walk along with the tour times.

Ryan saw a pretty fair-sized group of people standing by the sandwich board while they were still half a block away. "Pretty big group, don't you think?" That ball of ice in his stomach, the one that showed up just before he'd start giving a performance appeared like an old friend.

Melanie peered ahead. "Yeah. I changed my mind; I can go to my hotel later. You want me to come with you on your premiere?"

"Thanks, I could use the moral support."

They continued down the block to the corner that was opposite the group. "Looks like the old people's home is having an outing," he said. There were eight people standing waiting, and not one of them looked less than seventy years old. One of them had been watching them approach and said something to the others, because they all turned and faced him. A few of the women in the group smiled at him as they waved.

They were an interesting group, to say the least. Three of the four men were in military uniforms. One guy was in a dark brown tunic and khaki pants with an officer's hat on his head, another one was wearing sailor's whites, and another man was wearing what looked like battle fatigues. The fourth man was wearing work clothes—denim overalls and a tweed cap.

The women were a collection straight out of a 1940's movie. One was in a nurse's uniform—a crisp white dress and a stiff cap perched on her head. A second woman, despite her age, was wearing saddle shoes and an A-line skirt. The third woman had on an elegant rich gold satin cocktail dress, and beside her was a woman wearing a plain dark blue cotton dress with white polka dots and her hair in a bandanna. As a group, they waved and smiled at him excitedly as he stood at the street corner waiting for the light to change.

But everyone's face fell when he and Melanie crossed the street together and walked up to them.

"Hello, I'm Ryan, and I'm going to be your guide tonight," he said. He took a quick head count. There were four couples.

"That's wonderful, dear," one of the women said. She was the one in the satin cocktail dress. Well, an *old* satin cocktail dress. It hung from her frame like a weeping willow. She looked over at Melanie. "This is a private party, hon."

"You won't mind if she tags along, would you?" Ryan asked. "She's my sister and—"

"Absolutely not," one of the men chimed in. It was the guy in the military uniform wearing the peaked cap. Ryan noticed a pair of silver wings on the chest of his tunic. "Like my wife just told you, it's a *private* party." He looked with stern eyes at Melanie. "You don't belong here."

The woman in the polka-dotted house dress hushed him. "Now Robert, you've always been so abrupt. Ryan's not one of your pilots, you know."

When the Army officer shot her a look, the workman in overalls stepped to her side and took her hand. "We all made the agreement, Helen. Robert's right."

The woman named Helen pursed her lips, becoming silent. She looked at Melanie with a shrug that said *'I did what I could, dear'*.

Melanie looked curiously at the group, taking in one person at a time, looking them up and down. When Ryan tried to protest, she hushed him. She pointed at the Army officer. "Are those pilot wings?" she asked.

"That's correct, miss."

"I see." She gestured at his shoulders. "And those things on your shoulders. You're an officer?"

Robert brightened. He dusted off his shoulder pins. "Lieutenant Colonel, to be precise." At a nudge from the woman in the gold dress, he added, "but that was a long, long time ago..." Ryan knew it had to be; the guy's hair was pure white, and his skin looked like parchment. Parchment someone dribbled tea on, judging from the liver spots on his cheeks.

"I see." She looked over at the man in sailor whites. He was holding the hand of the woman in the nurse's uniform. Pointing with her chin at the woman she said, "You're dressed as a Navy nurse, aren't you?" she asked.

The sailor interrupted. "That's how we met!" he said with a grin. "She couldn't resist my charms, even though I'm just a swabbie and she's an officer!" The guy gave a short salute and the woman beside him did a mock curtsey. Ryan saw that she had a terrible case of varicose veins. He hoped she'd be able to do all the walking that was involved.

Melanie nodded. "And this is a private party..."

The woman in the saddle shoes and dark skirt came over to her. "I'm very sorry, hon. We've planned this as a family reunion. You wouldn't want to be a butt-insky would ya?"

Melanie nodded with her lips firm. "Not at all." She turned to Ryan. "I don't belong here. I'd just be a distraction."

Ryan was flummoxed. What the hell was with these people? Who did they think they were? "Hey...I'd really like her to come along, you guys. It's my first night on my new job!"

Robert the Colonel replied in a sharp voice. "Well son, we all paid to be here, and it was a special request."

"But—"

Melanie shushed him with a wave. "They're right, Ryan. I'll leave you all to it and catch up with you tomorrow, okay?" She gave him a quick squeeze and walked back the way they came.

This job was definitely starting off on the wrong foot. Ryan looked over the group, the annoyance on his face plain to see.

Helen, the woman in the house dress came up to him and patted him on the shoulder. "Don't fret, dear. Robert's right, and your sister agrees."

Her touch was soothing for some stupid reason. He couldn't resist a jibe. "You're pretty good at calming ruffled feathers, aren't you?"

"Well...blessed are the peacemakers, I suppose..."

Her husband, the guy in the overalls added, "She raised six kids, fella, and ran a great house. She hardly ever had to raise her voice!"

Helen put her head on his shoulder. "I had you for that, Dick." His hand automatically came up and stroked her hair.

"Dick? Why's he a dick?" Ryan asked.

"That's my name," Dick replied. "I mean, that's my nickname. I never liked 'Richard' and 'Rich' or 'Ricky' just wasn't my style."

"And you're cool with being a Dick."

"Sure! Why not?"

Ryan decided to let it go. "Nothing...just wondering, that's all. I don't know many Richards I guess...."

Dick stuck out his hand. "Pleased to meet cha'. We've looked forward to this for some time."

Ryan took his hand. Dick's grip was firm and the calluses in his hand felt like he was wearing a burlap glove. "I hope you enjoy it." He let go and addressed the group. "Now, I'm the new guy. I just got hired, and I'm not positive if I have all the tales committed to memory." He pulled out his manual. "So, if it's alright with you, I'll be doing a fair bit of referral to the guide. Is that okay?"

They all stared silently at him. Shit, that was unnerving. Even the pushy Lt. Colonel was silent. Ryan sighed. "Okay, look—if you want a more experienced tour guide—"

"No!" They all exclaimed at once. The women then laughed lightly, and most of the men chuckled.

Robert tipped his cap. "No son, we're perfectly happy with you, just the way you are."

The phrase spoken just that way sparked a memory for Ryan. "You like me just the way I am..." When Robert nodded, one of those sharp darts that is grief pierced his heart. He cleared his throat. "You're a fan of Mister Rogers Neighborhood like my dad used to be, huh?"

Robert looked at him with puzzlement. "Don't think I know that man. Is he an actor?"

"You don't know Fred Rogers? Don't you own a TV?"

"Can't say that I do."

Oh. A cultural elitist, huh? Ryan shrugged. "Never mind." He brightened. "I'm glad you guys are cool with me reading from the script." He glanced down at his manual. "Hmmm... our first stop is just up the block." He looked up. "Well, our first ghost story begins right here at the St. Regis Hotel! If you'll follow me..." He turned and headed back up the side street, with his group following...

⇝⇝〉 〈⇜⇜

Melanie watched the group as they set off. Not one of the people on the fairly busy street paid any mind to them or the 1940's themed costumes they were all wearing. Passersby skirted around them, intent on whatever journeys they were on, not even giving them a second glance.

It had been a hell of a day for her; she was wrung out before stopping by Ryan's place. A wave of sheer exhaustion rolled over her. There was no way she was going to be able to follow them as they went on their tour. If she didn't find a bed to crash onto in the next few minutes, she'd pass out on the street. She hailed a cab. She'd get her car back at Ryan's place tomorrow night or something.

"The Sheraton hotel please," she said getting in.

Chapter Four

The Tale Of Claudia Wheeler

R yan led the group up a side street to the back of the St. Regis Hotel. He glanced again at his manual and then addressed the group.

"If you look up at the top of the hotel, you see those dormer windows sticking out on what would be the fourth floor. The one at the very end is the first stop on our tour." They all looked up. At the top of the four-storey building, a row of dormers jutted out from the mansard roof. They were all dark. "Originally, those were the cheapest rooms in the hotel. Not surprising, as guests would have to climb up a long way to get to them." He glanced at his manual. "Back in the day, around 1870, a young woman arrived in Villmore, her name was Claudia Wheeler. She was seventeen-years-old, the eldest of seven children." Seven kids? That's insane! How the hell could a woman give birth to seven children? He shook his head in wonderment.

"Go on, Ryan...love to hear what happens!" He looked over, it was the woman in the saddle shoes and skirt. Damn...what was her name? She smiled when their eyes met. "She's practically my age!"

"What? You're nowhere near seventeen."

She rolled her eyes and her fingers grasped the edge of her skirt, lifting it out in an arc. "I was eighteen when I married John!"

The guy in battle fatigues put his arm around her waist. "Whirlwind romance and best honeymoon ever!" He looked up at Ryan. "I met Doris at a USO dance in New York city just before we shipped out back in the day. Fell for her like a ton of bricks, let me tell you. Got married the day after meeting her!"

"Good thing you did, too!" Doris rubbed her stomach. "Knocked me up that very weekend!"

The woman in the polka dot dress gasped at her phrasing. "Oh my!" she said, bringing a hand to the side of her face.

John ignored Helen's outburst and gave his wife a squeeze. "Yeah, well one kid's better than six, don't ya think?" he said with a wink.

Ryan coughed, getting their attention once again. "Well, Claudia came from a terribly impoverished family, yes. Her parents made arrangements for her to marry a local businessman. He was much, much older than her and wanted a healthy woman to sire an heir. He paid what was..." he glanced down at his manual, "well, they say here a 'princely sum' for a healthy young woman who knew her place." He pointed up at the darkened dormer window at the end of the roof line. "She was to reside in that room before their wedding so that the local church could publish the Banns of the engagement." His face furrowed. "I don't know what a Bann is, but it sounds like something important."

"She was Catholic, then," Helen said. "Just like Dick and me. They're announcements made at the church on Sunday of an engagement. I'm not sure why, but every Sunday they'd announce marriages for a few weeks before the wedding. I suppose back in Claudia's day no respectable person would dream of eloping after..." she shot a quick grin at John and Doris "just a day."

"There was a war on!" John said with a laugh.

"I'm not passing judgment here, dear. I'm explaining to Ryan. You and Doris are a couple of pistols, believe me!" she added with a smile. Turning back to Ryan, she added, "So it's not a surprise that she would be put up in such a fashion. I'm surprised she didn't have a chaperone as well, guaranteeing her purity…"

Ryan shrugged. "I don't see anything about chaperone's here. Well…here's the rest of the tale: Apparently, she didn't want to go through with the marriage. She became dead set against the idea of marrying a man as old as her own father I guess." He pointed with his chin back to the window. "One night, she leapt from that window, falling four stories and killing herself, smashing into the cobblestone street."

He let that hang in silence for a moment. "And it's said that if you stare at the window long enough, you will see her standing there, holding a candle pondering her fate."

He let the silence hang again. It was a pretty good story.

"That's a horrible lie!" Doris spat out.

Chapter Five

Embellishment

N ow Doris..." Mildred, the woman in the cocktail dress said.

"Damn it Mildred! You know it's the truth!" She strode out to the middle of the street and jerked a finger up at the hotel. "That poor, poor kid had been stuck up there for two weeks when it happened!" She turned around to Ryan. "Anything about *that* in your handbook, Buster Brown?"

Ryan's eyes shot wide. "Uh...no?"

"You're damn right!"

"Doris, language..." Helen murmured.

Dick put his arm over her shoulder. "Let her go hon, she's on a tear."

Doris stalked over to Ryan. "Claudia was a poor farm girl from the backwoods. Her mother taught her to read and write, and that's all the education she ever received. She was *terrified* by all the hustle and bustle of this city!" She spat. "Ohhh Villmore considered itself a real metropolitan hub...if you compare it to the backwoods around it, but it couldn't hold a candle to The Big Apple, even way back then!"

She looked back up at Ryan. "When the steam train pulled into the station..." She pointed down the street to the lakeshore, "... that was just over there, Claudia was terrified out of her mind! She thought the clouds of steam and sparks from the engine and the *noise* was the end of the world!" She took a deep breath. "She had only met the man her 'intended' had hired and had never set eyes on the guy who she was supposed to marry."

She pointed back up at the garret window. "So, there she was, all alone in a strange new world, and the worst had yet to happen."

"Okay, I'll bite," Ryan said. "What happened?"

Doris' eyes were on fire. "Don't be cute, Buster Brown. You're not too old for a spanking young man!" She was still standing in the middle of the street; Ryan looked up the one-way street and was grateful there was no traffic. "That poor, poor child was trapped. She said her rosary every night, praying on her knees." Doris' eyes filled with tears. "She *knew* she had to go through with this horrid marriage—it was the only hope for her family's survival!" She glared at Ryan. "And she was *supremely* devout. That child wouldn't *dare* to kill herself and be damned to hell for it. In addition, she was of solid stock; she knew in her heart and soul that she'd be able to make the best of whatever her so-called 'fiancée' could throw at her. She *practically* raised her younger brothers and sisters!"

"Says here she jumped out that window, Doris," Ryan mused.

"Ooh!" Doris stamped her feet and marched over to him. "Enough comments from the Peanut Gallery, okay boy?" She jabbed him in the chest with a finger, making him back up a step. "You silly, silly boy. Put your thinking cap on for a minute, would ya! Claudia didn't jump."

Ryan felt his heart get cold. He stared into Doris' eyes. They were dark embers, a deep brown, but the flecks of gold at the edges sparked. He kept his mouth shut, and asked his question with his eyes.

"She. Was. THROWN!" Doris covered her face with her hands. "That poor, poor girl..." she sobbed, her shoulders heaving.

Watching the elderly woman be so upset, Ryan didn't have the slightest idea what to do. But he didn't have to. The rest of the group gathered round her. The woman in the nurse's outfit stepped forward and took her in her arms.

"Hey, Doris...it's long past now..." she said in a gentle voice.

Doris lay her head on the other woman's chest. "I know Betty! I know! I just...it's just not fair!" she replied.

"You've always, always have had such a big old heart, you know that?" Betty the nurse replied.

"Why do you think I married her?" John chimed in, hitching up his khaki pants.

Doris pulled away from Betty for a moment. "Because you thought I was the bee's knees, and we fell in love like a couple of coconuts!" She wiped her eyes and smiled. "Boy oh boy, wasn't that a pip of a week though, huh?"

"You betcha', sweetheart..." his cocky smile faded into an expression of wistfulness. "It wasn't nearly long enough..."

"Long enough to leave me with someone to remember you by, big boy," she replied, patting her midriff.

John leaned over Doris. "Hey doll...let me tell ya something." He whispered in her ear. She shot a look at Ryan and nodded to her husband, who pointed upwards.

Ryan glanced from them back up to the window. "Hole-lee shit!" he gasped.

The rest of the group looked up. In the window there was a figure. Ryan couldn't make out the details, but it was definitely a woman. In her hand was a candle holder with a single taper letting out a soft glow. She looked down at them, and then off into the distance.

The candle blinked out without warning.

"Did you see that?" Ryan gasped.

"See what?" Doris asked.

"The woman in the window!"

She gave her head a small shake. "Nooo…" She looked around to the rest of the group. "Anyone see anything?" A chorus of 'no's' was the reply. Doris let out a long sigh and turned back to Ryan. "Well, how did you like my embellishment of your story, Buster Brown?" She blinked at him with a Cheshire cat smile. "A lot more interesting than what you read out to us!"

"Embellishment? You made all that up?"

She just kept smiling at him.

Robert cleared his throat. "Well…perhaps you can continue our little tour?"

"Yeah, sure. Okay…" His brain was foggy from Doris' outburst. He looked back up to the window, but there was nothing there. He looked down at his handbook and said, "If you'll just follow me, there're more tales to tell on our tour." Screw it. It's an odd night, that was for sure. He tapped the brim of his top hat and made a flourish with his cape and led them on to the next stop.

Chapter Six

Tock Tock Tock...

The rest of the tour passed without any further outbursts from Doris. Although, at the cemetery stop, telling the story of the woman and her potion of youth, Mildred got a little antsy. She started to say something at the end of Ryan's presentation, but thank God, Robert the Lt. Colonel hushed her.

No big deal. Meh times a hundred. Ryan was too rattled from Doris' outburst at the start of the tour and then that thing with the woman holding the candle in the window, to give much of a damn about Mildred's level of satisfaction with his story told at the cemetery fence line.

When he led them all back to the starting point by the entrance to the St. Regis, there wasn't anyone there. He figured that the other tour guides that gave the tours would be hanging around; it was a beautiful night. He glanced up at the sky. The moon was just a day or two from becoming full; the white orb in the sky looked close enough almost to touch. He sniffed the air. He didn't feel chilly, but the smell of wood burning hung gently all around. Some people were getting a head start on their weekends by having romantic fires in their living rooms he figured. A crisp, autumn night with the scent of wood smoke in the air always gave him some sort of 'satisfied' feeling. Cozying up before a bright fire at night was always an image that popped into his head.

Too damn bad his place didn't have one. Sure, they were a pain to maintain, but it would have been nice to put one on at home. What the hell—maybe he'd find a YouTube feed or something.

"Penny for your thoughts, Ryan?" He started at the sound of Betty's voice. "Oh! Sorry I scared you!" she said, her lips betraying her fib. She got a kick out of making him jump!

Just like Melanie! He chuckled. "Yeah, you got me. That's one for you." He peered at her. "Did you used to do that with your patients when you were a nurse?"

Betty shook her head, then adjusted her nurse's cap. "Not a chance. I save the good stuff for healthy, young men." She tilted her head at him. "You seemed a million miles away..."

He shrugged. "I don't know..." he gestured at the meeting place for The Haunted Walk. "Looks like all my co-workers have gone home. I was hoping to chat with some of them about my first night." He peered into the window of the antique bar. "Hmph. Looks like the place's closed. Not a soul in the joint, but they left all the lights on."

Betty followed his gaze. "I guess they thought it was okay to close up?" She shrugged and gave him a nudge with her elbow. "You did fine, by the way. In fact, since there's nothing going on at this bar, why don't you join us?"

"I don't know...Doris really put me off my game tonight."

"What?" Betty adjusted her nurse's cap. The woman was at least 80, but she sure as hell wasn't any frail old lady. Her hair was jet black—almost blue, it was so dark. It was a great dye job. And despite her age, her eyes were clear; none of that old-people's rheumy eyes. He looked at her hands as she fumbled with some bobby-pins that was holding her cap on. The liver spots on her hands told the truth her hair was lying about. Betty was *old*.

She noticed his appraising look. "Yes, I know; it's a little strange wearing this getup, but all the others wanted to dress along the lines of when we first met back in the day."

"When was that?"

"Oh, during the War. Bill was one of the swabbies on the hospital ship I worked on."

"The war?"

She nodded quickly, then called out to the others. "How about Ryan joining us this evening?"

Ryan immediately looked over at Doris to see her expression. The others seemed pretty amenable, and what the hell, he hadn't gotten any tips yet, so maybe...

But while Doris stayed silent, Helen spoke up beside her. "Mmmm...Betty? I'm not sure that's a good idea tonight." Her husband Dick nodded in agreement. "I'm sorry Ryan, it's just that...well...I'm feeling somewhat tired, and I think it would be best if all of us..." she eyed the rest of the group, "... called it a night."

There were murmurs of agreement.

Betty let out a sigh as she nodded. "Yes, too soon. Sorry Ryan, I guess Helen's probably right."

"Umm... well that's okay." He was a little surprised at how a pang of disappointment brushed up against him. He kind of enjoyed their company, even if they were all older than dirt.

Betty caressed his arm. "Now don't you worry. We're all coming back here tomorrow for another go-round with you!"

"Whaaat?"

She called out to the others. "Isn't that right? Tomorrow night, last tour of the evening like we did tonight?"

"Absolutely!" Doris said. "The kids will be here tomorrow!"

"Whaaat?"

"The entire family's not here yet," Betty said. "Tomorrow night, my son's coming—"

"Along with his wife, our daughter!" Mildred called out.

"That's right." Betty pointed to Doris and John. "Their son's also coming, and he's married to Helen and Dick's daughter."

"Wait, a minute. You guys are all in-laws?"

"Absolutely! I told you it's a family reunion, didn't I?"

Well, one of them did; he remembered that from when they first met. "Yeah, I guess I forgot."

"So, you just make sure you're back here at the same time tomorrow. I can't wait for the kids to meet you!"

Kids. Ha. Judging from the age of this crew and what Betty said about 'the war' or something, their 'kids were going to be pretty damn old too if they're a day. The Baby Boom generation was getting on. "Sure, sure," he said. "Sounds like a plan."

"Maybe tomorrow night you'll get together with us?" Betty said.

"Okay." He tipped his top hat and left them gathered in front of the sandwich board sign.

It was a short walk home, just a few blocks up the side street from Main Street. He felt kind of cool in the top-hat and cape. Too bad the streets were so empty; he would have loved to have seen people's expressions taking in his getup. There were tons of lights on in the homes he passed, and once again, the aroma of wood smoke lifted his spirits.

The air was still, not so much as a whisper of wind through the branches, and there wasn't any car traffic to speak of. Which was why the sound of footsteps behind him snagged his attention. It was a tock-tock of heels on pavement.

He tried to be all casual when he glanced over his shoulder.

A shiver skittered along his shoulders. There was nobody there.

What the hell? He stopped and looked across the street. Nope, nobody on the other side either. Hmmm. He took a deep breath, bolstering his nerve and continued on his way.

Tock, tock, tock.

This time he spun around. His heart leapt in his chest.

Again, nothing.

Okay, now this was getting creepy. He retraced his steps, looking to his left and right, but didn't see anyone. He looked up the staircases leading from the sidewalk to the front doors of the brownstones, but again, nobody there.

"Hey!" he called out. "Is there someone there?"

His cheeks grew warm as he looked around, wondering if anyone had seen his outburst. Talk about looking like a jerk! What the hell did he expect, someone to call back, "Just me!" or something?

He threw up his hands as it hit him. Damn it. Wait!

"Mel? Melanie? You trying to weird me out? Well, it's not working, sis!" He stood in the center of the sidewalk, his arms akimbo. "Come on out!"

Nothing.

"Okay, have it your way. You're still down in the score."

As soon as he resumed walking, the tock-tock started again. And when he picked up his pace, the noise behind him responded in kind. Well, he had always been a faster runner than Melanie, so... He took off at a full run.

And heard his pursuer follow.

It was gaining on him! Damn that Melanie! If she thought she'd get a point for giving him the creeps, she could go to hell. He could practically hear her voice saying something like 'Ha! Gotcha! You ran like a little girl!'. At that thought, he flung himself around again.

And yelled.

It was like someone had sparked one of those disposable cigarette lighters in his face. An instantaneous flash of sparking orange and yellow light flared up in his eyes, making his head snap back.

He blinked a couple of times, whispering, "What the hell *was* that!"

But only the silent darkness answered. Had it even been there?

He shuddered. This was too weird for words. Like a madman his head darted from side to side, and quickly behind him. What the hell was that? A quick, sparky flash in his eyes, then nothing? Did Melanie have one of those lasers or something?

"Mel? This isn't funny!"

Again, nothing.

He was just a little over a block away from his place. He took off at a dead run.

Tock-tock-tocks followed him every step of the way.

And again, they were getting louder.

He rounded a corner at full blast, the steps to his house right in front of him and pulled up to a dead stop. And grinned.

The sound pursuing him stopped too. He didn't give a damn, what he saw was too cool, and besides he was home. "Hey Buster! How you doing?" he said with a smile.

Sitting on the middle stair of the entranceway to his building was the kitten he'd rescued from the tree. It was sitting up, his paws delicately in front of him, looking up at Ryan expectedly. It tilted its head at him, one ear flitting like a butterfly's wing, as if to say, *'You gonna ask me in or what?'*

Ryan shook his head, the spectral pursuit totally forgotten. He hopped up the steps and bent over. "You know, I've never had a pet; you good with that?"

"Meeewww…"

"I'll take that as a yes." He held his hand out. The kitten immediately snuggled into it. "Well, how about that…" he scooped the kitten up. "I'm naming you 'Buster'; the name just came to me when I got you out of that tree, but then one of my tour clients called me 'Buster Brown' a few times. You okay with that?"

"Meww…"

"Fair enough then." He cuddled the poor little thing into the crook of his arm like a football and went up to his apartment.

Chapter Seven

Oh Really...

Ryan let himself into his place, still holding Buster in the crook of his arm, the gentle purring acting like a narcotic on his frayed nerves. Maybe that's why people owned cats. You pick up a friendly one and when it purrs right away, the subtle drone's calming effects could be as soporific as any drug.

"You hungry, bud?" He opened the fridge. There was a half a quart of milk. His eyes scanned the shelves. There were some cold cuts, a loaf of bread and other stuff. He'd get something to eat later.

Grabbing a saucer, he put Buster on the floor and poured some milk into it.

Buster looked down at the milk and back up to him.

"Not peckish either, huh bud?" Wait. He picked up the saucer and popped it into the microwave for ten seconds. Pulling it out, he tested it with his fingertip; it was tepid. He put the saucer back down, but Buster just wasn't interested. "Okey-dokey, I'll leave it here for you in case you want it later on, okay?"

Getting up on his hind feet, Buster pawed at the leg of his jeans. "Alrighty then." Ryan scooped the kitten up and wandered into the living room. He slumped down onto the sofa, and Buster climbed up onto his chest and nuzzled into his neck.

The gentle purring's effect was almost immediate. Ryan's eyes grew heavy, and his breathing matched his kitten's rhythm until... with a sigh he dozed.

SKAAARRRTTTCH!

His eyes sprung open. "What the hell is that!"

Buster leapt off his chest to the arm of the couch. His back arched as he too was looking left and right for the source of the noise. He let out a low hiss.

"You heard it too? Or did I just scare the hell out of you?" Ryan asked. "Could have been dream—"

SKRRAAATCHHH!

It was the sound of a pissed off grizzly bear in a schoolroom attacking the blackboard. The sound filled the room, then rolled into a threatening, almost crunching noise making the hair on the back of Ryan's neck stand straight up. Whoever was causing that commotion meant business.

He glanced over at Buster. The cat's eyes were fixed on the apartment door. Still on all fours, its back was now relaxed as it watched the door to the apartment. "Meewww..."

SKKAARRRAAATCH!

Buster blinked twice, and his nose twitched. "Mew!"

SKAARTCH!

"Quit it, would ya?" Ryan hissed at the cart who looked up at him with arched eyebrows. *'You gonna get the door or what?'*

Ryan stepped up to the apartment door. He'd never felt more grateful for the steel construction of the door than at that moment. Whatever was out there wasn't getting in without a battering ram or a grenade.

THUD! THUD!

"Aaaiee!" Ryan jumped at the pounding on the door. What the hell was out there? He grabbed at his back pocket. God damn it! What a lousy time to lose his freaking phone! "Shit!"

He eased up to the door and took a quick peek through the peephole.

Nothing. Just the hallway. But it was a quick peek. He put his eye to it again. The fisheye lens displayed a wide angle view up and down the hallway. Sure, maybe there was someone pressed beside the door hiding, but all he saw was his neighbor's place on the other side of the hall and the edge of the stairs coming up at the end of the hall. He looked over to Buster. "I don't see—"

THUD!

He felt the vibration on the door and let out a yell. What the hell *is* that? He pressed his eye to the peephole again, but nothing was there. He kept his view on the peephole. "Hell-ooo? Who is it?" he called out. He wanted a look at whatever the hell that was.

Nothing.

"Nyah-nyah! You can't get in can you!" he yelled. Screw you for scaring the living hell out of me!

Nothing again.

"Come on! Is that all you got? Ring and run, you punk?" Okay, it was more THUD and run...

With a courage (recklessness?) he never knew he had, Ryan flung the door open and leapt backwards holding his fists up.

Nothing.

What the hell? He crouched low and slid forward to the open portal. He took a quick glance out. Nothing. He straightened and walked to the staircase looking down. It was empty. Listening hard and turning his head left and right, he didn't hear a damn thing. What the hell? He went back to his apartment and looked at the door. Not a mark on the damn thing.

He rubbed his hand over the surface; it was as smooth as glass. What the freaking hell! He let out a sigh.

Going back into the apartment, he looked over at Buster, now sitting on the arm of the couch. "Nothing doing. You heard it too, though, didn't you?" The kitten looked at him impassively, just blinking its eyes. *'You woke me up, Ryan'* look on its face.

"No, man. It wasn't no dream. I was *awake at the door* the last time it made noise!"

'Oh. Really.'

"Come on! Yes really! Don't look at me like that!"

"Meeew..." *'Come back to bed, okay? I was super comfortable.'*

Like a warm blanket, a sense of sleepy lassitude descended on him. "I really ought to go to bed you know. Tell you what—I'll lie down with you for a few minutes, then we can head to bed, okay?"

"Mew."

"Glad you approve." He flopped onto the couch and Buster jumped from the arm of it right onto his chest. Again it snuggled in, its purring immediate.

Ryan tucked it into the crook of his arm. "Anyone comes knocking, you get it okay?"

Buster just nestled in and he closed his eyes.

"That's a good idea." Ryan's eyes slid shut too.

Chapter Eight

Ask It In...

D on't you think it's time you got your butt in gear?" Melanie's voice
called to him.

Ryan's eyes fluttered open, and he looked over to see his older sister
standing in the middle of the living room.

He sat up and shook his head. "I must'a dozed off." The windows of the
living room were dark. He shot a look up at her. "What the hell are you
doing here so late?"

She snorted. "You won't be late if you get moving. It's ten o'clock."

"What are you talking about? I just got home." His head felt fuzzy.

"From where?"

"The Haunted Walk, silly!" He let out a sigh. "I'm glad you stopped by
though. Some weird shit's been going on." He looked around the living
room. "Where's Buster?"

"Who?"

"The kitten! The one I got from the tree when we were heading out earlier? It was waiting for me when I got home!" He stood up. "Psssst! Buster!"

"Ryan..."

"What?"

Melanie looked him up and down. "That was last night, bro."

"What the hell are you talking about?"

"You rescued that kitten *last* night. It's Friday night, not Thursday."

"Whaaa—?"

She nodded. "And you have to be at work in half an hour."

"Whaaaat? Mel, I just got home! I dozed off for a bit on the couch, and now you're here!"

She shook her head. "No... I just stopped by to see how you were doing, if you made it home okay and stuff." She smiled at him. "How did it go last night, anyway?" Ryan dropped down onto the floor, peering under the couch. "What are you doing?"

"Where's the damn cat?"

"What are you talking about? What cat?"

He stood up again. "The kitten! Buster! Where is the little guy? We dozed off on the couch, he was lying in my arms, and now he's gone!"

"You feeling okay?" Melanie's eyes narrowed at him. "Or are you messing with me like you did last night?"

"Wait! I can prove it!" Crooking a finger at her, he went to the kitchen. "See?" He pointed at the saucer with the milk in it. "I tried to feed the little guy last night. There's the milk I gave him!"

Melanie looked down at the floor and back up. "Okay... maybe it got out. You have any windows open?"

"In October? You nuts?" He went through the apartment, checking under his bed, looking in the bathroom and again in the kitchen. "He was here, now he's gone..." he ran a hand through his hair. "Oh shit, Melanie, I don't think I should have taken that damn job..."

"Don't say that!"

He recoiled a bit at the vehemence in her voice. "You don't understand; weird shit's been going on since I did that stupid tour."

"I don't care!" She pointed at him. "YOU said you wanted to go for that job! You told *me* it would be a good thing! It's not my fault!"

"Whoa, whoa...take it easy...I didn't say anything was *your* fault..."

She stared at him, her eyes sparking. "*I* wanted you to just head to New York! *I* was going to pay your expenses for two damn years! But noooo..." She jabbed a finger at him like an ice pick. "*You* said you needed professional experience in your resume before heading down!" Her eyes teared up. "Why didn't you listen to me?"

What the hell was with her?

Melanie covered her face with her hands, and her shoulders quaked. "It's not my fault!" she said, her voice muffled by her palms.

"Hey...Mel...it's not your fault, I get it..." he went to her side. "I mean... last night was weird, yeah, but you weren't even there!"

"I know... they said I didn't belong..."

"Yeah, they're some kind of odd group, that's for sure."

She looked at him side-eyed. "Oh? How so?"

"Well, for starters, they're like a million years old, but they don't act like it."

"They looked pretty old to me."

He shook his head. "Nope. One of them told me they met during 'The War'."

"Which one?" She gasped. There's been wars going on as long as she could remember. Afghanistan, Iraq... she looked at Ryan. Pretty much his entire life had taken place while American soldiers were joining up and shipping out to go overseas to kill people. How did the 'war on terror' become a normal state of affairs?

Ryan looked thoughtful. "At first, I thought maybe it was Vietnam or something... but then their clothes..." He shook his head slowly, his eyes wide in amazement. "I think they're from the Second World War, man...."

"No way. They'd be over a hundred years old, Ryan! For heaven's sake, it *ended* like sixty years ago!"

"No...it *ended* in 1945...*seventy-five* years ago!" He scratched his head. "That would make them all about a hundred years old. *At least*! And that crew I was with last night... not one of them so much had a cane, let alone a walker! They did that tour with no problem." He tilted his head at Melanie. "They got to be on some kind of youth drug or something. I think I saw something online about some old rich guys trying to get some bio-company off the ground to do age reversal..."

"Age reversal?"

"Yeah, or something like that. Or maybe it was some Netflix movie?" He shook his head. "Damn, I can't remember. But I *think* there's something like that..." He sighed. "Beats me."

Melanie pointed at the dining table. "Well, get your hat and cape, because your second performance starts in less than half an hour. I'll walk you down, okay?"

"Yeah, okay..." Damn good thing Melanie had stopped by or he would have missed his second day of work. Or night of work. Or whatever... Man, he felt weird. He slept all night and all day? What the hell was up with that? As he gathered up his show duds, he took an inventory; nope, he felt fine and dandy. He was a little out of it when he woke up, but now he felt as right as rain. Oh, well...

He tied the collar of his cape together, put on his top hat and patted it in place. "How do I look? Super-naturally enough for ya?"

"Yeah, a genuine ghost tour dude." She went to the front door and opened it. "Let's go get 'em tiger!"

Ryan bent and checked the surface of the door. No, there were no marks on it at all.

"Now what?" Melanie asked.

He straightened up. "Last night, someone was trying to get into my place. They banged on the door, and then scraped on it really, really hard. But when I looked, there wasn't anyone there." He paused for a second. "I think...now don't go nuts on me, okay?"

"What? You think what?"

He blew out a huff of air. "This sounds stupid. I think it was a ghost or something."

"Why do you think that? I could have just been some kids, right?"

He shook his head. "No. Because when I looked out the peephole, there wasn't anyone there..." He looked at Melanie. "Am I losing my mind?"

She shook her head. "Nope. You're not losing your mind."

"You sure?"

She nodded. "Come on, we'll talk on the way, okay?"

He followed her outside. Melanie looked up at the sky. "Full moon tomorrow..." she said in a wistful voice.

"So what?"

She lowered her gaze to her brother. "On nights with a full moon the boundary between our world and the next is the thinnest."

"Oh, yeah?" When she nodded, he asked, "How do you know?" His eyes bulged. "Wait, a damn minute!" he jabbed a finger at her. "You actually believe in ghosts! You think they're real!"

Melanie shook her head. "No, you're wrong. I don't think they're real at all." She held up her hand to silence his retort. "No, Ryan, I *know* they're real."

"But..."

She crossed her arms. "You can believe me or not, it doesn't change the facts. I've had direct and genuine experiences with spirits." She dropped her arms and walked away.

"No way!" Ryan caught up with her.

Melanie kept walking. "Way." She looked at him. "Do you believe me? Or do you think I'm crazy?"

"I don't think you're nuts...but...man, Mel! Ghosts?"

She nodded. "So I know a thing or two. So I just want to give you advice. If that thing bangs and scrapes on your door, ask it in."

Ryan stopped dead in his tracks. "WHAT? Are you outta your mind? What if it tries to hurt me! It sure wasn't knocking all that gently you know. The noise it was making? It sounded pissed off!"

"I suspect that it's frustrated. It's really hard for them to interact with mortals. It's trying to communicate with you by getting your attention, but doesn't really understand anymore how to interact. If it really wanted to hurt you...if it could hurt you...it already would have, I think." She gestured at him. "Let's keep going. You need to be at work."

He followed her. "You sure about this? Ask it in?"

"Yes."

"How about you come with me? Stay at my place tonight. So if it happens again, you can show me what you mean."

She shook her head. "No... I don't think I should."

"What's that supposed to mean?"

"My gut tells me you need to handle this on your own." She pointed down the street. "Just like yesterday... your clients told me I didn't belong, right? I think this is the same thing."

Ryan huffed. The really shitty thing about Melanie's take on it was that it felt kind of 'right' or whatever to him as well. "Okay." They headed down the block in silence until once again they were across the street from the gathering spot for The Haunted Walk.

His eyebrows shot up. "Crowd's a little bigger this time," he said. He did a quick count. The eight people from last night were back—and they were all wearing the same getups they had last night. Betty the nurse and her husband Bill the sailor, Dick the plumber and his wife Helen, Doris the Bobby-soxer with John the soldier... and he couldn't forget Mildred in that gorgeous satin cocktail dress and her husband 'Col. Robert'.

There were two other couples with them, in their 30s or so. One couple looked like they just escaped from a hippie commune. The guy had long dark brown hair that went halfway to his waist held by a beaded bandanna and was wearing a fringed buckskin vest. His partner was the epitome of 'Earth Mother'; a long flowing dress with a black and orange pattern that almost went to her feet and hair in braids. The other couple, about the same age, was the exact opposite. The guy was in a gray flannel suit and his wife was in a polyester yellow pantsuit, her blonde hair short in the front, down to her shoulders in the back with a flip at the ends.

"I'm gonna need a roster card to keep track of these people," Ryan said.

"I'll leave you to it," Melanie said. "See you tomorrow?"

"Okay, sure."

Crossing the street, he knew deep down that this was going to be one hell of a night.

He had no idea...

Chapter Nine

We Don't Bite!

They all gathered around him smiling when he crossed the street. He scanned the group. Yeah, everyone from last night was back, and they were all wearing the same outfits, thank God. That way he'd be able to keep track of who's who.

Nurse Betty and Sailor Bill had paired off with Dick the plumber and his wife Helen. The strait-laced younger couple was with them.

Betty spoke first. "Ryan, I'd love to introduce you to our kids. This is my son Troy, and his wife is Helen and Dick's daughter Angie."

Without warning, Angie stepped forward and grabbed him in a firm hug. "I'm so, so happy to see you, Ryan!" she said. "You're such a handsome young man!"

He wouldn't lie; her welcoming embrace felt genuine, if unexpected. Even so, he hugged her back. "How do you do?" he said.

She stepped back and held his shoulders. "See? Ever the gentleman!" she smiled at the others.

Before he could recover, the other new woman, the hippie lady in beads grabbed his arm. "My turn!" she said and enveloped him into a hug as well. "Oh Ryan! This is super groovy!"

Okay... being hugged by two women about twenty years older than him, right out of nowhere was *weird*. But how the hell could something so damn out of left field feel so wonderful? His mind was yelling 'back off lady!' but his heart was doing a happy dance. What the hell; he hugged her back, saying "Pleased to meet ya."

The partners of the women—hippie dude and mister suit and tie—stepped in and shook hands one at a time.

Troy, the suit and tie guy said, "Nice firm grip, son" nodding in approval. And damn it, hearing that voice of approval felt good.

Hippie dude held his hand up, and instinctively, Ryan high-fived him. As soon as their hands touched, his hand became enveloped into a palm wrapping 'brother' handshake. "Smooth man, you're really smooth!" Again, the words were great to hear.

"Now Ryan," Mildred said, holding the Colonel's arm, "that's my daughter—"

"Call me 'Star' tonight, okay Mom?" the hippie woman interrupted. "That's what I went by back in the day!"

Mildred rolled her eyes and sighed. "Very well, dear."

Star grabbed her husband's arm. "And you're going to go by 'Moon Dog' again."

He shook his head. "Well, I'm dressed for it, aren't I?" He pointed over at Doris the Bobby-soxer and her husband John who was still in battle fatigues. "I'm their son."

Doris added, "Only child, too!"

Ryan's head was spinning. He really needed to write this all down.

Once again, they were the only people waiting for the tour. Well, it was kind of late—it was moving on towards 11:00. He looked up and down the wide street that skirted the lakefront. Beside their small crowd on the corner, he couldn't make out anyone else on the street. "Is there a big game or something on TV tonight?" he asked. "Aside from us, I don't see many people out tonight."

"Why, you got something better to do?" John said. "Got someplace else you'd rather be?" His expression was a little peeved.

"Whoa, no... just asking, that's all." That was pretty much the first time the guy spoke to him; and he came across prickly.

Doris shushed him. "Now honey, we're all happy to be here." She jabbed her husband in the chest. "Even you! Am I right?"

"Yeah...I guess so..." the cloud on his face passed. "Sorry, son. I guess I'm just itching to get this show on the road."

Ryan pulled his manual out. "Do you guys want to do the same tour as last night?" He was flipping pages. There was a list of other stops they could do instead.

"Absolutely," Helen and Mildred said at once. They looked at each other and giggled.

"Great minds think alike, hon," Mildred quipped.

Ryan looked the crowd over. Okay then... well he was familiar with the route. "Then let's be off!"

⇢⇢⇢⟩ ⟨⟪⟪⟪⇠

Just as in the previous night, they stopped below the window where Claudia's room was. Ryan gave his little spiel, keeping an eye on Doris as he told the tale from his manual. When he finished, he added with a nod in Doris' direction, "Now there's a strong opinion that Claudia did not jump to her death, but was thrown..." he let that sink in as Doris nodded.

"By who?" Moon Dog asked. When Ryan shrugged and pointed to Doris, he turned. "Who did it, Ma?"

Doris pointed up at the window. "I don't know..." they all looked up, and again a candle appeared, silhouetting someone holding it. "But she does!"

Moon Dog cupped his hands around his mouth. "Hey! Why don't you come down and solve this mystery already! We don't bite!"

As soon as he said the words, the light in the window went out.

They all watched the side of the building.

This was insane. Ryan didn't know who was up there doing the candle in the window bit, but to expect a ghost to appear just because you asked it?

Wait, a damn minute. Wasn't that just what Melanie said? Invite the ghost?

Ohhh shit...

He stood with the group watching the building, not daring to breathe.

Chapter Ten

Move Along...

"H mph!" Doris snorted. "Some people got no class!" They had all been waiting silently for a couple of minutes.

Ryan let out a whoosh of air. That was a relief. He shook his head at himself. Damn it, he was being played! He stared at all the people on his tour. Did Melanie set this whole thing up to jazz him? He knew she came into 'some money' as she'd put it. Some kind of inheritance from a girl she went to college with a couple of years ago. There had been a period where she had lived pretty large, her visits to him at school suddenly went from sharing a pizza and Netflix to classy dinners at the best restaurants in town. And she always slipped him a couple of hundred bucks when she left.

Mom and Dad had died during his first year in college. Stupid ice patch. Melanie absolutely refused to let him drop out or even take a leave of absence. When the funeral was over, she insisted he get back to school. "You focus on your work," she said as she sat crying that night after the burial. "It'll be easier to deal with if you have responsibilities."

He relented, and she made it a point to visit him twice a month all during his undergrad. It kind of felt stupid going to acting classes and studying drama from the olden days that first year. But Melanie had insisted. She told him that if he let his studies slide, he'd be dishonoring the memory of Mom and Dad. Sure, there had been a big insurance payout and stuff, but Melanie had taken steps to put his share into a trust fund until he was twenty-nine. She had told him that too much money too quickly could really mess you up. Whatever. He'd be worth a few hundred K from his share of their estate before he was thirty. And that was with his college all paid for.

Melanie didn't want him to take this job, but he knew having some kind of professional performing experience—even if only a tour guide—would give him an advantage when he started auditioning in New York next year. She really argued the point. He gave his head a shake. His memory was fuzzy, but what she had said back in the apartment tonight fitted in. Yeah, she didn't want him doing this...

Waitaminnit...

He looked the group over again. The period clothing, the people looking a hell of a lot younger than they ought to be if they were telling the truth, stuck in his mind. "Are you guys actors or something?" he asked the group. "Did my sister hire you for some kind of prank?"

"No, dear," Mildred said. "Melanie did not hire us. We're here because we want to be here!"

Doris chimed in. "We told you yesterday, silly! It's a family reunion!"

He rolled his eyes. "Yeah, whatever..." He gestured at the hotel's edifice. "Well, I guess we won't be joined by the ghost of Claudia whatever her name is—"

"Wheeler, Ryan. Her name is Claudia Wheeler." This time it was Helen who spoke. Her mouth was turned down. "A little respect, okay?"

"Jeez! Sorry! And just for the record, it's her name *was* Claudia Wheeler. She's kind of dead, you know."

Helen blinked at him. "Yes, Ryan... we know."

"Okay, okay! Sorry! Can we continue with the tour now?"

The tension in the group had risen. Last night, after Doris' outburst at this very spot, everyone was kind and solicitous to her, but tonight... everyone, including him, was on edge. He sure as hell wasn't overtired—shit, he slept for eighteen hours! Or more! But the exchange between him and Helen was like flipping a switch; they were watching him with a different attitude now.

He sighed. "Okay...look, I'm sorry, for being snippy." He gestured at the hotel. "This is getting a little strange for me, you know?"

Doris scoffed merrily. "It *ought* to! It's a haunted walk after all!" That broke the tension. Everyone either chuckled or laughed out loud.

Dick came over and patted Ryan's shoulder. "We're definitely getting our money's worth, son. If this gives the *tour guide* the heebie-jeebies, then it's a good tour, right?"

"Yeah, I guess so... Thanks Dick."

"No problem. Let's move along, huh?"

Chapter Eleven

The Tale Of Ronald Grafer

T he tour traced a box pattern in the city's streets. At each of the stops, the entire group did the 'ooo's' and 'ahhh's' as he related the different tales. Just as they came around the last section, one of the last stops, Ryan told them the tale of 'The Hanged Man's Ghost'.

They were in the back of the courthouse building. Back in the 1800s, when it had been first built, it also served as the local jail. In fact, the basement windows along the back of the building still had iron bars over the openings where the cells had once been. There was a parking area for city officials in the back of the building, an oval plaza that opened out on one side to a fairly large city park the size of several football fields.

"This plaza is now a parking lot," Ryan said, glancing at his manual. "But back in the early days of our fair city, it was a public gathering place." He pointed to a stone extension that jutted out from the edge of the courthouse. "That over there is the... 'cell for the condemned.'"

A quick gasp followed before he continued, "In those days, this courthouse served a huge part of the state. Criminals of all stripes were brought here to trial." He eyed the group in front of them. "Also back in those days, the death penalty was meted out...in swift...and absolute terms."

"Not long after this courthouse opened, it heard its first death penalty case. A man named Ronald Grafer was arrested and charged for a robbery in which three people were murdered—a woman, her child, and the butler of her home—were all slaughtered in a burglary that went bad."

He looked up from his manual to see his audience listening raptly. "An eyewitness from that night said they saw a man leaving the home wearing a peculiar coat and running at full speed. The coat was peculiar because it was inset with shiny brass buttons all up the sleeves and down the back." He dropped his voice for effect.

"There was only one man in the entire town with a coat like that—Ronald Grafer. The sheriff went to his home, if you could call it that. Ronald Grafer lived in a hovel on the property of one of the largest farmers in the county. He looked after the farm and he had six children. Times were hard, and his children were starving, as their mother had died giving birth to the youngest earlier that year. Ronald's coat was recovered, hidden in a barn along with the blood-stained knife used to slay the victims."

"Throughout the trial and afterwards, Ronald proclaimed his innocence. He claimed that his coat had been stolen, and he was being framed. That defense crumbled when a search of his lodgings turned up jewelry stolen in the robbery. He was sentenced to death, and his children were shipped off to orphanages."

He pointed at the courthouse extension. "That room over there was where a convicted man spent his last night on earth before being hanged in the morning until he was dead. This parking lot was a cobblestone plaza back then. The town folk would come out and witness the cruel hand of justice."

He took a deep breath. The next part gave him the willies. "From the moment he was brought from his cell, until the hangman's noose strangled him, Ronald Grafer proclaimed his innocence as loud as he could. To this day..." he paused and looked down at his manual and quoted the text, "...reports of a man wandering back and forth in this very plaza have occurred. He strides back and forth proclaiming he didn't do it, and calling for his children."

Ryan choked up a little. "He called for each of them by name... Caroline... Abigail... Festus... Garvey... Harry... and wee babe Anna... These names have floated in the air around this building for over a hundred years." He looked around to the faces before him. "And many, many times the people who reported these sightings, said the last they heard was 'I'm an innocent maaaaan!' before it faded away."

Ryan turned and looked at the courthouse. "Sometimes people see him on nights with a full moon..."

"He WAS innocent!" Helen cried out. "That poor, poor man!"

'Oh shit, here we go again!' Ryan thought.

Helen stepped away from the arm of her husband and stood under one streetlight. Ryan thought the woman must be freezing to death—it was late October, and she was only wearing a cotton dress. Those polka dots weren't going to provide any extra warmth, were they? Nope.

Didn't matter a bit. Helen's lips drew back in a snarl as she stabbed a finger towards the courthouse. "The local newspaper found that poor man guilty in its pages the day he was arrested! For days and days stories were printed in The Villmore Standard about the so-called 'loutish layabout that was Ronald Grafer'!" She turned to the group; her eyes tight. "He came from far away and in those days, it was enough to condemn him."

Mildred piped up. "Tell them the rest of the story, hon."

With a sharp nod, Helen continued. "Ronald Grafer did not kill those people. It was the twin brother of the man who owned the Villmore Standard who murdered everyone. His name was James Burns. He was in love with Florence Baxter... and had been in a jealous rage when she married another man. And when she gave birth to her son, it drove him over the edge." She folded her arms. "He was also the landlord and employer of one Ronald Grafer. He bribed a local drunkard to identify the coat and framed Ronald. Why Ronald? Because the poor man had been so overcome with grief at the death of his wife he hadn't worked in a month."

She looked up at the moon above. "He felt that he was 'killing two birds with one knife'... that's what he told his brother, the owner of the newspaper years later." she said in a faint voice.

They all remained silent after she finished. Ryan's eyes darted to the rest of the members of his group. Several of them were nodding in agreement with Helen's tale. Well, the hell with that, he wasn't going to upset the apple cart, so he said, "That's a tragic story."

"It's also true." She looked at him with a steady gaze.

No way he was going to get into an argument. No. Freaking. Way. So, he simply nodded.

Mildred spoke, her voice a soothing balm. "I think... I think we should say a prayer for that poor lost soul." She turned. "Don't you think so too, Doris? We should have done it last night when you spoke of Claudia..."

Doris nodded and stepped up to Helen and took her hands. "Eternal rest grant unto him oh Lord, and may perpetual light shine upon him..."

The group responded 'Amen' and Doris released Helen's hand. She took a deep breath. "I think that's enough for tonight..."

They headed back to the gathering spot in silence.

Chapter Twelve

Crazy Real Fast

I t was a short walk to return to the St. Regis Hotel. The group proceeded in silence as Ryan led the way. He didn't know why, but he was convinced that Helen's tale of woe back at the courthouse was true. His heart felt heavy; he couldn't help but think about the terror and absolute rage that poor man must have felt as they tightened the noose around his neck. He could practically feel the scratching bristles of the rope that bound the man's wrists, and the wave of horror when the hangman's door beneath his feet popped open.

He shuddered. In his mind's eye he saw the bright morning sun, the crowd of onlookers staring at him with mirth as he was led to his doom. They all knew that Ronald Grafer was a lying, murderous bastard—the papers said so! No protest from him would erase that conviction.

Fake news was a hella lot older than the internet...

When he got to the rostrum beside the hotel's entrance where the 'The Haunted Walk' signage was, he turned to the group. Despite his heavy heart, he saw them all smiling at him.

Betty spoke first. "Kind of a Debbie Downer back there, huh?" She slid her gaze over to Helen and Doris. "You two are some pieces of work you know—you ruined the poor kid's tour."

"It's the truth, Betty," Helen replied.

"So what? It's ancient history too!" Betty pointed at Ryan. "He's got enough on his plate; he doesn't need to hear that stuff. Do you, Ryan?"

Ryan let out a long sigh. "I don't know... I mean, sure it ended on a pretty crappy note..." His voice faded and he looked up at the stars and just-about-full moon. "But at the same time, I'm kinda glad to know the truth about the poor guy, y'know?" He took his top hat off and looked at it. "I mean...my *job* is to tell that guy's story, right? And even though it's a terrible thing that happened to him...it's the truth."

"Oh, yeah?" John, Doris' husband had his arm around her shoulders. "So watcha' gonna do about it, bud?"

Ryan looked over at the man. He'd been fairly quiet both nights. Of all the guests there, for some reason he was the most stand-offish. He glanced at John's hand around Doris. His fingers were splayed over her shoulder, pressing in. Come to think of it, with the exception of her antics in the middle of the street last night, he was always, always touching her. A hand around her shoulder like right now, pulling her close, a hand around her waist as he listened to his stories on the walk, and always, *always* holding her hand as they walked around the town. Two old people, and yet he was still really into her.

John held his gaze. His eyes glittered like pale grey discs. "Asked ya a question, bud."

Ryan was a little taken aback. A part of him wanted to snark back at him 'What's it to you?' or maybe 'None of your business'. He wasn't worried about mouthing off to a guest. But instead, he spoke with his heart.

He took a deep breath. "I don't know why... but..." He paused and looked at all of them before returning John's stare. "...tomorrow morning, when I wake up... I'm going to find Ronald Grafer's grave and visit him." He felt the back of his eyes burn and sniffled. "I'm... I'm gonna stand at the foot of his grave and tell him I *believe* him all these years later. And..." his voice broke for a second. "And I'm gonna tell him I'm so sorry for what happened to him."

Shit. He was getting all verklempt here! He brushed his hands over his face and looked up at John. "Good enough for ya?"

John pressed his lips together into a tight white line and nodded. "Yeah. That's really good, Ryan. Really, really good."

Helen took her daughter Angie's hand and together the women stepped up and cupped Ryan's face. A sense of 'Okay' flowed through him. He was surprised that their invading his space so intimately didn't bother him in the slightest.

Angie spoke. "When you do Ryan, bring a rose and leave it for him." Her eyes glistened, shiny with feeling. "That was his wife's name."

"Rose?"

She nodded and leaned forward and kissed his cheek. "I'm so very, very proud of you!" She looked back to the group. "He's bitchin', isn't he?"

Everyone in the group agreed. A chorus of quiet, 'Yeah', 'Yes' and 'Uh-huh' floated up.

Helen rolled her eyes. "Language dear," but she couldn't help but smile.

Angie's eyes sparked. "Hey Ma! I got an idea! Why don't we visit ol' Ronald's grave right now!" She tugged Ryan's hand. "That would be so groovy! We'd *all* go together and wish him well!"

Now her hand was icy. Ryan jerked back, but she held onto him. "No way!" he said. "I'm not walking around a graveyard in the middle of the night! Are you nuts?"

Helen was watching their exchange with interest. "Oh, I don't know... there *is* safety in numbers in case you're scared of a boogie man or whatever dear..."

What the hell? He shot a wild-eyed look at her. "Are you out of your mind too?"

"Oh, honey...it's okay..." She reached out and took his other hand.

"NO!" He leapt back, breaking both their grips.

But both women advanced on him. "Now Ryan," Helen said, "you need to open your mind more. Angie's got a wonderful idea..."

An old woman, in a navy-blue house dress with white polka dots was advancing on him, smiling as if she was asking if he wanted a glass of milk with his slice of freshly baked apple pie was trying to get him to go to some graveyard? At midnight? *With a full moon?* His jaw dropped in shock.

Dick came up behind Helen. "Now, now...you're scaring the heck out of the lad, hon." He tapped Angie's shoulder. "That's enough of that, young lady."

"Awww Daaad!" She tossed her head insolently and put a hand on her yellow pant-suited hip. "You're being a real drag, man!"

From behind them, the other younger couple giggled. "Get a load of her, Moon Dog!" Star chuckled. "Ol Angie's going out there! Hey hon!" she called out. "You drop acid or what?"

Angie spun and glared at the woman. "That's more your style than mine, Star! I'm just trying to help."

Moon Dog hooked his arm around Star's neck. "Be cool, babe. Ryan's okay, and he doesn't wanna." He looked to Ryan. "Ain't that right, man?"

"I gotta go." Ryan replied.

"We'll see ya tomorrow, my man!" Moon Dog replied. He looked over to Angie, who had rejoined her husband. "How about we bring the kids, what do you say?"

"I guess so..." Angie said with a sullen look.

"See you tomorrow, Ryan!" Star called out.

But Ryan was already halfway down the block. That had gotten crazy real fast. It went from sad for poor Ronald Grafer to creepy as hell. He wasn't going to run. No, he wasn't. He was...

He broke into a dead run.

Chapter Thirteen

You Okay Man?

He looked behind him when he turned the corner. Nobody was coming after him. Even though they were all pretty old, if Moon Dog or even Angie for that matter, decided to come after him, he didn't know if he'd be able to get away. He was no runner. Still, he wasn't taking any chances. He kept going for another half a block before slowing to a walk.

Man, adrenaline was great. He wasn't even winded in the slightest.

He must have been a sight to behold. A guy dressed in black, wearing a top hat and black flowing cape... yeah, Jack The Ripper after a hard night's work! He couldn't help but laugh.

That Angie! What the hell was with her? He figured that 'Star' or whatever her real name was would have been the flake, looking like she just stepped out of auditioning for a role as an extra as a hippy in 'Once Upon A Time In Hollywood', but noooo...it was the woman who looked like some 70s sitcom mom who was the nut case.

'Wouldn't mind a damn bit if they decided to not show up tomorrow' he thought to himself. How many more members of that nutty crew were there, anyway?

Oh damn, he wished he had his freaking phone! He ought to call Melanie and fill her in on the insanity of this night! Well, if he was lucky, she'd show up tomorrow, right?

He threw another glance over his shoulder, grateful to see that it was empty.

And quiet.

Really quiet. He cocked an ear and listened. He couldn't hear a damn thing. There was no sound of cars, no wind whispering through the trees. Looking in the living rooms of homes he was passing, he could see the blue hue of TV screens, but couldn't hear anything.

He looked up and down the street. He was the only person on it.

Wait.

Up ahead he saw a figure walking down the sidewalk on the opposite side of the street. A rush of relief washed over him. He kept his pace, watching the figure approach from the corner of his eye.

It was some guy around his age in jeans and a t-shirt, carrying a backpack. Okay, a student from Villmore College. Usually, the sidewalks would have a bunch of undergrads hustling around; even at midnight. They'd be coming from or heading to house parties; it was Friday night for crying out loud!

But just the sight of another person was a comfort.

As the guy drew closer, he noticed Ryan. He slowed his progress down, staring at him as he came down the street. When they were opposite one another, across the street from each other, the guy called out.

"Are you real?"

What the hell? The poor guy must be high on something.

Ryan nodded, but the guy asked again, this time his voice almost a whine.

"Yeah!" He called back. Under the streetlight, Ryan saw the guy looked pretty messed up. His navy-blue polo shirt was stained with what looked like puke, his hair was a tangle of cowlicks; standing out in all directions like he had stuck his hand in a wall outlet. This guy was having a perfectly, shitty Friday night. "You okay, man?"

"I'm fine! I just can't find my house!"

Ohhh... a strung-out student who forgot where he lived. First year undergrads had to live in dorms per university regulations, but most of them moved into apartments in the student ghetto in their second year. Stoned and lost second-year students was a standing joke, especially early in the semester.

"No problem, bud." Ryan stepped into the street. "I just gotta tell you, you're a sight for sore eyes. I haven't seen *anyone* out until you."

"Stop! Stay over there! Don't come near me!"

Ryan froze. The kid's eyes were wild. "I'm just trying to get home! Stay away from me!"

"Hey dude... I'm just trying to help, okay?" Ryan kept crossing the street.

"Noooo!" The kid let out an even louder wail and backed away from Ryan, heading down the sidewalk.

"Hey man!" Ryan called.

"Aaaa!" The kid turned and fled down the block to the corner, turned it and disappeared, screaming every inch of the way.

Ryan stood transfixed. The back of the kid's head was an oozing, red mass. Flaps of his scalp were peeled back and an oozing mass pulsed with every step the kid ran. A shining reflection of skull greased with tissue reflected in the streetlights.

"Holy shit, he's messed up!" Ryan sped off after him. "Hey! Buddy! You're hurt man!" he yelled, running as fast as he could.

But when he rounded the corner, the kid was nowhere to be seen. He ran down to the next corner, calling out "Hey, I'm trying to help you!" At the next corner, again, the streets and sidewalks were completely empty. He yelled at the top of his lungs, "Help! Help!"

But nobody came out. Some of the houses had open windows, techno rock throbbed from one home, another had a smooth reggae beat with party lights flashing and changing colors in sync with the music. Typical Friday night parties, for sure.

But Ryan didn't see a single soul. He went to the house that had the lights flashing on in the second-floor apartment, but the front door was locked. He pounded on it, shouting for help.

Nobody answered.

He stepped out onto the sidewalk again, looking up at the open second-floor window. "Help! Someone's hurt out here!" he shouted over and over.

What the hell is wrong with those people? He hopped up to see if he could catch anyone's eye, but wasn't able to see a single person. That's idiotic. The keg parties he had gone to during his years at Villmore College had always been wall to wall with other students.

Shaking his head, he went to the other residence that was blaring music.

Same damn thing. He couldn't see anyone, through the windows, the front door was locked tight, and he didn't see a single person inside.

With a sigh, he looked up and down the street again for any sign of that poor, poor kid. Lost in the night without a clue how bad of a shape he was in.

'I did all I could, didn't I?' he thought to himself. Probably not, but what the hell else could he do? By all that's holy, when he saw Melanie again, he'd be getting that goddamn phone!

Holy shit.

Chasing that kid had taken him back to the rear of the St. Regis hotel. Where that ghost of Claudia Wheeler was supposed to be.

As if guided by remote control, he crossed the street opposite it and looked up to the dormer window.

As soon as he looked, a candle appeared.

He stood there silently watching.

And it went out.

Chapter Fourteen

Invite You In

"Damn it," Oh, what the hell. Ryan cupped his hands around his mouth. "C'mon down! I'm not scared of you, Claudia!"

What the hell was he doing? He dropped his hands and looked up and down the street. Well, the emptiness of it was some kind of blessing now, right? He called out again.

He was losing his mind. No question about it.

Did he even *see* that kid with the gaping head wound? Did he actually try to get those unseen partiers to help? With the events of his night, everything was more than a little fuzzy.

"Self," (cuz that's what he always says when he talks to himself), "we gotta get you home, have a stiff drink and go to bed." He was beat to hell and back. Shaking his head, he turned from the hotel and wound his way back to his place.

"Mew."

Ryan jumped at the sound by his feet. He was just half a block away from his flat. Looking down, he saw the white kitten from the night before. "Buster!" he laughed, scooping the poor little thing up in his hand. Cuddling it, he scratched its ears, immediately getting a purring response. "How the hell did you get out of my place, huh?" Shit, he had never really been all that into pets, but holding that stupid cat infused him with such a sense of comfort and wellbeing. "You stick around tonight, okay?"

More purring. *'Fair enough'.*

He walked the rest of the way home cuddling and petting the creature, cradling it to his chest. It was asleep already, its ribs rising and falling with each hypnotic purr.

He turned in to go up the steps to his building's entrance and sprang back when he saw what was waiting for him.

"Hello," she said.

∽≫≫ ≪≪ぐ

Sitting on the steps leading up to the front entrance was the most beautiful and frightening woman Ryan had ever seen.

Dressed in a white cotton nightgown, with her feet tucked up, her arms folded over her knees, she looked up at him. Her eyes were deep-set, two pale blue lights peering out at him. Her auburn, almost brown hair was in a tight bun at the back of her head. Beside her was a brass candle holder with a lit taper mounted in its single cup.

She looked at him curiously, her head slightly tilted. "Did I frighten you? I'm sorry."

Ryan's mouth hung open in shock until he felt Buster stir in his hands. The kitten hunched its shoulders and relaxed again. But it wasn't purring now. It lifted its head, looked over at the girl, yawned and nestled back into his hand.

She looked like she was Ryan's age, maybe a few years younger.

Her eyes though... there was something about them that unnerved him. How the hell were they so bright?

She was still studying him. "Are you unwell?"

"What? No, I'm fine. You startled the hell out of me."

Her eyebrows knotted. "Why should you be startled? You asked me to join you." She looked from side to side. "I'm not sure how I got here, I must say; but you looked quite dapper from the street," she nodded at him. "Your hat and cape are rather dashing."

Ryan couldn't help himself. "What, this old thing?" he replied with a smile. "At any rate, I'm glad you approve."

Her lips turned down in a frown. "You were also by my chambers last night as well, weren't you? With a group of people? And you all came by this evening too, didn't you?"

"Yes." He should be terrified out of his god-damn mind. The fact that he wasn't was what frightened him the most. Buster nestled into his palm again, this time its claws pressed against the skin. He absently stroked the back of its ears until it stopped. What the hell was going on here? "I was leading a tour group."

"They were the same people as last night, weren't they?"

"Yes. There were a few new ones, but yes."

She nodded. "Yes, one of them called to me to join you." Her eyes narrowed. "I did not care for that man's tone, though." She looked up at Ryan. "But when you called to me, it felt..." she nodded slowly, "... correct somehow, I suppose." Her eyes flew wide. "I hope we're not spied upon! I am betrothed after all!"

Ryan squatted down so his eyes were level with hers. "Not to worry, ma'am. Your honor is safe with me."

Again, she tilted that head, just so. It was charming as anything. *'Charming? When did you ever use that word to describe a babe?'* shot through his head. Well, when he came up with something that captured innocence and attraction, he'd use that damn word. For now, 'charming' was just fine.

Waitaminnit. Just wait one damn minute!

He was having a conversation with a ghost.

And it didn't bother him a bit.

"You're Claudia Wheeler," he said.

With a mischievous smile, she nodded. "Have we met? Forgive me if we have," she closed her eyes and re-opened them. "Sadly, my mind has been somewhat addled of late."

"No, we've never been introduced. My name is Ryan Walker."

She held out her hand. "How do you do, Mister Walker?"

He stared at her hand. It looked real. Not ghostly or spectral; it was as solid a hand as his own. He took it and pumped it twice before letting go. He stared at his own hand. Nope; felt as normal as any handshake. Her hand was dry, not sweaty and her grasp had been firm.

"May I join you?" He said, pointing at the step beside her.

She giggled and moved over. "Of course! After all, you called to me!"

He sat beside her, still cradling Buster. Any thoughts of sleep he'd had were tossed under the bus. He nodded. "I suppose I did. Thank you for coming."

She tilted her head at him. He noticed that her deep-set eyes were almost like a doe's; the outside corners were slightly cast upwards; almost Asian. They didn't appear nearly as deep set as they had been at first sight. "Now Mister Walker, why did you call to me?"

"I... well... I thought perhaps you were lonely in your room. You've been there for quite some time, no?"

"It feels like years and years sometimes," she agreed, nodding. "But the n..." and a look of puzzlement clouded her face, "it feels to me that I'd just arrived in your city." She shook her head slowly. "If I sound confused to you, please believe me that I'm even more confused inside!"

"My lady, we're all confused by this life at one point or another."

She put a hand on his arm. "That's a comfort to hear." Her head jerked. "Oh! You have a kitten!" It was the arm he had been cradling Buster in. Buster lifted his head and turned to Ryan, then back to Claudia, watching her. She lifted a finger to his face and traced the outline of the little guy's whiskers. "And such an adorable creature! I believe I shall ask my fiancé to provide me with such an adorable animal as a pet."

"Did you have pets growing up? I believe you lived on a farm?"

"I'm…" that baffled look flitted across her face. "I'm not quite sure. My memories before arriving in this city elude me. I believe I have many brothers and sisters, and yes, we did live a hard life on a farm…" She looked up at the sky. "But it feels so, so long ago to me." She shot her gaze to Ryan. "Which is strange, because I've only arrived from there within the last fortnight." She put a finger to her mouth and chewed on the tip. "Why do you suppose that is?"

"Uhhh…. well… time can be slippery, don't you think?"

"Slippery? Whatever do you mean?"

Ryan recalled a high school teacher in a physics class explaining relativity. "Well… let me put it like this—if you accidentally brushed up against a hot stove, every second would feel like hours, correct?" When she nodded, he added, "And yet, if you're in the arms of your beloved, every hour would seem like a minute!" He hoped he got that right.

"Well… I don't have a 'beloved', sir. I'm betrothed by an agreement between my father and Mister William Mayhan."

"Uh… that's the best I got, Miss Wheeler."

"I do, however see your point," she nodded. "Time *can* be a slippery thing." She let out a sigh. "Betrothed. More like sold as chattel."

"You didn't enter your engagement willingly?"

She shook her head silently before saying "My parents told me that Mister Mayhan intends to be very generous to my family on my wedding day... and then even more so upon the birth of my first son." She looked at him with sadness. "My father is far from a talented farmer. Despite repeated attempts at farming his crops failed..." Her voice faded. "Each failure was harder to bear."

Ryan nodded. "It only looks easy on TV."

"TV? What is that?"

Oh boy. Culture shock to the max. "Uhhh... sort of like picture books?"

Claudia shrugged. "Oh. Well..." She sighed again. "This last farm my father worked was for Mr. Sullivan. He owns many, many acreages in the area. He offered generous terms to my father several years ago." She shook her head. "But... after the latest crop failure he now owes a debt to the landlord and intends to seek work elsewhere. His arrangement with Mister Mayhan will settle the owed debt and give my family an opportunity for another chance to make a life."

"Hold on, you just said it was a guy named Sullivan your father owes money to."

"Yes. And it was Mr. Sullivan who made the arrangements on Mister Mayhan's behalf." She looked around them. "He's the wealthiest man in Villmore."

"So you're some kind of mail-order bride?"

She nodded. "It's quite common I've learned. But more so out in the western territories than a city such as here. But I suppose that is the case." Her face fell. "I am from humble beginnings, but I am nimble with needle and thread and not afraid to put my back into work." She looked up at Ryan. "Although, I must confess—even if it's to a stranger—I'm quite afraid of the...

"Wedding night."

"Oh!" She covered her face with her hands and nodded.

"Well, don't be."

"But..."

He took her hands. "It's as natural a thing there is, Claudia. How in the world do you think we all got here?" He added with a quick grin.

She huffed a sigh and looked away.

At that moment, it began to rain. No drizzle warning; it was as if someone turned a valve. A steady, heavy rain began to drench the streets and walkways.

"Oh! How will I return to my chambers! I'll be soaked through and through!"

Ryan doubted very much that she walked here. He looked down at her candleholder. They had been speaking for a while, yet the candle hadn't burned down in the slightest.

His jaw dropped when he recalled his conversation with Melanie earlier in the evening. He stood and held out his hand.

"Miss Wheeler? I think I'm meant to invite you in."

Chapter Fifteen

How Odd...

S he tilted her head. "You're *meant* to?" A bemused smile stole across her lips for a second. "By whom?"

Ryan shook his head slowly. "I have no idea. But I think I should." She remained seated on the step; her mouth closed looking at him expectantly.

The silence lingered, Ryan feeling more and more stupid with each second that passed.

Finally, Claudia said, "Well? When will you invite me?"

Oh shit. He smacked his forehead and stood. Opening the front door to the house, he said. "Please come in, Miss Wheeler."

"Why thank you!" Grabbing her still burning candle, she hopped to her feet and brushed past him into the entrance foyer. She looked from side to side at the closed doors of the two apartments on the first floor. "Is this some sort of inn?"

"Well...it used to be a home for a family, but they broke it up into apartments years ago." He gestured to the staircase. "My flat's on the top floor. After you."

She hiked her nightgown up and Ryan followed. He watched the flex of her hips under the fabric. This girl was a ghost, but looked and felt like a regular person. *Does she even know she's dead? She sure didn't look it.*

He opened the door to his place, and she swept past him again.

When he turned on the lights in the living room, she jumped. "What is that?" she asked, pointing at the ceiling. "Having a flame so close to the ceiling—is that not dangerous?" She shielded her eyes. "And such a bright light!"

Shit. He fumbled with the dimmer switch. "Uhhh...it's a new invention. It's called... a light?" Well, that sounded stupid. But then... what the hell could he call it?

"A light? What a magical thing to behold!" She gestured at the wall switch. "And that controls the height of the wick like an oil lamp? Like some kind of pulley?"

He was *not* going to explain how electricity worked. Hell, *he* didn't know how electricity worked. Ryan took a deep breath. "Yes, it's something like that. This controls the light."

"May I..." she looked at the dimmer switch in wonder and reached out a hand.

"Of course." He stepped away. "Just turn that dial, and the light will grow brighter or lower."

With an open mouth, Claudia reached for the dimmer and twisted it. The living room dropped into darkness. She turned it the other direction, and it bloomed brightly. "A miracle!" she whispered.

No way. No freaking way was he going to turn on the TV.

Buster stirred in his hand. "Make yourself comfortable," he said, pointing at the couch. "Would you care for something to drink?"

"No, thank you."

Claudia sat at one end of the sofa, and Ryan sat at the other. He put Buster on the cushion between them. Buster sat back on his hindquarters, scratched the back of an ear for a moment, then slowly stepped over to Claudia. They both watched in silence as he stepped up onto her lap, circled once and lay down.

She immediately began stroking him. "The purring of a kitty is a relaxing tonic, is it not?" she said absently.

"Yeah." Ryan leaned back against the arm of the couch and stretched out his legs. "So... why exactly did you come here?"

Claudia dropped her head for a moment and shook it slowly. "I don't know..." she raised it and looked at him. "I think *I'm meant to.*"

"Well, I know *that* feeling!" He paused and added. "So, tell me about yourself."

She held up her index finger. "Not yet. Tell me about yourself." She looked around the living room. "I'm an unescorted woman in a strange man's home. I believe I should know more about you."

"You're pretty slick." When Claudia's face registered confusion, he added, "That's meant as a compliment. It means that you're capable of handling yourself in uncomfortable situations."

"Thank you. Now who are you, sir? You've told me your name, but that is all I know of you."

Ryan stood. He doffed his top hat and bowed. "My name is Ryan Walker. I am a recent graduate of Villmore College where I studied the craft of acting and the dramatic arts. I was born and raised in Utica, New York, and have lived here in Villmore for the last four years."

"And your family?"

Family. Shit. She had to go there, didn't she? Ryan let out a long sigh. He tossed his top hat onto the coffee table and undid his cape. He flopped back down onto the couch. "My family is quite small. It's just me now, and my older sister Melanie."

She brightened. "An *older* sister? She must love you very much!"

"Yeah, she sure does..."

"Your parents? They've passed on?"

Shit. "Yeah. They were killed in a car wreck a few years ago."

"A railroad car?"

He waved at her quickly. "No, an automobile." Before she could ask anything more about that, he went on. "They were driving home from the airport after their winter vacation in the Caribbean and hit a patch of ice in a snowstorm. The car rolled several times and... they died."

Oh, man it was close. He tossed off Mom and Dad's senseless deaths just like that. Ever since that night he found out, he'd kept that in a box. But here, with Claudia, that box almost exploded. He closed his eyes.

In his mind's eye, he imagined himself taking two photographs of Mom and Dad, putting them in a steel box and closing it. With a heavy steel padlock, he tightly sealed that box. There was no way he was going to revisit that agony. There would be no point in wallowing in that shit. It was ancient history. He nodded sharply and opened his eyes again to see Claudia watching him wide-eyed.

"You...you sealed up their memories in your heart," she said in a low voice.

He just nodded quickly at her a couple of times; his lips pressed tightly together.

She leaned over to him, staring wide eyed. "You've never wept for them."

"How the hell would you know!"

She blinked at his outburst. "I don't believe I'm mistaken. Were they evil people?"

"Hell no!" In the pit of his stomach he felt a roiling; a pool of bubbling, hissing lava. He shot a hand out at her. "Stop, okay? Just quit it! They died and life moves on, alright?" Shit, she's worse than Melanie. All during the stupid wake and funeral, Melanie had nagged the hell out of him to 'let it out' or some such bullshit. Like he owes the world something?

Claudia sat back. "Very well." She continued stroking Buster. "I find it odd. Do you love them?"

"Yes! They were fantastic people! Dad worked hard, and was a great father! Mom was the absolute best!"

"And yet, you don't weep. How odd."

Ryan huffed out a breath. "Different strokes, how about that?"

"Strokes?"

"People handle stuff in their own way. One artist might like to paint in oils, another in watercolor. Different strokes for different folks." He shook his head. "Jeezuz, you sound like my sister."

Claudia stared off into the distance. "It was a two-day journey by train for me. I'm sure I cried every waking moment, missing my family. I must have been terribly afraid I'd never see them again and was heartbroken. The clack clack of the train's wheels on the tracks were like the sound of hammering of nails into my heart." She swallowed. "It would have been unbearable..."

THE TALE
OF

CLAUDIA WHEELER

Chapter Sixteen

'I Have A Proposal'

The clack clack clack of the wheels of the train were pinging hammers on Claudia Wheeler's heart. She stared out the window of the railcar, seeing nothing as the trees clad in fiery autumn slipped past. Her body ached from being seated in her third-class seat for the last twenty-four hours. Even sighing was painful; her corset prevented her from breathing deeply —it was the first time she'd worn one in all of her seventeen years.

Just seven days ago she lived a completely different life. Eldest of the seven Wheeler children, she was the 'Captain to Mother's General' as Papa put it. The farmhouse needed sweeping out daily, water from the well brought in every morning and night, the young'uns dressed every day and set about to play in the dooryard, away from the chickens and pigs nearby.

Looking after a family of nine people was grueling work. But being able to give Mumma respite was a reward in itself. Mumma and Papa did the very best they could with the cross the Lord asked them to bear. Whilst it was a boisterous home, it was a happy one.

Lucas and Larraby, her next brothers, helped Papa in the fields every day, and suppertime at the huge pine table was always filled with chatter and tales. In the evenings, after supper, Mumma would darn socks and mend clothing by the fireplace and Papa would work with the twins teaching them the fiddle.

Papa was always a much better fiddler than he ever was a farmer. For the last five years they scraped and barely got by on the acreage they tended for Mister Sullivan. He had been kind enough to forebear his claim to harvest the first year—after all, Papa had never farmed before, and there was a poor harvest.

But from the time Papa had arrived in the village of Crocus, his different accent set him apart from the townsfolk. Always polite as small-town people are, they also kept their distance from the Wheelers. And kept any advice and council on how to raise corn and rye on the land to themselves as well.

Papa spent that first winter studying books he managed to get from the Agricultural Library way out in Albany—a two-day journey each way. He had to leave a deposit of five whole dollars in cash when he borrowed the books. Five dollars was a small fortune. He returned them proudly five months later, but returned home empty-handed. The college informed him that the books were in terrible condition and would need to be re-bound, whatever that meant.

So, the five whole dollars they were relying on to tide them over had disappeared.

And poor Papa remained a terrible farmer.

Again.

Years earlier, when he learned that Mumma was expecting their firstborn, he made a decision to leave the tenements of New York city. The five corners were no place to raise children. He found a newspaper advertisement that was looking for tenant farmers upstate and decided to give it a go.

But that first farm had been lost when the landowner sold the property. The second time Papa hired out, there were now two children. That farm was taken by the bank after two years—the landowner had lost everything in a stock market crash whatever that was.

They had rejoiced five years ago when Papa and Mister Sullivan had come to an agreement, but the land was poor. No matter what Papa tried, he had no talent for it. He should have given up after the second year, but Papa was stubborn.

Only the boys were permitted to go to school. Eventually they would grow into men and be the masters of their own homes. They needed to be able to work with sums and read somewhat. For Claudia and her sisters, they would be better served to learn to properly sew, cook and clean to be able to manage a household after marriage. Mumma had looked after teaching them to read and write enough.

By the end of his fifth growing season, Papa was a beaten man. The harvests were barely enough to keep body and soul together for his family, with nothing for Mr. Sullivan to collect as payment. Each year he informed Papa that in 'lieu' of his rightful share, Papa would sign a promise note. In that note, he promised Mr. Sullivan the sum of one hundred dollars for the season.

In five years, Papa had now owed Mr. Sullivan five hundred dollars! For rent! And then interest on top of that! Papa needed to raise almost six hundred before he'd be able to leave the farm! Or else it was debtor's prison for him, and the workhouse for his family! They'd be trapped until they produced enough to pay off his debt! And the workhouse was in Albany!

One evening a week earlier, Mr. Sullivan had stopped by their home.

He arrived in an elegant shiny black coach pulled by a team of two black stallions. His driver shooed'd the other children away and called to Claudia.

"You there, girl! Fetch your father from the fields. Mister Sullivan would have a word!"

Mumma came to the door of their cabin. At the sight of Mr. Sullivan's carriage, her face went white. She put a hand to her chest and approached.

The driver flicked his carriage whip in her direction, making a snapping sound like a pistol shot. "Away with you woman! Fetch Mister Wheeler!"

It took no time for Papa to appear. He approached the carriage, and Mr. Sullivan's hand jutted from the window on the door. A single crook of his finger beckoned father.

The rest of the family stood in the dooryard watching as Papa stepped up and into the carriage.

They couldn't make out the words, but heard Papa's voice rise in protest, only to be silenced with a sharp word from Mr. Sullivan. Their conversation continued until silence fell over all.

And Papa climbed out. His feet were unsteady as he closed the door. With not a word of fare-the-well, the driver snapped his buggy whip at the horses, and with a lurch, they departed in a cloud of dry October dust.

The air was still as they all watched Mr. Sullivan's carriage turn onto the road and disappear around a bend.

Papa turned to Mumma; his face gaunt. "We've been told to leave. Immediately. And I'll be off to prison."

Mumma let out a soft groan, put her hand to her mouth, and collapsed to the ground like a deflating balloon. She stared blankly at her husband; her eyes wide.

"I... I'm so sorry Kate." His voice was barely above a whisper. "I thought I'd get the hang of this farmin', but I'm just no good at it." He spread his hands like he was upon a cross. "I... I wanted the children away from that jungle in New York... but..." he looked about himself in a daze, "... I've made everything so much worse..." His knees went weak. "Three times I tried to farm! Three times! And now..."

"What of the children, Louis?" Mumma keened, as sharp and high as a squealing pig as the slaughter knife was drawn. "What will become of the childrennnn?"

"I... I don't know... Mister Sullivan said that the sheriff will be a'comin' here this week to take me away and ensure you're off his property..."

"What would the sheriff want with you? What have you done Louis?" Mumma's voice was so far away. The past five years had beaten her down; no, that's not right. She was beyond being beaten down; a person beaten to the ground could rise up, but Mumma had no rises left in her. "What did you doooo?"

"I signed a paper when we took the place over, Kate. A promisery note or something like that. I'm in debt to Mr. Sullivan. And with that, he can have me tossed into prison."

Claudia's back straightened, like the backs of all young people, protected from the cruelties of the world, she stood tall. In hopeful ignorance she said, "You did nothing wrong Papa! They can't do such a thing!"

Papa went to Mumma and lifted her to her feet. "They can and they shall, my dear. Mr. Sullivan is a wealthy man, and the world bends to his will, it cares not for the likes of us." Holding his beloved, Papa guided her to the door of their cabin. "Fetch the children home, lass."

That evening Claudia looked to feeding the children. Mumma and Papa sat in chairs by the hearth, holding hands and staring off into space.

The youngsters were frightened at the condition of their parents. Claudia soothed their fears as best she could. "Mumma and Papa had a piece of bad news that befell dear friends from far away and are sad," she lied to them. "They've had a terrible shock, but all will be well on the morrow."

The twins didn't believe a word of her spiel, but kept their silence for the sake of the smallest. As the eldest, Claudia had authority second only to Mumma's, so when she shooed everyone to an early bedtime, that was that.

As she climbed the ladder to the sleeping loft they all shared, Mumma and Papa were still side by side at the fireplace, the logs now glowing embers.

Seeing them there, joined hands gave her a sense of comfort that enabled her to finally drift off. Tomorrow's another day after all.

⤞⤜

Mister Sullivan returned at first light.

They were still at their meager breakfast when the clopping of his horses stirred the chilly morning air. They were approaching at a quick trot; by the time Papa had the door open, the carriage was already at the front of the house. As Papa came out the doorway with cautious steps, Mr. Sullivan bounded out of the carriage with a huge smile and open arms.

Mr. Sullivan was a stout man, round of belly and florid faced, but as light on his feet as a ballerina. "Louis my good man! I have solved all your difficulties!" he called in a voice of hearty friendship.

Papa stared at him dumbly as Sullivan approached.

"I was quite concerned after leaving you yesterday, Louis," Sullivan continued. "I'm a man of business, and it's absolutely imperative I cut my losses with you as my tenant." When he was toe to toe with father, he patted him on the shoulder. "I wish you had been more forthright with me about your total ignorance of agriculture, man! It would have saved all of us..." He gestured at the family who had followed Papa out the door, "... all of us such heartache." His voice dropped. "And myself to such terrible costs."

At the mention of his losses, Mr. Sullivan's face turned dark. "We can not have losses, man! Not in these times!" He poked Papa's shoulder. "And with you in prison—as justified as it would be—I'd never recover those losses!" He shook his head from side to side. "No. Absolutely not acceptable. Not. Acceptable. Louis." With each word, he poked Papa's shoulder again, each jab of his meaty finger driving Papa back a step.

"I don't understand, Mr. Sullivan. What can be done?" the word 'forlorn' would not come near Papa's voice. He was bereft.

In that moment, Claudia saw her Papa differently. He was no longer the bastion of her home, the person with all the answers, light of heart when things were well and dark of mood when the children tried his patience. His voice was as wheedling as the youngest child begging for a taste of jam.

She saw her father as merely a man. And it was unnerving. If Papa could be reduced to a child by a man as bluff and phony as Mr. Sullivan (wealthy as he was) ...how dangerous was this world in truth?

She kept her own counsel, but watched the events unfurl before her carefully.

"Ahhh Louis, what *can* be done indeed?" Sullivan's eyes slid over to Claudia. His heavy mustache twitched as his gaze washed over her; from her heavy shoes, up her cotton apron, past her bosom to her face. He pursed his lips and beckoned her with a crooked finger. "Here girl. Now."

Claudia was bewildered. Mr. Sullivan wanted her to step—

"Now, girl!" he barked.

"Now Mister Sullivan, there's no need to shout," Papa said. He turned and gestured to her.

Another man got out of the carriage's coach. He was a slight man, thinning hair and a sharp nose. He also eyed Claudia up and down. With a quick nod to himself he went to the back of the carriage and opened a trunk lashed to the rear.

Claudia stepped forward hesitantly, like a skittish colt, she approached the men.

"Yes, yes...I believe she will do nicely..." Mr. Sullivan muttered. He walked around Claudia like she was a horse at auction. She could sense his eyes climbing up and down her body as she heard his breathing deepen when he was behind her. "Yes... yes...." A bolt of fear shot through her. Fear of what, she didn't have the slightest idea; but her instincts were telling her in no uncertain terms that she was in a precarious position. She looked at Papa whose face was as confused as her own mind.

"Mister Sullivan!" Mother's voice came from the doorway. "What are you doing?" Mother's voice was not shy at all. Claudia looked over her shoulder to see mother gather her skirts, step off the veranda and storm up to where they were. "You're looking my daughter over like a prize mare, sir! And I don't like it one bit!"

Sullivan ignored Mumma as you would a gnat. A slight distraction, but no more. "How old is the lass, Louis?" he asked.

"Seventeen, sir." Papa's voice was wispy.

"And is she betrothed?"

"What!" Mumma shouted. "Mister Sullivan!"

He gave the slightest of waves with his hand. "Louis?"

"Katie, hush now..." Papa said. "No sir. She's no beaus, either."

"Very good. Very, very good." Sullivan looked over his shoulder. "Are you ready Lenahan?"

The other man had set up the oddest-looking contraption. It was a wooden box, about the size and girth of a tomato crate, set upon three spindly wooden legs. From the back of the box a shroud of black fabric hung down. The man was at the back of the box, half covered by the cloth, fidgeting with something Claudia could not see. He pulled the cloth from his head. "Just one moment, Mr. Sullivan," he said. He stared up at the sky. "The light is quite good, but I'll be needing to use the flashing powder to augment it."

"Very well."

"That shall be an additional fee, Mr. Sullivan."

Sullivan heaved a sigh. "Of course, Mr. Lenahan. Why am I not surprised? I'll want one of the lass and then another of her with her family."

"Yes, sir." Lenahan resumed whatever he had been doing under the cowl.

"Flash powder?" Papa said. "Is that a camera obscura?" His voice was now filled with wonder.

"Yes, yes... Lenahan's going to take some photographs."

"But why?"

"I have a proposition for you Louis. And I believe it will be in your best interest, and that of your family to accept it." Sullivan said those words while watching Claudia.

He then licked his lips.

⤞⟫⟫ ⟪⟪⤝

Seven days later, Claudia was on this train, bound for the city of Villmore to become, after the appropriate time, the wedded wife of one William Mayhan.

She barely had enough time to weep for leaving her home before becoming absolutely terrified at the fate that awaited her.

Mr. Sullivan had laid out their choice matter-of-factly. He had a business associate, Mr. William Mayhan of the city of Villmore, who was in need of a wife capable of bearing children. He had never married and was without an heir to his fortune. With the Wheeler family falling on hard times, he was willing to make good Papa's debt to Mr. Sullivan, and also give the family enough funds to settle in the factory city of Syracuse in exchange for Claudia's hand in marriage. Her ignorance of schooling was acceptable, as long as she was a girl who knew her place in the world.

And the arrangements were made.

Otherwise, Papa would be off to debtor's prison, and his wife and children were in the workhouse.

Her departure at the railroad station (after an interminable wagon ride) was a blur. She cried the entire trip. At least Mumma accompanied her and

Papa. Their local church provided someone to look after the younglings for the time they were away.

She was in a daze at the railroad terminal. They arrived several hours before the train would depart, and while Papa kept a stoic appearance, she and Mumma cried nonstop until she watched them drift away on the platform as the train departed.

Now, an eternity later she was in Villmore, New York. She took the bundle of her belongings from the rack overhead when the conductor informed her she was at her destination.

The railroad station was a tumultuous and roiling ocean of humanity. She had never seen so many people in one place in her entire life!

Her knees knocked as she disembarked her railcar. She was told to 'look for a tall man in a black frock coat by the name of 'Hester'.

Practically every man on the platform was wearing a black frock coat!

As a wave of terror—lost in an unknown city, alone and without a penny—began to wash over her, she heard someone call her name.

She turned to see a tall bald man looking at her.

"Are you Claudia Wheeler?" he asked.

She nodded silently.

"Do you have a tongue girl?" he asked sharply.

She nodded again.

"Then speak damn it!"

"Oh!" And began to cry.

Chapter Seventeen

William Mayhan

William Mayhan's payroll of bribes to local officials and police was greater than the city's entire budget for road repair . And well worth every penny; he was left alone to do as he pleased.

He started out young, working as a stock clerk in the dry goods store. Originally it was named 'Stein's', but when he bought out the founder's grieving widow, he changed it to 'Mayhan's'.

His home was by far the largest estate within the city limits, a wooded property that bordered the great lake, over twenty acres. At the age of thirty, when he banked his first million, he consulted with an architect, decided an overall design and had his older sister Meredith look after its construction.

For the first ten years of her life, Meredith wanted a baby brother. When William was born, she loved him more than their mother did. From birth, Meredith looked after William, doting on the boy and now caring for the man. She never married; the life of a spinster was all she needed as long as that life was shared with her William. As children, neither of them had any need for others—even their parents were but beings in their lives to be tolerated. The world was harsh, but together they bent it to their will.

On his fortieth birthday, Meredith informed William it was time for him to take a wife.

They were travelling to their offices at the start of a workday. Meredith was the dictator of Mayhan's, and William's offices for his other ventures occupied the top floor of their block-long enterprise.

As the carriage rolled down the cobblestones of Washington Street, Meredith cleared her throat.

Opposite her, William lowered his copy of the newspaper and eyed her. That little 'ahem' his sister made had been her signal to him to pay attention since he was a toddler.

"Yes, dear?" he said.

"You need a wife." She was an impressive woman despite her frail frame. Shining steel, devoid of rust or impurities of any sort, Meredith sat perfectly still on the padded seat of the carriage. When it jostled over one of the many ruts and gaps in the roadway, pitching side to side, she barely moved. She stared at William from under the brim of her hat, her eyes holding his.

"Hmph. I've gotten along quite nicely so far without such a distraction."

"Companionship, William. A wife is a good companion for a man."

He snorted. "Companionship? And what pray tell do you think you provide me with, dear sister?" He tossed his paper aside and bent forward, taking her hands.

William was the only man in the entire world whose touch did not make Meredith flinch. She pressed her fingers into his palms, feeling and reveling in the warmth and strength. "You must have a wife, William. You're a man... after all..." She was unafraid of speaking frankly. "Men have needs beyond business."

He nodded. "I know that, and those needs find solace at Mrs. Beddin's."

"But—"

He shushed her. "Any other needs in my life you provide my dear. My refuge from the storms of enterprise, my light to guide my way." He raised their joined hands and kissed hers.

Of course Meredith allowed it. Yes, it was from her brother...she was always safe and sound with him. It did sometimes feel... somewhat unsettling at times. She huffed a sigh and released his hold. "Now William, listen to me. You need a son, and shortly. A boy we could raise, who would care for us in our dotage, but also inherit your estate. What would you otherwise do? Divide it up amongst those toadies you employ?"

When William tried to protest, she sharply waved him to silence. "I've given this substantial thought, brother. I considered you adopting some child, but discarded that idea because the lad would not be our blood relation and I won't have that. I considered giving birth out of wedlock myself—"

"Meredith!"

His reaction was shock at her frankness mingled with... was that a twinge of jealousy? No mind. She continued, "But a bastard child would also have society's scorn, no matter our wealth." Shaking her head, she said, "No. The answer to this dilemma is for you to wed and father two sons at least."

"Two."

"Yes. It's how royalty across the world do it, darling. 'An heir and a spare' is how they put it."

William slowly shook his head. "I can't believe you're actually promoting such an idea."

"You're not getting any younger, William. This situation needs addressing as soon as possible. I won't let this fester."

"Very well, what do you propose? Sending me out in the world on a quest for a bride?"

"That won't be necessary. I've already taken care of that."

"What?"

Meredith rummaged in her bag and pulled out a small leather-bound folder. "You remember James Sullivan, don't you?"

"Of course. We've made substantial profits together on several ventures. Why? Does he have a marriageable daughter?"

"No. And I wouldn't want to unite our family with his anyway. Jim Sullivan is a man better kept at arm's length. But... he has a solution to our dilemma." She opened the small folder and held it out to William.

He took it from her and looked it over carefully. "So, this is who you advocate on behalf of?"

"No, this is the breeder I've chosen." Meredith's voice was even as she watched William's face carefully for any sign of him being smitten. Thankfully, there was none. "She's seventeen, a country bumpkin, but in excellent health according to Sullivan. For a simple fee of a thousand dollars, she'll wed you and become your wife."

He glanced up quickly. "Her hair...it looks almost white..."

"Mr. Sullivan told me in his letter it is the color of fresh corn; quite blonde."

He looked back down at the photo and nodded. "She appears quite healthy and buxom. Is she biddable?"

"Quite. Mr. Sullivan has taken pains to assure me on that front. Her family is in dire straits and she'd do anything on their behalf." Meredith shrugged her shoulders. "And being the wife of a man of such means as yours will be a vast improvement over her current life of sharing a log cabin with the mob of her family out on some patch of dirt in Oswego County."

"Very well."

Chapter Eighteen

Elegant And Urbane

C laudia was seated in an open two seat surrey, pulled by a single horse. The strange man assisted her huffily into her seat, lashed her box of belongings to the back and with a touch of his buggy whip proceeded down Main Street to the St. Regis Hotel.

Claudia wept the entire journey. She was at the mercy of this hulking, strange looking man! Was he the man she was supposed to wed? He must be quite wealthy, as this carriage, shining and new, was of a better quality than the coach Mr. Sullivan had come to their farm in! The wheels were much higher, the horse much, much better looked after, and there were gold trimmings on the wheel spokes. It even had two lanterns on either side, also golden!

But the man... oh dear. He was barrel-chested, and it was no doubt his arms were powerful, as they filled his topcoat to the point of straining the seams of it. He gripped the buggy whip with large meaty fingers, holding the reins to the horse with his other. His eyes, like those of a rooting pig, kept sliding over to her, looking her up and down and making her feel uncomfortable to the point of being afraid.

But what frightened her more than anything was that he did not have a single hair on him! No eyebrows, no eyelashes even. And when she stole a glance to his heavy face, she saw not the slightest hint of a beard. She looked back at his thick fingers. They were as full and thick as a sausage, and as hairless.

When he noticed her examining him, his face turned pink. He snapped at her. "Do I look odd to you?"

Oh dear. She sniffled. "Are you Mister Mayhan?"

He barked a laugh that sounded more like a noise an attacking dog would make. "No, I'm not the man who will share your wedding bed."

"Oh!" How inappropriate!

"I'm Mr. Mayhan's manservant. He sent me to fetch you to your quarters until your marriage." He turned to her as they weaved down the cobblestone street. "You'll be in the 'Ladies Section' of the St. Regis Hotel until your wedding three weeks hence."

"Why three weeks?"

He shrugged. "Something to do with the Church. They need to announce your engagement for three weeks before your wedding. I really don't know those details as I'm not one to waste time on such matters."

"You don't go to church?"

He brayed a laugh. "Sunday is my only free day! I spend it recovering from my Saturday night at Mrs. Beddin's House!"

He looked at Claudia again, this time making her skin crawl. "You could earn a pretty penny at Mrs. Beddin's establishment, I think," he licked his lips wetly, then caught himself. "... but you're to become a fine lady, aren't you? Mr. Mayhan's the wealthiest man in the city!"

It wasn't long before they arrived at the St. Regis Hotel. A white, wooden framed establishment that took up a large part of the block, it loomed over Claudia as Mr. Mayhan's man tied the horse's reins to one of the stand posts. He quickly grabbed her belongings, and she followed him inside.

At the check-in desk, a tall thin man watched as they entered.

"I'm here to place this lass in the Ladies Section," her escort said to the clerk.

"Hmmm...name?"

"Hester. What business is it of yours what my name is, man?"

Claudia's eyes widened as her escort finally had a name. Only one name, but still, she hadn't even thought to make proper introductions prior to joining him on the carriage.

The man behind the counter sighed theatrically. "Not your name, you dolt. The lady's name—" he quickly gasped when Hester's hand lashed out and grabbed him by the vest, yanking him across the desk.

"Who are you calling dolt, you simpering twerp!" He violently yanked the man against the desk two more times.

"Stop! Stop it!" Claudia cried out. She stamped her foot. This was insane!

Hester released the desk clerk, pushing him away with a quick shove. "The lady is Miss Claudia Wheeler. She's to be Mr. William Mayhan's bride. Show a little deference, you."

The desk clerk was ashen faced from the quick assault by Hester, yet his eyes grew wide at the mention of Mayhan. "My apologies, sir." He rooted at papers on the desk. "Ah yes, she's to have the suite... very good." He looked over to Claudia. "You may take your meals at our dining facilities over there," he said pointing. "Just sign your name to any bills; Mr. Mayhan will be looking after everything." He snapped his fingers at the bellhops who had watched wide-eyed the entire scene from their station in an alcove beside the front desk.

Two of them came over. The taller one was around Claudia's age, and the shorter one looked no more than twelve. They both wore bright orange uniforms; two rows of shining brass buttons ran down the front of their tunics.

The older boy tugged his forelock at her and Hester, not meeting their eyes. "We'll take your bags up, ma'am," he said, keeping his eyes downcast. He gestured at the wide staircase. "Ladies rooms are on the top floor." He easily lifted up her suitcase. His eyebrows furrowed, and he looked around. "Just the one?" he asked.

Claudia nodded.

"Is there a trunk outside on your surrey, sir?" He asked Hester. When the man shook his head 'no', the bellhop tested the heft of her bag again.

Everything she owned in the world was inside. She had never felt poor up until that moment. Claudia felt her face warm at the pitying look from the bellhop before he turned and headed to the stairs.

"Let's go, lass," Hester said, grasping her elbow. The touch of his hand made Claudia shudder inwardly.

"You can't go up sir!" the man at the desk called out. "Only for ladies..." his voice faded at the sight of Hester's face when he spun around. While his face was relaxed, Hester's eyes were narrow as he glared at the man behind the desk.

The man took a step backwards from the desk and put his hands up before him, palms out. "I... I suppose we can make an exception, sir."

Hester turned to the bellboys and Claudia. With a sharp nod, he told them to get moving.

On the landing to the top floor there was a desk where a woman was sitting. She looked up from the book she had been reading as the group ascended the final flight.

She had a rounded face, but thin lips. Her dark eyes watched as they ascended. She held a hand out to Hester. "No men allowed," she said.

Hester smirked. "I'll go where I want."

"Then I'll summon the police."

Hester shrugged. "And I'll notify my employer. I'm in charge of this lass. Her name is Claudia Wheeler. She's to wed Mr. William Mayhan."

Hester was empty-handed, but Claudia could not help but see his hand open and flex tightly into a fist, making his knuckles white. This man ached for a fight. With anyone. Again she shuddered.

Glancing down at a sheet on her desk, the woman pursed her lips as she picked up a pencil and marked off a name. Claudia's was the only name on the paper. "Then I'll join you." She stood and swept by them. Taking a key from around her neck, she unlocked a set of double doors and swept them open. "You have the suite at the end, Miss Wheeler," she said as she led the way. She looked over her shoulder at Claudia. "My name is Mrs. Pynchon. I'm the concierge for the women's quarters." She tilted her head to the nearest room. "My own room is here."

It was a plain gray hallway with not a single decoration. Claudia felt like she was being led down a prison corridor to her cell.

The woman opened a door at the end of the corridor. "You have the suite," she said, entering. "It has its own bath, but you'll need to call for hot water to be brought up," she said, pointing to a small room to the right. "This is your sitting area, and your bedchamber is over there." A set of glass French doors separated the other side of the room. Turning to the bellhop, Mrs. Pynchon gestured to one of the dressers where he placed her belongings.

Unlike the hallway, her chambers were exquisite. The walls were a delicate shade of pink, decorated with paintings of lakeside sunsets, downtown scenes and a ship sailing on the ocean. There was a pair of overstuffed armchairs, separated by a small round table beside a small fireplace. On the dresser was an oil lamp and beside the dresser was a china washbasin with a large pitcher. There were two rich white hand towels hanging from a bar at the side of the stand.

Claudia had never seen such elegance in her life.

Mrs. Pynchon then turned to Hester. "Your charge is settled in. You may leave now." She was a short, stout woman. She stepped up to Hester, her neck craning to look him in the eye. "I'm of no concern who your employer may or may not be, sir. She is in my care, and men..." she smirked and looked him up and down briefly before catching his gaze again, "... are forbidden."

The two of them stood silently glaring at one another until Hester smiled like a hungry crocodile. "Very well," he said. He looked over to Claudia. "Your intended will be by some time for introductions." With that, he turned on his heel and left, the bellhop trailing behind him at a safe distance.

"I'll show you your bedchambers now, miss," Mrs. Pynchon said. She leaned forward and sniffed. "You have the stench of the farm on you. I'm going to engage a lady's maid to come and attend you. You'll have a good scrubbing from head to toe, and we'll have something done about these locks of yours." She spun Claudia around and began picking at her scalp. "No lice, thank heavens." She spun Claudia around again until they faced one another.

"Where are you from, child?" she asked gently.

Claudia felt her chin tremble. She took a deep breath and said in a rush, "My parents tended a farm in Oswego County," she said. "I'm to wed Mr. Mayhan...to keep my father out of debtor's jail and my family to go to a workhouse!" She began to cry.

"Stop that!" Mrs. Pynchon said, shaking her shoulders. "Stop that right now! You're about to become the wife of a wealthy man! There's nothing there to cry for!" Her voice softened. "You're far from home, and I under-stand that." She gestured at one of the windows. "Come here." She tugged Claudia to the window.

Claudia almost got dizzy looking down at the people in the street. She grasped at the windowsill for balance. She'd never been this high off the ground before. When she collected herself, she watched the busy comings and goings below her.

Horse-drawn wagons, men pushing carts laden with vegetables and goods all competed with one another and pedestrians in a hullabaloo of activity below her.

"Many of those people below, especially the poorest ones," Mrs. Pynchon said, pointing at a group of men dressed in the shabbiest of clothing, "Left their own homes across the ocean to come here. Many do not even speak English. And when winter comes... some of them will freeze to death in the street below..." She turned to Claudia. "While you shall be drinking tea and sherry in the most elegant home in the city. Your family will never know hunger, nor cold again. You have naught to shed tears for."

It was like a sun rose in the back of her mind. Mrs. Pynchon was absolutely right. Now she didn't have the slightest idea just *how* she could ensure the well-being of her family...but how on earth could a man let his wife's own kin starve or freeze?

A cloud passed over her new dawn. "Is he... kind?" She took Mrs. Pynchon's hand in hers and grasped it tightly. "Is he... is he a good man?"

The older woman looked away, chewing her lower lip. "I really don't know, Miss." She took a breath and smiled wanly. We're not members of the same social circles if you know what I mean." She saw the crestfallen expression on Claudia's face and quickly added, "I also don't know if he's a bad man..."

With a sigh, Claudia replied, "Well there is that, I suppose."

"Wait! I forgot! There was an article in the newspaper last week about how he gave a handsome sum of money to the hospital!"

"Truly?"

"Yes! They want to build an additional wing in the hospital! And the story in the paper was how..." she paused. "The elegant and urbane Mr. Mr. William Mayhan simply wrote a check for the needed balance."

"I know what elegant means, it means refined, does it not? But I don't understand 'urbane'. Is that a good thing?"

"Hmmm…I think so. The article was quite laudatory in its nature." Mrs. Pynchon tilted her head. "Do you read, child?"

"Yes! Mumma taught us all to read the Bible! I can quote you many verses from it!" Mumma had told her to not let on that she read. *'You're going to a strange land, Claudia; let them underestimate you,'* she had said. But Mrs. Pynchon was already treating her like she was her own. Still… "Please don't let on that I do."

Mrs. Pynchon waved a hand. "None of my affair. I just want you to know that the hotel has a library of books in the lobby for you… and a dictionary. I'm curious myself to determine just what that word urbane means too!" Mrs. Pynchon felt proud. The scared rabbit that had ascended the stairs now looked like an excited puppy. "Now let's clean you up, feed you and put you down for the night. I'll summon a lady's maid to help you with your bath."

Claudia's eyes sparked with annoyance. "I know how to bathe myself ma'am."

"Oh my darling, I know you do! But a lady's maid will rid your hair of any knots painlessly and ensure that your appearance will be quite suitable. After all, you have a big day tomorrow, do you not?"

"Oh yes! Mr. Mayhan will formally propose marriage tomorrow! And I'll accept!" Claudia clapped her hands. Her life would also be elegant! And 'urbane', whatever that meant—it would be grand!

She would never be more wrong for the rest of her short days ahead.

Chapter Nineteen

Urgent

While Claudia was being bathed and groomed by a ladies' maid engaged by Mrs. Pynchon, Meredith Mayhan was putting the final piece of her plan in place.

Her younger brother, bless his heart, had a keen ability in business affairs, but alas Michael was a mere stock boy when it came to family matters. Her first part was successful; Michael was open to settling down and creating heirs. And now her final goal was about to be reached.

She was sitting in the office of Harlan Melincourt, the majority owner of Atlantic-Pacific Railroad. His combined interests in the railroad, and Nazareth Steel, along with significant Wall Street holdings made him one of the twenty wealthiest men in the country. Let the Rockefellers, Carnegies, Mellons et al. fight it out for the title of richest; the newspapers hounded those men without fatigue. Mr. Melincourt and Meredith had in common the philosophy that it is a more peaceful life to live and thrive in the shadows of so-called 'titans of industry'; there is much to profit from in remaining un-noticed.

And honestly, what difference does it make if one's wealth is one hundred million or one fifty million? One couldn't spend it all in either case.

When she was ushered into his spacious office overlooking the New York Stock Exchange, he stood up from his desk as a gentleman should. He was no Andrew Carnegie; rather than being a bloated whale, Melincourt was wasp thin, and graceful as a circus tumbler as he came around his massive desk to take her hand and guide her into her visitor's chair.

"A delight to see you, Meredith as always," he said. "To what do I owe the pleasure of this visit? Your telegram said it was of the greatest urgency. Is everything well? Please tell me your brother is healthy."

"My brother is in wonderful spirits and health, Harlan, thank you for asking."

Melincourt took his seat behind the desk and tilted his head at her. "Is this a social call then? I normally conduct business with William..." he let his voice trail off.

Meredith tilted her head from side to side. "Somewhat social, I suspect, but there is an element of business as well."

"Hmmm...now you have me quite curious."

"And how is your family, Harlan? Is your wife well?"

"Thank you for asking. Lilibeth is happy and healthy. She's organizing a benefit ball next week for some charity or another. I'll tell her you've inquired."

"Please do." Now to see if there was a prospect for her plan. "And Maribel?"

At the mention of his only daughter, Melincourt's mouth turned down for a moment. "Maribel is Maribel, Meredith." His eyes snapped up at her. "Interesting you asked about my youngest child and only daughter and none of my sons."

"Well... I'm sure they're happy and healthy, are they not? All wed with families of their own, working with you in your business." She made a fluttering gesture with her hands. "Alas, I feel as if Maribel is a sister to me. Unwed, with no suitors..."

"Not for lack of effort on my part, I'll admit." He shook his head ruefully. "The only potential beaus that have shown any interest in her have all turned out to be charlatans and carpetbaggers looking for a share of my wealth." He let out a deep sigh. "That riding accident she had as a child cost her more than her leg I'm afraid... what sane man of means would be interested in an amputee?"

"You make it sound like she's one of those men who wander the streets from the Civil War! It's but from below the knee, I've been told."

Harlan sat back in his office chair, the springs barely squeaking. He folded his hands behind his head, his eyes watching Meredith carefully. "Your sources tell you the truth."

"I've also been told that she's quite bright and of good spirits nevertheless."

"Her faith in God and His plan has been a comfort, yes."

"It's a terrible burden for you, Harlan. To see a loved one looking down a future alone." When Harlan didn't reply, she continued. "I had been terribly concerned for my brother's own future. William is now forty years of age." She made a small shrug. "Thank goodness he's a man; he's many healthy years before him. I've made arrangements for him to be wed shortly."

"*You* made the arrangements."

She nodded. "Yes. Thank goodness we're not residents of New York city. The social circles you inhabit have no impact on us in far away Villmore. My brother needed a healthy woman, God-fearing of course, who will abide to her husband's needs and wishes. I've found a suitable candidate."

"Oh? Has a date yet been set for the wedding? I hope to be invited to the celebration." His voice held no timbre of joy; he was watching her like a hawk.

"Shortly, I think. She's a mere farm girl."

"A *farm girl*? You can't be serious, Meredith."

She shrugged. "It's important that William have heirs, sir. I think an arrangement such as that would be fruitful. After all, she has many brothers and sisters."

"Each of my own sons have four children at least, Meredith. And my dear wife bore five children, all who survived infancy."

"Hmmm... healthy stock, I'd say..."

"And although she wears a brace and artificial limb, my Maribel *still* rides. And hikes. Quite the healthy lass."

"I see..."

"And she's but twenty years old."

The two of them held one another's eyes in the ensuing silence.

Finally, Harlan nodded slowly, and Meredith nodded in reply before he even asked, "Is there any possibility that your brother might reconsider his intentions with this country bumpkin? It sounds to me like she's somewhat handicapped." He flipped a hand carelessly. "Poor education, no breeding, probably has never had servants...." He looked up at her. "Are you certain dear William is acting wisely?"

"*Dear* William? Harlan, I had no idea you held my brother in your affections!"

He shrugged and made a moue. "I've done business with him, of course; he's been honorable and we've both profited. The times we entertained together had been quite enjoyable." He nodded sagely. "William is a good man, one I'm proud to call a friend..." His eyes darted to her again. "But is this a wise choice? Is he smitten with this country lass?"

Meredith laughed lightly. "He's yet to meet her. I'm the one who has made the arrangements."

"Really."

She remained silent for just a moment before replying with a nod of her head. "Yes, really." She leaned forward and put a hand on the edge of his desk. "Do you think I could make better arrangements, sir?"

Harlan leaned forward. "I think so. I truly do."

"Tell me more."

❯❯❯❯❯ ❮❮❮❮❮

An hour and a half later, with a check for a full million dollars as the down payment of Maribel Melincourt's dowry in her handbag, Meredith burst into the offices of Western Union. She pushed her way to the front of the line unapologetically, exclaiming "It's a matter of life or death! I must send a telegram immediately!"

When she got to the clerk, she filled out the form:

TO: WILLIAM MAYHAN, VILLMORE NEW YORK

URGENT URGENT URGENT

UNDER NO CIRCUMSTANCES PROPOSE TO MISS WHEEL-ER TOMORROW.

WONDERFUL NEWS. I'M RETURNING HOME FROM MAN-HATTAN AND SHALL TELL UPON ARRIVAL

LOVINGLY, YOUR SISTER

MEREDITH

Chapter Twenty

To Plots And Schemes

When Meredith got off the train at Villmore Station, it was William, not Hester, who was waiting for her at the First Class carriage. Before he could say a word, she shushed him by holding a finger to his lips. "We'll speak of matters when we get home."

He called to a porter to load her bags on the back of the carriage and helped her up and onto her seat.

His face was stern, but Meredith didn't care a whit. He'd come around as soon as she gave him the news. And she certainly was not going to do it while riding in a surrey!

Presently, they arrived at the manor. William instructed the staff to see to Miss Meredith's belongings and beckoned her into the study.

Closing the heavy door, he turned to her and said, "What in the world is going on?"

Smiling at him silently, she opened her handbag. She removed the envelope and handed it to him. "Open it."

His eyes almost fell out of his head when he looked at the check. "A million dollars? From Melincourt?" He shot a look at her. "What did you do?"

"I saved you from marrying a farm girl, my dearest! And got you millions in cash on top of that!"

"Whaaat?"

She explained to him her trip to New York city was to see Harlan Melincourt and make an arrangement for William to wed his youngest daughter in place of that country bumpkin Claudia Wheeler. Harlan, in turn welcomed the prospect of his crippled daughter finding a husband of William's caliber to be a perfect idea. As a goodwill gesture, he sent the cashier's check, and promised to add millions more to it on his daughter's wedding day.

In addition to a dowry worthy of King Midas himself, William was also going to become an informed insider on Wall Street's most profitable dealings through his new father-in-law. The inner sanctums of Wall Street make for a walled off granite fortress, and by marrying Maribel Melincourt, dear William was no longer on the outside looking in. The Mayhan fortune was going to explode in titanic proportions.

"Now pick your jaw up off the floor, William, it gets even better than that!" she said smiling.

"But... she only has one leg!"

"Just from below the knee, dear boy."

"But..."

"William! Of course, she's flawed! But don't you think a girl from a tenant farm won't have flaws? Oh, dear me! I haven't even met the poor thing, but I'll guarantee you that she'll not have any musical abilities, won't be able to read a word, nor will she be welcome in proper homes in Villmore, let alone New York! Yes, yes, she has legs and arms, but you must understand that she's not nearly as good a match for you as Maribel!"

William had to sit down. With a sigh, Meredith poured whisky into two tumblers and handed him one.

"Why in the world did you do this?"

She snorted. "It was my plan all along. I wasn't going to have you call on Miss Melincourt and attempt to woo her. You'd be terrible at it. No, I planned to have Harlan Melincourt snatch you away from that country girl at the last second—feeling a sense of victory as it was—and finally marrying off his only daughter." She raised her glass in a toast. "Marrying her off to a fine, fine man if I may say so."

"I see. You planned this all along." When she nodded, he added, "Without saying a word to me!"

"That's right. You're only a man. You'd be too soft-hearted, and soft headed to go through with this. And, to be honest, I wasn't sure it would work at all." She tapped the check William had placed on the desk. "But work it did!"

He shook his head slowly. "Plots and schemes..."

She shrugged. "It's how women in this world advance, darling."

A cloud passed over William's face. "And what of the girl?"

Meredith laughed lightly. "You just referred to her as 'The Girl'. She was to be your intended wife and you do not even recall her name."

William's mouth opened, then closed with a sigh. "You're right. I cannot recall her name. What is it again?"

Meredith made a short wave with her hand. "Her name is of no matter, my dear. The name you need to know is Maribel Melincourt."

He nodded slowly. "Of course. But what is to happen to the farm girl?"

"Does it matter?" When William didn't immediately reply, she added, "I'll send her back to the bosom of her family with letters of reference for her to gain a position of one sort or another in Syracuse. That's where her family is resettling. She'll also have a generous honorarium for her troubles and disappointment for not becoming 'Mrs. William Mayhan'. Does that sound fair?"

"So, you'll go and see her?"

Meredith burst out laughing. "Absolutely not! I'll dispatch your man Hester to rid us of this problem!" She blinked her eyes at her brother. "Your man's quite adept at that sort of thing, is he not?"

William stared at his glass. "Yes, Hester's... adept, yes." He shivered slightly.

Meredith caught her brother's hesitation. "Then it's settled!" She held her glass out. "Let us toast to your new fiancée!"

William clinked her glass with his own. "To plots and schemes..." he said.

"To plots and schemes!"

Chapter Twenty-One

Call Me Meredith

Late that Saturday night, as Hester Grolsch walked down Governor Street on unsteady legs he heard the church bells toll twice. Two AM... not too bad; he usually fell into his bed with the sun peeking up on Sunday mornings. Ahhh but dear Sophie was as exquisite as always entertaining him in her chambers at Mrs. Beddin's house. She wore him out thoroughly and completely. She even graciously led him to the door to make his departure rather than remain in her chambers!

Who was he kidding? That wench moved him along so she could 'entertain' other clients that night. He couldn't really blame her; after all, it was money that made the world go round and round...

He let himself onto the grounds of the Mayhan estate through the steel door set into the eight-foot-high walls. Only he and the drayman had keys to that lock. Fair enough. He'd be able to get to his quarters easily. His loft dwelling over the storehouse afforded him enough privacy; no prying eyes would be able to follow his activities set back this far from the main house.

He'd take his breakfast tomorrow while the rest of the servants were sitting down to their luncheon.

He loved his Sundays off. Not because he'd be in chapel or a church moaning prayers or bleating their hymns. No, Sundays were meant to recover from his enjoyments of his Saturday nights. A few hands of poker at Milligan's cellar, then out to the warehouse section to watch a bare-knuckle fight, and ending his evening in the billowing charms of dear Sophie. Ahhh...another night well spent.

He glanced up at the window of his dwelling and stopped. He could see the light of an oil lamp glowing through the glass.

Someone was up there.

Who the hell could it be? He hadn't any 'disagreements' with anyone in months! And the last one was just teaching that Chinaman a lesson in minding manners. Still... with a gesture of habit formed by years of a hard man's hard life his hand patted the back waistband of his trousers to ensure his sheathed blade was in place, then wandered to his back pocket where he kept his leather-bound lead cosh—a six-inch bar of lead wrapped in leather ending in a loop ended many, many difficulties before they got too far out of hand.

He entered the main door of the warehouse and looked to the stairs leading up to his accommodations. Yes, there was a lamp glow, not a candle; the light was too strong. He closed the door quietly, not latching it for fear of noise and stepped softly to the stairs. Every squeak and groan of that staircase was well known to him; he'd be able to ascend as silent as a ghost. If whoever was up there wasn't watching the stairs, they'd have a quick and dirty surprise.

Like a fleet-footed shadow he glided up the steps, crouched low, holding his cosh in one hand and his blade in the other.

He was a big man. If one saw him seated at a bar, they'd make the mistake of thinking him a lumbering ox, judging by his size. But as a boy in Wales, he was called 'Dancer' on the rugby fields. He had an almost preternatural ability to skip, slide, pivot, jump and spin like a ballerina on a stage. As he matured in size and bulk, he retained those gifts. Many a man was shocked at his cobra quickness; he usually got the first blow in, and his heft more often than not ensured it was also the last.

In a single hop he leapt to the top landing, clearing the half wall beside the staircase.

"Hello Hester," said Meredith Mayhan. She was sitting in his wing-backed chair by the fireplace, the glow from the oil lamp surrounding her with a golden aura.

She was perched on the edge of her seat, her back perfectly straight. She was wearing a deep blue, almost black taffeta dress with a high collar buttoned at her neck. She was hatless, her auburn hair flowing over her shoulders in ringlets.

Her always stern demeanor belied the fact that she was a great beauty.

And in his quarters. Alone.

My my, this situation was pregnant with possibilities! Hester smiled as he stepped over to the sitting area. Beside her she had an open bottle of whiskey and two glasses already poured. My, my...

"To what do I owe the honor of this late hour visit?" he asked, standing before her.

"Put those things away," she replied, her finger gesturing at his blade and cosh. "I'm certainly no threat to your well being." She primly rested her hands on her lap, holding him with her gaze.

He secreted his weapons and put his hands on his waist, looming over her. "How did you get in?"

Meredith tilted her head at him. "I own this building, sir."

"Your brother owns it."

"There's no difference." She held up a key. "We have keys to every lock on every property we own."

"How romantic."

Meredith's eyes flared at his audacious insinuation, but remained silent.

"In the still of the night you come to my rooms," he took a step forward. "Any normal man would take that as flattering. So, tell me, my dear; how long have you longed for me?" He was upon her, reaching out to grasp each of the chair's wings. There. She's not going anywhere.

Meredith had stayed completely still during his approach, holding his eyes as his thick hands held the back of her chair. The woman was rather absolutely fearless, or else deeply attracted.

"Step away, Hester," she said, her voice even. Not a shred of fear in this one.

"Oh, I don't know, *Meredith*..." he lowered his head.

"Stop." She shifted in her seat.

Ahhh... finally a crack in the facade! He loved it when they feared him. "I don't think so." He lowered his mouth to hers.

"Then you'll die where you stand."

The metal point easily slid through his coat and shirt, digging into the flesh of his chest just below his ribcage. Hester stilled.

"I'll drive this icepick up into your heart if you do not step back. Now."

He felt the pressure increase. She had him!

Hester pushed away from the chair with a light laugh. "Well now, well played Meredith!"

"That's Miss Mayhan!" she snapped.

"Oh no, my dear, not at all. Perhaps, *perhaps* in public. But you're still sitting in my quarters; I'm entitled to that familiarity." He was still smiling, but felt a small trickle of blood on his skin. He shook his head. "You're the only person to draw blood from me in twenty years and yet be still able to walk, Meredith."

She let out a sigh. "Fetch yourself a chair from your table, you oaf. I have a proposal for you."

Well now... "Really? Of what sort? It's certainly not for my affections." He stepped to his table and retrieved one of the chairs around it. Flipping it backwards, he settled across from her, the whiskey between them.

"It's along the lines of the special tasks my brother has given you in the past." Her mouth was a thin line. "Such as when that banker Seymour Cohen attempted to purchase a majority stake in our lumber mill by calling our line of credit?"

"Poor Mr. Cohen. What a tragic accident that befell the poor man." Falling down that flight of icy stone steps coming out of his offices that night. Of course, he had been brained as he came out the door of his building by the cosh, and *then* pitched down the stairs. "Tragic accident, I've heard."

"Or that harlot from Mrs. Beddin's house?"

Hester's head shot up. "You know of poor Lorena?"

"I'm aware of every activity you've performed on William's behalf. Who in the world do you think encouraged him to engage those services?"

"Was her hanging *your* idea or your brother's?"

"Poor lass thought she could accuse good William of putting her with child," Meredith replied. "It's good to know she kept her condition secret prior to going to William, yes?"

"Aren't you curious as to if she suffered?"

Meredith slow shook her head from side to side. "My only interest is that the deed was done quickly... and quietly."

"And I'm sure, having her pen that note before hanging, under the pretense of being paid to leave town? Was that your idea as well?"

Meredith's eyes looked up at the ceiling. "Let me see... *'I'm moving on to better things than here in Villmore. Farewell all...'* did I quote that correctly? I wanted her words to be just right, so she'd write them as a farewell note in her own hand..."

"And the investigation would conclude it to be a suicide note. Well played Meredith."

With a satisfied smile, Hester continued. "And those four souls who made the mistake of hijacking your payroll delivery to the sawmill?"

"A month's wages for seventy-five men? That was an expensive loss, Hester."

"And was it your idea that their hands be severed and strung around their necks?"

She leaned forward with a glint in her eye. "You *did* follow your instructions to amputate them prior to dispatching them, correct?"

Hester let out a huff of air, nodding. That moment with her at the wingback chair? She would have certainly killed him if he didn't back away. This woman was no spinster. She was stone cold. "Well then, Miss Mayhan, what can I do for you?"

"There's a young lady at the Regis Hotel."

He nodded. "Yes, Claudia Wheeler is still awaiting your brother's proposal. It's been almost two weeks, and she's yet to see him."

"She needs to go away, Hester. Tomorrow night." She reached in her bag and withdrew a stack of bills. "This is two thousand dollars. Give her what you think is necessary to have her leave and never return." She passed it to him. "And *do* whatever you think is needed to ensure that she never breathes..." she stared at him. "Never, ever *breathes*... a word of this to anyone." She resumed her perch on the edge of the chair, back as straight as a flagpole. "You may keep as your fee whatever is left over."

He riffled the bills. This was by leaps and bounds much, much more than what William had paid him in the past. "Never breathes a word," he said. "I can assure you that will be the case."

"Good!" She passed him a glass of the whiskey. "A toast to your successful completion!"

He took the glass and downed its contents in a single gulp while Meredith took but a small sip. He winced. "This has a coppery taste to it."

"Yes it does! It's a special ingredient they use. It makes it smoother over the tongue, don't you think so?"

He shrugged. "If you say so. I can handle my liquor no matter."

She tilted her head towards the bottle. "I'll leave this with you tonight. And..." Her eyes were dancing now. "I'll be awaiting you here again tomorrow night for your return." She leaned forward. "And who knows what could transpire then?" she asked, brushing her arm.

Who knows indeed! "It will be my utmost pleasure, Ma'am."

"Tomorrow...call me Meredith."

Chapter Twenty-Two

'Dear Mumma And Papa...'

Dearest Mumma, Papa, Lucas, Larraby, Iris, Daniel, Mary and little George:

I write to you with a heavy heart.

I arrived in Villmore Monday last, and have been in my hotel room for almost two weeks now. The journey was quite tiring. The novelty of boarding and travelling on a train wore off much faster than I imagined it would. I had so looked forward to watching the world slip by as we travelled on the rails, but in all honesty, the towns and wilderness we passed through quickly became a blur.

I'm quite afraid that disappointment was an omen of further and deeper disappointments to come.

When I arrived in Villmore. I was met by Mr. Mayhan's servant Hester. I do not know the man's full name, just 'Hester'. He's a quite big man, Papa; as tall and broad as a circus strongman that we have seen pictures of in Harper's Weekly. But unlike those illustrations, Mr. Hester has no mustache.

Nor sideburns. In fact, he must suffer from a disease I imagine, because I was not able to see a single hair on his person! No eyebrows, nor lashes, no shadow of a beard; and when he was driving the carriage to take me from the station, I was able to see that the backs of his hands were as free of hair as a newborn's as well. How curious, no?

As I said, further disappointments…

Since my arrival, I've been a guest at the St. Regis Hotel. It is quite smart! It's four stories in height! My chambers are on the top floor, and it's as if I were on a cliff overlooking the busy streets below. There is a restaurant and saloon on the main floor, along with a small newsstand and a place where gentlemen can get their shoes shined.

My chambers are impressive, Mama! I have a room just for sleeping, and it is in a magnificent featherbed. There is also a room they call 'the water closet'. It takes the place of our outhouse! With a pull of a chain, a thunder of water roars, and the chamber pot is washed as clean as a whistle. I hope to be able to show it to you all one day.

I also have, separate from my 'bed-room' (as it's called) a 'parlor'. It's a separate room entirely where I can sit by a fireplace and read if I so desire. The hotel has a collection of books available for their guests to read at their leisure. At the time of this writing, I've already read an entire book!

This establishment is quite grand.

I've been taken under the wing of Mrs. Pynchon. She's an employee of the hotel, whose job is to ensure that the section where women who are travelling alone can reside with a sense of dignity and propriety.

She's been like a fairy godmother to me. She's taken me shopping for new clothing for after the wedding. She calls it a trousseau; it's done by all of the fine people she says. She has told me that I wouldn't be needing all of the other items such as linens or chinaware as Mr. Mayhan's home has all those things.

Mama, I have a hat! Several, actually. No more bonnets such as we wore on the farm.

Now despite all this bounty, I am rather concerned.

I was supposed to meet with Mr. Mayhan the day after my arrival in Villmore. But alas, I had been told that he was away on a business emergency and to await further word. Now today is Sunday (and yes, I did attend services with Mrs. Pynchon Mama!) and it's now been many whole days since my arrival. I was last told that I ought to hear from Mr. Mayhan at any moment. He needs to 'officially' propose marriage or something, and then our betrothal needs to be read at church for three weeks, and only then will we be permitted to marry.

I'm quite on pins and needles to see him soon.

What if he decides that I'm not suitable? I'm terribly worried. I've had a smattering of the taste of a fine life and I do like it very much. But more importantly than that, as a woman of position I'd be able to help you all get on better than it has been for the last years and years.

But alas, I have a deep sense of foreboding about all these matters now. I'd be completely distraught if I would be unable to assist you all in these difficulties. Were our arrangement with Mr. Mayhan not to bear out, I'd return home to just become another mouth to feed, and I won't have that.

There. She'd finish the letter in the morning. During the last five days, Mrs. Pynchon had been as supportive as an oak for her feelings of despondency and fear of it not working out. In fact, what Mrs. Pynchon told her after church today gave Claudia a great deal to hope for.

⟫⟫⟩ ⟨⟨⟨

"My dear," she had said in her most serious tone. "If Mr. Mayhan has a change of heart, you will still be well. You'll still be able to provide assistance to your family."

"How ma'am? I've a strong back, yes; but how?"

The older woman laughed lightly. "How many younger brothers and sisters do you have?"

"Six. I'm the eldest of seven."

The older woman nodded sagely. "So, you're telling me that all your life you've looked after children."

"Yes."

"Well my dear, there is ample work for an honest and kind young lass in this." She patted Claudia's hand. "You can become a nanny, and if it works well, you would be able to move up to become a governess." She gestured at the grand homes near the church. "All these houses have children in them; some of them have as many as five young ones. A good nanny is a godsend to the wives of these men. Having one such as yourself would be a blessing to them." She winked an eye. "A blessing they are willing to pay handsomely for."

"For what? To look after children?" Claudia couldn't believe her ears.

"Yes, you silly goose!" She grasped Claudia by the elbow and arm in arm, they walked away from the finer homes for several blocks. A while later, the great houses gave way to more modest homes. Where there had been sweeping homes built of oak, limestone and brick surrounded by high stone walls and iron fences, there were now small door yards and clapboard walls.

"What do you think of these homes, my dear?" she asked.

"They're quite lovely. Not as elegant and grand as the other homes, but lovely houses."

Mrs. Pynchon nodded. "These are the homes of the shop-keepers, the draymen and millwrights." She pointed at a quaint two-story home with a peaked roof. "Isn't that a nice home?"

"Yes…"

"That home is where the nanny to the Haliburton family's governess lives. The children, there were three, are now all grown and with families of their own. Her work is now done, and she lives there. The three children love her dearly and look after her quite well." She laughed lightly. "She's but forty-five years of age and is comfortably retired now!" She pointed to another home further down the street, a lovely home of white clapboard. "That's the home of 'Miss Skeffington'. She's the retired governess of the Wainwright family. She raised not one but two generations of children. Again, she lives comfortably." She stopped and turned to Claudia. "These women live as well as any woman in those great homes, my dear. They do not have servants, no. Nor do they have philandering spouses, however. What they do have is independence."

"What does this have to do with me, ma'am?"

"Well, when it had been three days and no Mr. Mayhan, I took it upon myself to make inquiries with these two women. They've each assured me that a young woman such as yourself would be a valuable asset to any home." She waggled her eyebrows at Claudia. "I did sing your praises loudly, my dear, yes; but I told them the truth about you." She patted Claudia's arm again. "So fear not if Mr. Mayhan has a change of heart. The world will still be at your feet!"

⋙ ⋘

So perhaps things weren't as dark as they seemed but a day earlier. She'd tell her family that she wouldn't be returning home, and explain why. She picked up the pen and began writing.

If things don't resolve with Mr. Mayhan, Mama and Papa, I won't be returning home. I'd just be a further burden.

Before Claudia could write another word, a knock at her door startled her. It was late, the brass clock on the mantle over the fireplace showed it as being almost midnight.

She scampered to the door of her room and stopped. Mrs. Pynchon had always said not to open the door without asking first who is there.

"Who is it?" she asked.

"It's Mrs. Pynchon, dear. I have Mr. Mayhan's manservant with me. He needs to see you on a most urgent matter."

Claudia flung open the door. Mrs. Pynchon was at the fore in a dressing robe and her head wrapped in a cotton scarf, with Mr. Hester looming over behind her. Both of them wore expressions of grave concern on their faces.

When Mrs. Pynchon moved to enter the room, Mr. Hester placed his hand on her shoulder and pulled her back.

"The news I have is for Miss Wheeler first, ma'am," he said. "I'd appreciate you giving us privacy as I relate it to her."

Mrs. Pynchon spun around. "I won't be having men in the ladies' rooms without a chaperone sir!" She had to arch her neck to look up at him.

"I... I understand, ma'am, I truly do," he replied. "But this is an extremely sensitive matter that Miss Wheeler needs to be informed about. I was given clear instructions that they were to be for her ears only." The expression on his face was almost comical in that he looked so supplicating. He let out a sigh and shot a glance to Claudia. "If I'm unable to discuss this with her in private, then... I should leave." He began to turn away.

"No, Mr. Hester! Please don't go!" Claudia said. She opened the door wide. "I'll see you in the sitting room!" She looked at Mrs. Pynchon. "Please ma'am! You can wait just outside the door!"

Mr. Hester let out a soft sigh. "It won't be but for a few moments, ma'am. And with you just outside the door..." He looked from one woman to the other. "I think that would be best—for you to be here for Miss Wheeler after I deliver the news."

"Very well." The older woman stepped aside. "I'll be right here for you, Claudia dear."

"Thank you, ma'am!" Claudia stepped back from the door and bade Mr. Hester to enter.

He stepped into the room and stood beside the door as she shut it. His fingers found the latch and flipped the lock silently. He gestured to the sitting area beside the fireplace, and Claudia went and sat down.

"Please sir, my heart is racing," she said as she took her seat, making sure to perch on the edge as Mrs. Pynchon told her that fine ladies did. Her fingers knotted together with a mind of their own.

Hester stared down at her; his eyes full of sympathy.

"Oh, dear!" she cried. "Has something befallen Mr. Mayhan?"

He glanced down at her writing table. "Oh, you're composing a letter?" he asked.

Claudia was baffled. "Yes, to my parents! Please, tell me the message!" She felt her voice crack. All of the dreams of her fine life... was she now to waken and realize they were but a fantasy? A cruel prank played upon her by a cruel world?

Chapter Twenty-Three

The Rabbit's Eyes

H ester read the last line of Claudia's letter:

If things don't resolve with Mr. Mayhan, Mama and Papa, I won't be returning home. I'd just be a further burden.

It was a gift from God. He smiled to himself and turned to face the poor girl.

She was looking up at him with the most innocent eyes; their look inspiring a memory…

Once, as a child back in Wales, his family on the brink of starvation, he had snuck into the grounds of the Evans Estate. They were the landowners of the entire area, some sort of Lord or Earl or something; he couldn't recall.

But there was game on those grounds, and a ten-year-old boy could easily remain unseen by the gamekeepers. He knew where they lay their trap lines for rabbits—a constant scourge on the crops grown on the grounds. If he could find one, or even an unfortunate hedgehog or something, Mum would be happy and they'd have meat.

He came across a rabbit, snared by its back leg. It looked up at him with soulful eyes, almost pleading. Claudia's eyes held him in the same gaze, confused by what the world is doing, fearful of the outcome, but with a spark of hope for better times faintly glimmering.

He had crushed that rabbit's head with a rock, reveling in the look of surprise and horror as the stone crashed down.

"Please Mr. Hester, tell me the news!" Claudia implored.

Hester nodded sadly. "So I shall." He shook his shoulders. "Quite close in here, isn't it? I can barely catch a breath."

"Excuse me?"

He stepped to the window behind her and as quietly as he could, raised the sash as high as it would go, up to his shoulders. He breathed in a deep draught of the late night air. A crisp and clean Autumn night. Leaning his head out, he looked up and down the deserted streets. Very good.

"Mister Hester!" Claudia's voice was like the mewl of a hungry kitten. "Please tell me!" She was leaning over her chair facing him.

"So I must," he said to the night and turned. His hand snaked to his back pocket for his cosh.

❧❧❧

"NO CLAUDIA DON'T!"

Mrs. Pynchon almost jumped out of her skin at the sound of Mr. Hester's shouting inside. She grasped the doorknob and flung the door open.

At the window, Hester was leaning out, his face a pallor of shock. Claudia was nowhere to be seen.

"What's happened!" she shrieked, running to the window.

"That poor, poor girl!" he said, pointing to the pavement four stories below. "She was so quick! She was up and out of her chair before I could move a muscle!"

Mrs. Pynchon looked down below. All the life went out of her, seeing Claudia prone face down on the street below. Her hair splayed out around her head a halo, but much too small to cover the blood and gore flowing beneath it.

Hester's voice rasped in her ear as he said, "She... she didn't say a word! I told her the bad news from Mr. Mayhan, she nodded and as quick as a cat, leapt out the window!"

Mrs. Pynchon had no words. She gulped air, staring down at the body below.

"We should call the police, ma'am!" Mr. Hester said. "This is horrible!"

She shot a look at him. Hester wants the police here? She knew enough about the man's reputation to know that any involvement on his part with the constabulary was something he'd avoid at all costs.

"Woman! Summon the police!" he barked at her.

Chapter Twenty-Four

Done And Done

Hester's stomach had been rolling all day, damn it. His bowels felt like water as he made his way back to his garret. Which probably served him well, he thought. His reflection in the dresser mirror in that girl's room showed him to be pasty faced, all the better for him as he told his lies—the stupid coppers bought his tale of a distraught Claudia taking 'the widow's leap' hook line and sinker. Especially when one of them found her letter on her writing table and that exquisitely worded and timed last line:

If things don't resolve with Mr. Mayhan, Mama and Papa, I won't be returning home. I'd just be a further burden.

Now THAT was a gift from God if ever there was one! His own pale and clammy face only served to support the theory that a poor farm girl, at her wit's end, having the promise of a life of wealth and opulence snatched away had killed herself rather than return home in shame and destitution.

Hell, even that old biddy, Mrs. Pynchon seemed to buy his story in full. The battle-axe actually broke down in tears! She prattled on about how she tried to help the poor thing; she was going to get her a position in service if Mayhan backed out!

He shook his head. He even comforted *her* in her grief!

Approaching his quarters, he saw the glow of the oil lamp through the window.

Meredith.

Ahhhh...

Last night they became familiar; first name basis and all. And she told him that she was going to bestow her gratitude upon him when the task was done! He patted the money she had given him. He had kept in on his person since receiving it; he'd put it in his deposit box at the bank first thing tomorrow when he had a few moments to spare. A few more assignments such as this and he'd have ample funds to open that tavern he always wanted to have.

He'd finally be his own man; beholden to no one for his daily bread.

He made no attempts at subtlety as he climbed the stairs. Coming around the half wall he saw Meredith again, calmly waiting for him at his sitting area. Oh, she looked positively scrumptious sitting there. A different dress this time; a flattering burgundy number, complimenting her flowing light brown hair. The light from the oil lamp made parts of her dark hair almost red in color at the ends. And was that a hint of her décolletage in her bodice? Oh yes, this was going to be a night to remember!

If his damn guts would calm down! His stomach rumbled again as he crossed the room, and a sense of needing to vomit filled the back of his mouth with a coppery taste.

She looked up at him, her eyes glinting. "Well?"

"Well, well, well indeed, *Meredith*," he replied as he grabbed a chair from his table and set it beside her.

She watched him as he took his seat. "Is it done?"

He nodded. "Like sugar and water." He made a small snort. "Better than I could have possibly hoped for."

"You must tell me everything!" she said, clapping her hands. "But first, a toast!" She already had two glasses poured and handed him one.

He took the glass and eyed it. "I don't know...my stomach's been unsettled all day..."

"Nonsense!" She got to her feet and held her glass out to him. "This will be fine medicine for what ails you! Drink with me, man!"

What the hell. Maybe a hair of the dog or what have you. He clinked his glass with hers and drank. "Hmmm!" he said, smacking his lips. "A fine whiskey!" Better than the rotgut she left him last night.

"Twenty-four-year-old single malt from Scotland, sir!" she replied brightly after taking a sip. "My father's favorite, and now it's yours!" With her free hand she grabbed the bottle and poured him another. "Drink up, man! You saved my family! I'll have a case of this sent to you at my expense!" She gave him a lubricious look, her lips slightly parted. "And that's just the beginning... a man such as yourself... I'm sure you have many talents with the ladies..."

How bloody forward! And how enticing! He downed his second glass and held it out for another.

"But first my dear Hester, tell me everything!" she exclaimed as she filled his tumbler again.

He downed half the glass, the scotch warming his belly nicely. "It really wasn't much to do at all. As soon as I entered the room, I threw the lock on the door as silent as a mouse. I didn't want anyone barging in as I did my work; that old lady Mrs. Pynchon almost didn't allow me in to see her alone and was standing guard just outside the door." He shrugged in mock humility. "Once inside alone with the girl, I complained of it being stuffy and opened her window that was looking out onto the street four stories below." His stomach rumbled, and he took another generous swallow and held his glass out for another refill. The scotch was as smooth as honey, even so, there was a hint of that metallic taste...

"Go on, sir!" Meredith's eyes were gleaming. This woman is actually *enjoying* hearing this tale! No phony vapors from this one. He eyed her figure with frank appraisal. She saw his eyes slide up and down her and blinked saucily at him. "Please, sir!" she said.

"Well... she looked up at me... with such innocent eyes..." he watched Meredith's face carefully.

She licked her lips. Oh, yes...

"And as quick as I could, I came from behind her and bopped her in the head with my cosh. She fell back in her chair and didn't move. I then slipped to the door and undid the lock." He stepped back and forth in the room pantomiming what he did. "Quick as a bunny, I grabbed the lass and pitched her out of the window, yelling and shouting as she fell!"

"Did you... did you hear her strike the ground?"

"Oh yes. A crunching splat like a pumpkin tossed from a barn loft!"

"Oh, you brave man!"

He made a grimace at the pain in his gut. "No need to be brave with a simple farm girl." He nodded sharply. "But not afraid to get my hands dirty, that's for certain."

A sharp pain pierced his stomach. A pain so sharp and true it was a red-hot poker charged with electricity. Hester doubled over with a loud moan. "What the hell!"

Meredith remained seated. "Oh Hester! Whatever is the matter?"

He fell to his knees, clutching his stomach. "Oh god! What is this?" He began to cough, each spasm wracking his body with agony. Was that blood splattering on the floor? He wiped his mouth and looked at the crimson stain on his hand. He shot a look at Meredith. "What did you do?"

"Are you unwell, sir?" Meredith replied, her eyes steady watching him.

"You poisoned me?" Another wrack of coughs shot through him. The pain went from his stomach to his chest and back again. He felt his nethers begin to loosen. Oh, no! He scrambled to his feet. "What did you do!" he shouted. "You've poisoned me!"

Meredith sat back in her seat, no longer the prim well-to-do lady. "You look ill sir! Shall I call for the doctor?" Her eyes were watching him like a hungry eagle.

He took a step towards her and began to cough again. His legs gave way, and he fell flat onto the floor. He continued crawling towards her.

Meredith stood up. "I don't think you're well, sir. I'll leave you to it." She picked up her glass and left a bottle of pills by his whiskey bottle. "You're so distraught over that girl's suicide, I believe. You're guilt ridden that you couldn't save her and decided to do away with yourself it seems. Poor man..." She swept from the room. "I'll make sure the investigation leads to that conclusion. You'll be mourned as a caring man Hester."

Another rage of coughs filled Hester. He couldn't breathe! He gasped for air, feeling his life begin to slip away.

The last sounds he heard over his panting, before the darkness settled in was the sound of Meredith on his staircase. The steps squeaked and groaned at her descent.

When he heard the door slam shut behind her, he let himself slip into the billowing darkness.

⇒⟫⟩ ⟨⟨⟪⟸

Meredith stopped still in her tracks after closing the door and let out a sigh. *The money.* She turned and looked up at the window of Hester's room. Where would he have hidden it? She quickly let out a sigh. An amount that large he wouldn't take his eyes from it until he got to a bank. It was a substantial amount...

She re-opened the door and as quietly as she could, ascended the stairs.

He was on his back, his form still. He *was* dead, was he not?

A familiar thrill swept over her as she gazed at the still form. The first time she did away with someone was frightening, but like Hester, a deed that had to be done. She wasn't as thrilled as afraid of the consequences the first time. The second one, however—now that was a thrill. Silly chambermaid, stealing her diamond and gold broach as if Meredith wouldn't notice? Telling her to her face at the top of the stone stairs at the outside balcony just as she shoved her? That expression of surprise then terror as she began to tumble backwards was absolutely intoxicating. And now...to put down a man of Hester's size and ability...a shudder of pleasure passed through her.

She made her way to his body. What a gentleman! He was on his back, making it Simple Simon to go through his pockets. In a trice she had the packet of bills.

Done and done.

As she descended the stairs again, she was humming a tune.

THE
FINAL TOUR

Chapter Twenty-Five

A Catnap

Ryan watched Claudia's eyes film with tears. "You still miss them?" he asked.

She nodded slowly. "Yes. One day I hope for them to come for me," she replied, a faraway look in her eyes. She turned to Ryan. "But... for some reason, I'm afraid they may never come for me...." She let out a sigh. "It's become quite strange staying at the hotel. I seem to stir and look about, but it's only at nighttime." She let out a rueful laugh, the sound like a small dove crying. "I've seemed to lose a sense of time. Earlier tonight, Mr. Hester came by..."

"Hester?"

"Yes. He's my intended fiancée's manservant. He picked me up at the rail station earlier this week and told me to expect to meet the man who intends to wed me—Mister William Mayhan—the next day. But the entire week passed, and I've not seen Mr. Mayhan yet." She shivered slightly. "He came to my rooms to tell me important news... but I can't recall what it was. I doze in my chair, and when I awaken, everything is the same." She looked up at Ryan. "But then...you and your group of friends came by the hotel and stood outside."

A look of fear swept over her face like a wave on the shore of a beach. "You were at my hotel tonight, is that correct?" She gave a small shake of her head. "For some reason it feels like it was last night as well... but that cannot be right..." She shut her eyes tightly and held the sides of her head. "I don't understand! Am I losing my wits?"

"Hey...hey...don't fret. You're not losing your wits."

"Everything seems...so unreal..." She reached out and patted Ryan's arm. "You feel real...you're the first person I've spoken with since Mr. Hester came by this evening, but at the same time, it feels like it's been years and years since he came to my room." She shook her head sharply, back and forth, her hair creating an auburn halo around her head. "I can't recall what message he gave me!" She brought the heel of her hand to her forehead. "My head aches so sometimes... I wonder if I'm ill."

Ryan grasped her hand. "No. I promise you, you're not sick Claudia." That's for certain. No way she was sick. Dead, yeah; but sick? Nope.

Buster had rearranged himself on Ryan's lap, watching the woman intently. "That's Buster," he said, "he finds you fascinating."

"What a lovely kitten," she replied. She scratched the back of his head, and he began to purr. He pushed his feet against the cushions, nestling snuggly. "I so love the sound of a kitty purring..." she said as she stroked his fur. "Such a tiny thing."

But then another expression filled her face. "This is not proper, me being here, but why then does it feel so right?" her voice small in wonder. "I should leave," she said, holding his hand back. "If anyone learns, I'm at a man's home, there will be such gossip!"

"Don't worry, I'm not going to make a move on you Claudia."

"A move?" She looked around. "You want to play checkers?"

Ryan huffed a sigh. "Figure of speech. Your honor is as safe with me as it could ever be."

"Truly?"

He nodded.

"We can hold hands, can we not?" she asked. "I'll be wed shortly. Back home, there weren't many opportunities to be with other boys. Our farm was so far from town, and the neighboring farms... well, they had no children I believe..."

"Holding hands keeps fear at bay," he replied. Damn... that was what Melanie had said to him growing up when they'd be scared. "It makes you stronger than the fear." When Mom and Dad died, he and Melanie spent their first night together sitting on the couch holding hands. Keeping the woe at bay.

Taking her free hand, he turned it over to look at the back of it.

She had such small delicate hands. The poor thing should have had a life, but no, she died ages and ages ago. And yet, here she was, innocent as a ten-year-old, but yet so brave to seek him out. Without thinking, he raised the back of her hand to his lips and kissed it softly.

"Oh, my!" But Claudia didn't pull away, her voice floating over them.

He brought her hand away from his mouth and rested them between them. With his free hand, Ryan reached over and tucked a flyway lock of auburn hair behind Claudia's ear. The moon had set, but there was still plenty of light coming in the window. He wondered just how her hair would look in the light of a full moon tomorrow. "Tell me stories about your family growing up, Claudia. Tell me about you."

Her eyebrows knitted. "I... I cannot." They widened. "What's the matter with me? I can't recall my own family?"

"Whoa...take it easy...it's okay..."

"Are you sure?" She looked about the room, alarmed. "There must be something wrong with me!" she said, her voice barely above a whisper.

Uh-oh...the last thing he needed was a panicked ghost! "Hey, let me tell you about my family, how about that?"

She immediately brightened. "Oh yes! Please do!"

"Well... I was born at a very young age..."

She rewarded him with a small laugh, and he continued. All through the night his voice floated in the room as she stroked the back of Ryan's hand with her thumb, engrossed with every word. The night crept along through their window, the moon passing over his window and away.

When he paused she let out a yawn. "I'm terribly tired, Ryan. May I just close my eyes for a moment?"

"Sure." He snuggled next to her and wrapped his arm around her shoulders, tucking her to him. As natural as rain on a summer's afternoon, she lay her head on his shoulder, a perfect fit.

He was beat to a snot as well. He'd just close his eyes... just for a minute... then figure out how to take her back to her hotel. That's where she belonged right? Okay, that's a good idea. But just after their little catnap...

The last thought he had was what a waste of a good Friday night this was...

Chapter Twenty-Six

Good Evening All

Ryan found himself in his bed when he opened his eyes. A quick glance at the window told him it was still nighttime. How the hell did he wind up here?

Where the hell was Claudia?

He sat up in a shot.

"Ahhh... there you are."

He flung his eyes to the door. Melanie was leaning against the jamb, her arms crossed in front of her.

"What the hell...?"

She cut him off with a wave of her hand. "It's your last night, bro. You'll have to decide what you want to do."

He hopped out of bed. Oh maaaan... he slept in his clothes. Again. "Where's Claudia?"

"Who's Claudia?"

He elbowed past her and went into the living room looking around. Again, all the lights were off, and moonlight was pouring through the far window. Wait a damn minute, he saw it set already!

Melanie had followed him from the bedroom. "Who's Claudia, Ryan?"

"She's..." he heaved a big sigh. "Look... rather I'm going crazy, or I just spent the night with a ghost." He looked at her face. It remained impassive. "Doesn't that scare you?"

Melanie snorted. "If you've seen half the stuff I've seen in the last couple of years, Ryan there's not a lot of stuff that scares me anymore."

"Wait, a damn minute—*you* told me this already, right? Are you telling me the truth?" She'd always been into that New Age-y 'Astral Plane' kind of bullshit... but to just admit it as easily as telling him she had pizza for lunch?

She crossed the room to him. "I not only believe in ghosts, bro. I've *seen* them."

"Them?"

She nodded. "Yeah. I kind of always wanted to believe in the afterlife... especially after Mom and Dad died, you know? But having faith in something because you want to believe in it is a hella lot different from actually experiencing it."

"What the hell are you talking about?"

She rolled her eyes. "I didn't want to tell you any details the other night because I figured you would think I'm crazy."

"Crazy like I am right now? Telling you I talked to a ghost?"

She nodded with a cryptic smile. "Pretty much. I saw a ghost for the first time a few years back. Remember that weird reunion I had with my girlfriends from college?"

"The one at the abandoned resort in the Catskills?"

"Yeah..." She looked away. "Shit, it was just a couple of years ago, and it feels like a lifetime..." She shuddered. "We went there as part of Dara's Last

Will And Testament. She died the previous year, and her will stated that if we spent a couple nights there on the anniversary of her death, me and the other girls would split her estate three ways. Well, there was a lot more going on, and to make a long story short... I saw and spoke to Dara that weekend.

"You talked to a ghost."

She made an odd smile. "And that was the easy stuff. A lot of stuff happened that weekend. A lot more. It convinced me that there's a lot more to this universe than you'd think."

"Really?"

She looked at him with sad eyes. "Yes." She reached over and stroked the side of Ryan's face. "Really. And a lot more than I'm able to explain..."

The gentle stroke of her hand against his face was a comfort. But... Ryan shrugged. "... maybe it was just some kind of group hysteria thing? Or you guys got some bad weed?"

"Nope. That weekend was just the first of strange things in my life. After that weekend, I got back in touch with a friend from high school... remember Paige Wright?"

Ryan nodded. "Yeah. You and her were best buds back in the day."

"Yeah, well, she became a lawyer and got her client out of trouble during a nasty divorce. Turns out as soon as she got him sprung, he murdered his ex and his own daughter!"

"Holy shit!"

"Yeah. And I got mixed up in that and saw the kid's ghost too."

"No way!"

"Way." She tilted her head at him. "So... maybe it runs in the family or something." She made that weird smile again and reached out and rubbed his shoulder. "You got the same kind of gift, maybe." She glanced out the window. "So who's Claudia?"

"Claudia Wheeler. She haunts the top floor of the St. Regis Hotel. It's the first stop on the tour." He pulled out his guidebook. "It says in here she killed herself by jumping out a window."

"Holy shit!"

Ryan shook his head. "Well, that's where it gets strange. The other night, one of the tourists—Dorothy—told everyone that she was *thrown* out the window."

"She was murdered?"

Ryan nodded. "And I spent last night with her ghost." He shot Melanie a strange look. "I took your advice when I met her waiting for me on the front steps."

"What do you mean?"

Ryan made a wan smile. "I did what you said. I invited her in." He had a wistful expression. "We spent the night talking and dozed off on the couch." He gave his head a shake. "I don't remember her leaving, and I don't remember going to my bedroom. Next thing I know is you're here..." He looked away. "This is really strange, Melanie. I'm kinda scared."

Melanie took her baby brother in her arms. Sure, he was a twenty-year-old young man, but he'd be her baby brother to the day she died. "Don't be. The Universe is good, and it is just. And it's kind. We people screw stuff up all the time, but the Universe is greater than all of us. Ghosts are just a part of being alive sometimes, sweetie." She held him in her arms, feeling her eyes well up. "So you met a girl, huh?" she asked with a smirk.

"Yeah. Claudia Wheeler." He took a deep breath. "She's cool."

"Well... maybe you'll see her again tonight..."

Ryan made a strange look. "I don't know if this job's right for me, Mel. Too much weird stuff is going on."

Melanie nodded. "I understand." She quickly wiped her eyes.

"Hey, are you crying?"

She sniffled. "I think it's allergies, maybe."

"In October?"

She shrugged. "What can I say? Just another weird thing about me, huh?" She flashed a cheesy grin. "Now about this job... maybe you make tonight your last night, okay?"

"Yeah, you mentioned that—tonight's my last night—how come?"

"We'll talk about it when you're finished. I think this is your last night doing this."

"But what about my resume? I need more than just three nights giving tours to impress casting people in New York!"

She threw an arm around his shoulders. "Don't you worry a bit about *that* bro! We'll take care of it, okay?"

"Promise?"

"Yup." She looked out the window at the full moon. "A full moon in October...no wonder you're seeing ghosts..."

"What's that supposed to mean?"

She let out a soft sigh. "Nights of the full moon are when the boundary between this world and the next are the most... I don't know... leaky?"

"Leaky."

Melanie nodded. "Yes. It's easier to move from this world to the next on nights with a full moon." She pursed her lips. "I think that's why you only see spirits during the night... the moon has some effect on the boundary or something. And a night with the full moon... that's special. And... I don't know why, but in October... that's the time of year when it's the thinnest."

Ryan snorted. "I *told* you I was scared! Now I'm freaking out!" He smiled as he said it.

"Suck it up then!" They both laughed.

Ryan let out a whoosh of air. "So, we'll talk after, right? About what I do next?"

She nodded and stepped to the window. The moon was fully up over the horizon. "It's time, Ryan."

"Time for what?"

Melanie's eyes filmed for a moment, and she cleared her throat. "You need to get to work, hon. It's your third night."

Ryan was confused. He'd just closed his eyes for a second! "What..." he looked around the living room. "It's Saturday night? You're telling me I slept all night and all day?" When Melanie nodded, he said, "What happened to Claudia?"

"I'm not sure. I think maybe she needed to be somewhere else."

"Back at the hotel?" When Melanie shrugged in response, he grabbed his cape and top hat. "Okay then, let's get to work." Melanie opened the door to the apartment to usher him out. He looked at the place and a sense of nostalgia flowed over him. "I love this place you know..."

"I understand."

~≫≫〉 〈≪≪~

Ryan and Melanie stopped across the street again from the St. Regis Hotel. He let out a light laugh. "It just keeps getting better, doesn't it?" he said, pointing at the group across the street.

Yes, the so-called 'Family Reunion' had grown.

Sure, the eight elderly people, four couples were there. Doris the bob-by-soxer and her husband John in his battle fatigues, Helen in her polka-dot housedress along with her husband Richard (call me 'Dick' and keep a straight face) in his denim coveralls, Mildred all spiffed up in a cocktail dress was on the arm of her classy officer husband Robert, and last of the group was Elizabeth in her Navy nurse whites on the arm of the Lieutenant William (call me 'Bill'). They were as old as Methuselah, but as spry as anyone he ever met.

Their four kids were there too—straight out of the sixties. Angie and Troy, looking like they just stepped off the set for *Leave It To Beaver* or maybe even *The Brady Bunch*, were with the other couple, 'Star' and 'Moon Dog' who were dressed like refugees from some hippie commune.

But the newest addition to this bunch were the kids in strollers. A boy and a girl were in chrome tubing baby strollers. Ryan knew it was a boy and a girl because one stroller had pink fabric and the other one had baby blue fabric. The munchkins looked like they were about two or three years old.

He felt Melanie's hand on the small of his back. She spoke in his ear. "I'll meet you back at your place," she said, giving him a gentle nudge to the street. "I'll love you forever, Ryan."

He stepped onto the pavement and turned around. "That's a weird thing to say."

"It's the truth." She gestured at the group on the corner. "Your audience awaits your performance, maestro."

"Okay... see ya..."

Once again, looking up and down Main Street, there wasn't a car in sight. Which was odd for a Saturday night? It *was* a Saturday night, right? He was sure of it, but his memory of the last few days was kinda cloudy. He might see a doctor or something. He'd been sleeping waaay too much. And not after getting high or drunk like his college days. Nope; last night he closed his eyes just for a second holding Claudia's hand and the next thing he knew he woke up in his bed. He sniffed his armpit. No matter that he didn't smell, he was definitely taking a shower as soon as he got back to his place. He must stink to high heaven.

He crossed the street watching the group watching him. Every single one of them were looking at him with welcoming faces. From the wide grin of 'Dick' to the crooked smile from 'Soldier John', through to the radiant smiles of spiffy Mildred and her high and tight husband Robert, all of them were looking at him like he was Brad Pitt or something. He had a great start to a fan club when he moved to New York, that was for sure!

When he got in front of them, he doffed his top hat, flurried his cape and made a deep bow. "Good evening, ladies and gentlemen! Welcome to yet another night of The Haunted Walk!"

Chapter Twenty-Seven

Okie Dokie

W ell, what's on the tour for tonight?" asked Mildred from the back. She stood in the same satin cocktail dress, her arm through her husband's elbow.

Just like him, they all were wearing the same clothes they had on two nights ago when they first met.

Ryan didn't answer, instead he looked down at the toddlers in strollers. The little girl was being looked after by Moon Dog and Star, and the boy was obviously the son of Angie and Troy. The Brady Bunch meets the cast of Hair, he thought to himself.

But the two children were...different. Their strollers were beside one another, tucked in close and the children were holding one another's hand. But the strangest thing was when he caught them looking up at them. They had the most interesting look in their eyes; they were appraising him or something. The girl was squinting at him, her mouth pressed tightly closed. The boy was also watching him, but was slowly nodding his head. Did the kid like his hat or something?

"What are your kids' names?" he asked the two couples.

Moon Dog shrugged. "Not a big deal, man. What's a name anyway? Just some mouth noise used to separate people, right?" He looked over at the other couple. "We don't need to get into that whole scene of names, do we Troy?"

Troy straightened the knot of the tie he was wearing. He nodded in agreement. "Yes, at this point it's not all that important." He smiled down at his son. "We call him 'Bigsy' right now."

His wife Angie chuckled. "Well, he was a bruiser at birth, that's for sure!"

Moon Dog stretched his arms apart, turning his attention back to Ryan. "See? That's Bigsy, okay?" He tapped the handlebar of the pink stroller. "An' since her momma goes by 'Star', we call this little one 'Twinkle'. How's that?"

Ryan chortled. "You guys must be up to no good if you're even giving your kids aliases! What are you, a crime family or something?"

Before anyone could respond, Mildred interrupted. "So, where to tonight?"

Ryan was a little perplexed. They'd all been on the same tour since Friday; they saw all the sights he had to offer. "Well, do you want to have one more go round?" he asked. He could probably do the tour from memory now.

"Well...I have an idea..." Mildred said.

"What's that?"

"Well...we've seen everything, how about we do it sort of a la carte?" When she saw the look of confusion on Ryan's face, she said, "There are a few of your stops that we'd like to see again."

"Oh? Which ones?"

Doris the bobby-soxer waved her arm in the air. "We want to visit the hotel where that young girl died..."

Helen added, "And then go to the place where that man was hanged unjustly..."

And Mildred finished with, "And lastly we want to go to the cemetery where that woman is said to haunt, and visit her grave." She bent a little at the waist. "The one who had that magic potion that gave her eternal youth."

Ryan folded his arms over his chest. He looked over at Doris. "You want to visit the stop where you told me that the girl who died there was thrown out the window." He pointed his chin at Helen. "And you want to revisit Ronald Grafer's hanging spot." He turned to Mildred. "I don't know about the grave you're talking about, we only stopped outside the cemetery."

Mildred made a sly smile. "It's not in your guidebook. We'll show it to you."

He knew this was going to be a strange outing. But what the hell... He tapped the crown of his top hat. "Okie dokie, let's get to it."

He had nooo idea.

Chapter Twenty-Eight

Sweetie

R yan didn't 'lead' the group so much as just be in the front. Everyone knew where they were going; just to the end of the block where Claudia's room was. He was hoping she would be up in the window. When they were only halfway down the street, he started to crane his neck, looking up in hope to see the candle glowing again.

A tap on his shoulder startled him.

"Ain't you going to ask how we fit into all this, man?" Moon Dog asked with a wry grin. He was pushing the stroller with his daughter in it.

"I don't know...nephews, nieces or something?"

Moon Dog shook his head. "Nahh..." he swept his arm at the group. "We're all kinda related."

"What do you mean?"

"Well, my parents are Doris and John," he nodded at them. "I grew up an only child, right ma?" he called out.

Doris nodded.

And my old lady Star is the daughter of 'The Colonel' Bob and Mildred."
He grinned widely. We got together in college out at UCLA. And boy oh
boy..." he chuckled again. "Her daddy really didn't like me much!"

"We're good now, son," Bob called out. "You made a hell of a man out
of yourself, even if you burned your draft card."

"Which, if I ain't mistaken, was your idea, pops!' Moon Dog laughed
back. "Took you awhile to come around, didn't it?"

Bob shrugged. "Better late than never. You never got called up either."

"Thank God," Doris added from beside him, walking arm and arm with
her own husband John. "The government was wrong, right down the line."

"What the hell you guys talking about?" Ryan asked.

"Water under the bridge man," Moon Dog replied. He pointed at Col.
Bob and Mildred and then his own parents. "What I was getting to is that
me and Star made in-laws of those four,"

"Oh."

"And ol' insurance man Troy," he nodded to the other couple pushing
the little boy's stroller, "Troy's the son of Betty and Bill."

"You mean the nurse and Navy guy?"

"Yup."

Ryan scanned the rest of the group. The only ones left were Helen
and Dick, the 'working class's contingent. "Yep, Angie's the daughter of a
plumber and a housewife who never missed Mass on Sunday to the day she
died."

As always, he was puzzled that the woman was only wearing a cotton
dress at night. But then, he didn't feel cold at all. It really was a mild night
for October.

"Uh-huh... does that ring any bells for you?"

"What?"

Star elbowed her husband in the side. "Moon Doggie...don't go down
that rabbit hole okay?"

Moon Dog's eyes slid from Ryan to his wife and back. "Yeah, sorry about that. It's not the time, huh?"

"No, it's not hon. Not yet anyway." Star tucked her long hair behind her ear as she looked up at Ryan. "Sometimes the acid he did back in the day scrambles his brain. Pay him no mind, Ryan."

"My head's fine, hon," Moon Dog replied.

"You hush now."

Ryan was looking at both of them totally confused. "What the hell are you two talking about?"

"Easy does it, man," Moon Dog replied. "Just getting ahead of myself. Sorry."

Star brightened. "What my addle-brained hubby is trying to tell you is that we're all kind of family here practically, that's all." She stood on tiptoe and kissed Ryan's cheek. "And family's a wonderful thing, don't you think?"

A wave of sadness washed over Ryan. "I don't have much of a family."

"What do you mean?"

"Well, all my grandparents died when I was really little, and my parents were killed in a car crash a few years ago…"

"That's pretty sad," she replied.

"Yeah. No cousins either. It's just me and my older sister Melanie left in the world."

Star's hand rose to and stroked the side of his face. "Well…I think your family's watching over you from the other side then."

He looked in her eyes as she cupped his cheek. The feel of her hand on his face gave him such a deep sense of comfort. He gave a little cough and replied, "Yeah, maybe, I guess."

"No, I'm sure of it, sweetie."

"Sweetie?"

"Yes.,"

Now he felt his eyes film and the world get all misty. "That's...that's what my Mom used to call us. She'd say 'My Sweetie Pie' all the time..." The memory this time didn't hurt. For the first time in years, he thought about his departed parents with fondness and not pain. The pain that was so bad he walled it off with a band of steel around his heart it scared him so much.

"That's nice," she replied. "Wonder where she got that from?" Star dropped her hand and rubbed the side of Ryan's arm and looked up at the side of the hotel. "We're at the first stop I think."

Chapter Twenty-Nine

Far Out

S tar was right. Ryan looked up to see a faint glow from the window on the top floor of the old hotel.

"Claudia!" he called out. "Claudia! Come down!" He darted into the street and looked up. He could barely make out a silhouette at the window. "Claudia! Why'd you take off last night?"

There was no response. Damn it.

He looked over at the group. They were all on the sidewalk and were watching him in silence.

"Hey Doris! You know all about her right? Why won't she come down?"

The woman looked at the others in the group before replying. They all gave a 'meh' sort of shrug to her before she looked over to Ryan. "I don't think she's able to leave the room, maybe?"

"That's nuts. She was with me last night!"

"Whoaaa man," Moon Dog replied. "You spent the night...*with a ghost*? Far out!"

"Wait a minute—you *believe* me?"

Mood Dog waved his hands. "Oh dude, the stuff I saw on acid trips..." he leveled a gaze at Ryan. "There are more things in heaven and earth Horatio..." and let it hang.

Ryan nodded. "...than are in your philosophy. Yeah, I studied Shakespeare in college too, bud."

"Like I said, man—*far out*!"

Well, now that he put it that way, it was far out. "I think it might run in the family," he said.

"Oh yeah?" Moon Dog tilted his head at him. "How's that?"

"Well...my sister's kind of a sensitive. She told me she's able to see ghosts and spirits sometimes. So maybe I got whatever gift she's got, right?" That sounded completely crazy as far as he was concerned, but it was the only thing he could hang his hat on.

Doris only responded with another shrug. "Well, all I can say is that Claudia was murdered the night she died. And didn't you say that she's only been seen in the window?"

"Until last night!"

Ryan looked up at the window again. The freaking light in the window was gone. "Claudia!" he shouted again. But there was no response. He called out, "Maybe you can stop by my place again? Please?" This was absolutely insane, but he genuinely missed her presence.

Colonel 'Bob' broke away from the group and went up to Ryan. "It looks like there's nothing we can do here right now, son. How about we continue on our way?" He took Ryan by the elbow and guided him back to the sidewalk and at the head of the group. "We'd really like to visit the old prison place where that poor man died."

"Why? What's it to you? You're just in town for a visit, right?" Ryan didn't really want to leave Claudia. He didn't know why, but that was that.

"Well...I believe that Ronald Grafer was unjustly convicted and wrongly executed. That's as terrible a thing as what happened here," he replied, gesturing at Claudia's window. "There's nothing we can do here right now for that poor girl…"

"So you think we can do something for that guy down at the old jail?"

"I think it's worth looking into."

Ryan shook his head. This job has turned into the weirdest experience of his life. Damn, he had to find his phone! He had to talk to Melanie about these crazy goings-on. Finally, he huffed a sigh. "Okay, let's move on then."

Chapter Thirty

We're On Your Side

For whatever reason, the limestone courthouse and jail was more imposing this night. Bathed in the light of the full moon on a partly cloudy sky, the stonework shone with a brilliance as if it was illuminated from within. As the group passed the front of the courthouse, the row of imposing columns over the entrance appeared to be leaning over them, taunting and threatening them the way a schoolyard bully would intimidate a preschooler.

Doris nudged Ryan. "You okay?"

Ryan watched the building with a sideways look. "This feels weird."

She dropped her head and snorted. "Getting a case of the willies? The heebie-jeebies? Whim-whams?"

Ryan looked at her closely. Doris looked *different*. Yeah, she was wearing the same white blouse, pleated black skirt along with saddle shoes and bobby-sox...but she didn't look nearly as old as she had the previous two nights. Her hair, which had obviously had a black dye job when they first met, flowed with the fullness and body of a natural color.

He stopped in his tracks. "Hey Doris, look at me."

She lifted her head, smiling.

What the hell?

She was still an old woman...wasn't she? Except her skin that had been almost papery in its appearance was now glowing with vitality. Her once rheumy eyes were now clear and steady. And her wrinkles had diminished! Along with that old lady waddle that had run from her neck to her jaw line.

"What have you been doing since last night?" he asked. "You go to a spa or something?"

She just replied with a crooked smile. "Just good living, I guess. I gave up smoking years ago, maybe that's it." She did a little twirl, the hem of her skirt lifting and flirting. "This ol' outfit still fits, isn't that grand?" She shot a look over to her husband John. "We decided to wear the outfits we wore the night we met at the USO club during the war."

"What war?"

John stepped up and put his arm around Doris's waist. "Look at the kid, wanting to hear about ancient history!" He twirled Doris again, humming and singing a tune. The two of them spun and shimmied like they were in a Hollywood musical, both of them now humming the same tune.

"Hey gang, can we keep moving?" Mildred called out. "It's getting late."

As a single unit Doris and John stopped. She stuck her tongue out at Ryan. "Not so much scaredy-cat anymore, are ya bub?" she said.

She was right. He looked up at the courthouse. It wasn't as threatening anymore. He heard of whistling past a graveyard, but dancing past a courthouse? "You got a point."

They went around the side of the courthouse to where the old entrance to the jail was.

Ryan addressed the group. "You guys want me to tell the story of Ronald Grafer again? 'Cuz I don't know what else to do or say."

"Who's calling me!"

Ryan jumped a foot in the air at the shout behind his head and spun around.

In front of him was a man in his forties. He was about Ryan's height, but much more filled out. Despite his size, he looked worn out; his face lined with grief and bags under his eyes. His hands were thick fingered, sticking out from the sleeves of a filthy topcoat. His pants were thin and worn, just this side of the Goodwill bin.

Ryan's voice cracked. "Ronald Grafer?"

"'Tis me. Who be you all? Are you to take me home to my wee ones?" He clenched his hands in front of him. "They say I murdered a man, but I did no such thing!" He turned his gaze up to the moon. "They'll be hanging me tomorrow..." A look of shock covered his face. "I was over there in the jail but a moment ago looking up at the moon! How did I get here?" The shock gave way to bewilderment. He began to hit the side of his head. "I'm all mixed up! They took me from the jail! They did! And they..." He looked around again. "Where's the gallows? They took me to the gallows! I remember! They took me to the gallows! There was a big crowd! All of 'em jeering me! I tried to tell 'em I was innocent! I hurt no one! But they all jeered and cat-called me like I was some circus clown!" He looked wild-eyed over at the now empty parking lot. "It was right over there! I heard the workmen building it all night long!"

He staggered away towards the spot, his arms flailing. "I can see an' hear 'em all screaming for me hangin'! Oh lord...oh lord I was so afraid...I was gonna die! And they were cheering for that!"

He stopped, his back to them, his hands covering his face, shoulders trembling. A keening moan rose into the air. "Oooohhhhhhhh....me wee ones! They're all alone in the world now...oooohhhh! Eleanor... Abigail... Festus... Garvey...Harry...and wee babe Anna... Their momma gone, and now their Pa hanged as a murderer! Oooooohhhh!"

He turned back towards the group, his hands still covering his face of grief until the sobbing ended. He dropped his hands and faced them. "You weren't there! Who are you? You here to see me swing on the morrow? Here for the show are ya?" He advanced on them. "There's no guards here now is there?"

"Hey wait a minute, buddy," John detached from Doris and stood in front of Ronald. "Ain't nobody here to do you wrong, okay? Just take it easy..."

"Easy! You want me to take it easy!" He jabbed a finger at the jail. "Waiting all night in there to die in the mornin'! You think that's easy?"

"No friend, it's not easy at all. I know what that's like waiting to die..." John replied in a gentle voice. "Been there, did that..."

Helen rounded around from the group, the polka dots on her housedress catching the moonlight like fireflies. She had her hands out before her. "We all *know* you're an innocent man, Ronald. That's why we're here." She took his shoulders, looking up into his rough face. "We're on your side."

"But..." he shook his head. "But I'm to be hanged!" He hit the side of his head. "No! I *WAS* hanged!" He clutched at his head. "What's happening to meeee! It's all mixed up!"

Helen, who was a big woman, was just about Ronald's height. She took the man in her arms, cradling his head to her shoulder. "It's all mixed up just for now, darling. We're here to make it alright for you."

He grasped her like a small boy. "I don't understand, I don't understand..." he repeated over and over.

"You will, hon, you will."

Ryan stood open mouthed, watching the events unfurl before him. Ronald Grafer was confused? That didn't hold a candle to his own bafflement.

As if she heard his thoughts, Helen lifted her head and looked at him.

"Everything will make sense before long, dear," she said, looking at Ryan while comforting Ronald.

A chill went down Ryan's back. That didn't sound good.

At. All.

Chapter Thirty-One

You're Cool

Helen continued to hold and comfort the ghost of Ronald Grafer for a few moments until Mildred spoke up. "The moon is moving hon," she called out. "We need to get going, don't you think?"

Helen nodded and pushed away from Ronald. Taking him by the hand, she said, "Will you join us?"

His face brightened. "You're really breaking me out?"

Helen made a wry smile. "I suppose. Will you come along with us?"

"Will I get me wee ones?" He looked around. "I don't know where they'd be. They probably took 'em to an orphanage or something when they arrested me!" He dropped his gaze to the ground. "Neither me nor me poor dead wife have any family to speak of..."

Helen took a deep breath. "They've been well looked after. They've had a good life...but miss their Pa every day."

His head shot up. "You speaking the truth?" He looked at his hands. "Sometimes I feel like I've been in the jail for ages and ages...but then I

look out and see the full moon, knowing they'll come for me at sunup."
He looked at Helen. "How long have I been in the jail?"

"Too long. You're an innocent man, love. A day is an eternity for an
innocent man in prison."

He nodded and looked back at his hands. "They don't seem to be an old
man's hands..." He looked back at Helen. "I don't know what I'll do now."

"We'll help you with all that. Now we have one more errand to run. We
need to see someone else. When we're done with all that, we'll unite you
with your wee ones."

"Truly?"

"Yes."

"Then let us be off!"

Ryan turned to the group. "Ummm...where do you want to go next?"

Betty, the woman in the Navy nurse uniform stepped away from her
husband Bill raised her hand. "I'll show the way," she said.

"Is it far?" Ronald asked. "I want to see my children."

"Don't fret, hon," Helen said. "It's been a long time, I know. But we
need to do this too. There's someone else we need to see."

Ronald looked at her with a confused expression. "Someone else in
prison for no reason?"

"Well...someone who's trapped in a way... so that's a prison of a sort I
suppose."

As Ryan watched the exchange, with Betty moving to the head of the
group, holding her husband Bill's hand still, he knew this was the last night
he'd be doing this job. He completely lost control of these people.

This guy Ronald Grafer... why did they hire an actor for this? And what
was up with Doris? Was she an old woman now with stage makeup to make
her look younger? Or...

"Wait a damn minute!" he said with an edge in his voice. He went up to
Betty and Bill, looking at them closely. Damn right. Just like Doris, the years

had fallen off them as well. Bill's grey hair was now just salt and pepper, and Betty's legs, which had one hell of a case of varicose veins were now as lithe as a Rockette's!

"You guys are all actors, aren't you?" he said, turning to look at all of them. "This is some crazy stunt Melanie's cooked up, isn't it? She's paid you all for this gig, right?" He walked among them, eyeing each of them up and down.

Every one of them—every single one—had a more youthful appearance than they had before. Even Mildred and 'The Colonel' Robert. On the first night, he had his trousers pulled up halfway to his god damn chest and now they sat snugly on his trim waist. Just like Bill, Robert's hair had been grey—hell no, two nights ago it was *white*. He looked closely. And he had liver spots on his cheeks two nights ago! And Mildred's cocktail dress? Brother! What had hung limply on her rail thin frame that first night—practically a caricature of an old lady trying to dress younger than she ought to—was now a snug, alluring fit that showed curves and flair that most certainly was *not* there before!

He was in the center of the group. "What the hell's going on here? What the hell are you guys really up to?"

Col. Robert pushed his officer's cap to the back of his head and gazed at him with a level expression. "What do you think we're up to, sonny?" he asked, irritation in his voice. "You think we're pulling something on you?"

"Did my sister hire you?"

He let out a snort. "Melanie? No, son. She didn't hire us at all." He looked around the group. "To tell you the truth, I never even had a chance to meet her until you showed up with her in tow." He looked over to his wife. "She's a fine woman though, isn't she Mildred?"

A kind of sad smile flitted over the woman's face as she nodded silently.

"So what the hell's going on here!"

Bob held up a hand. "Hold on son—"

"I'm *not* your damn son! Jesus Christ, I hate it when guys like you say that crap!" An explosive anger welled up and he wasn't going to do a damn thing to hold it down. "You people are up to something! Who was it you sent to my place last night?" He shook his head. "I can't believe it. I *actually* thought I hung out with a freaking ghost..."

"Whoaaa man!" Moon Dog elbowed his way up to stand face to face with Ryan. "Be cool, alright? Look man, nobody here is up to any funny business, okay?" He flashed a big smile. "You had some kind of freakout last night, that's all. Maybe this job isn't for you. But..." He turned and waved his arm at the rest of the group. "Nobody here would do a god-damn thing to hurt you. You can count on that."

The rest of the group with the exception of Ronald Grafer, who had stood off to the side staring wide-eyed at the confrontation, all murmured assent.

"Ryan, dear," said Betty, still holding onto the arm of her husband in the sailor uniform, "You must believe us that none of us—not one single person here—has anything but your best interests at heart."

"Why? What's it to you?"

Betty let out a sigh. "You'll find out, don't fret. Just try to trust us, okay? After all, we trust you!"

"Trust me? What the hell's that supposed to mean?"

A look of consternation filled Betty's face. Her eyebrows knitted and she looked away.

Her husband Bill spoke. "We trusted you to give us the tour, and to return each night, son—I mean, Ryan. So much that we brought our kids, and even our grandchildren." He looked over to the two tykes in their strollers. Despite the late hour, they too were watching the exchange intently, their heads pivoting back and forth between each person as they spoke.

As if they understood what everyone was saying... Which was, as far as Ryan was concerned a stupid idea. They didn't look more than two years old, if that.

"See man?" Moon Dog said. "Ol Bill's got that right, brother. I sure as hell wouldn't let ol 'Baby Bigsy' come along if I thought you were some kind of head case, okay?"

"I spend the night with a ghost, and you don't think I'm a head case?"

Moon Dog just shrugged and grinned. "You said you only thought she was a ghost. Now you say she ain't." He shook his head from side to side. "Don't matter to me, man. You're cool."

Ryan huffed another long sigh. This was, as Moon Dog called it, 'far out' for sure. But what made it completely off the charts looney tunes was what he said next. "Okay then. Where to next?" He was definitely losing his marbles now. He wasn't leading this Haunted Walk; he was now a customer! Sheesh...

"It's not far," Nurse Betty said, pointing up the street. "A few blocks away is that old church—"

"Saint Andrews." Ryan sighed again. "Of course, it would be St. Andrews."

"Oh! You know it? Are you a member of the congregation?"

Ryan shook his head. "No. It's a landmark in the city. The oldest operating church in the city. Everyone who lives here in Villmore knows the place. Why do you want to go there?"

Betty chewed her lower lip. "It's not just the oldest church in the city though, is it?"

"Huh?"

"It has another feature too, doesn't it?"

Oh man... Ryan dropped his head. "I shoulda' known." He lifted his head. "Yeah. Yeah, it does. Let's get this over with already."

"Oh goodie!" Doris clapped her hands.

And they set off.

To St. Andrew's Cemetery.

Chapter Thirty-Two

Emily Donahue

The group of them followed Betty and Bill who led them arm in arm. Each of them in their respective uniforms of white were a bright beacon for the rest to follow. The youngest ones, the toddlers in the strollers brought up the rear, pushed by their respective fathers. Trailing them was Ronald Grafer, with a determined look on his face to get this over with so he could get to his 'wee ones'.

Ryan was directly behind Nurse Betty and Lt. Bill. He pretty much believed what he had been told—Melanie wasn't behind this whole thing—but he sure as hell knew that there was something funny going on here. The oddest aspect of all these shenanigans was that he was more puzzled than afraid. He was more curious to see how this all ended up than worried about any harm could befall him.

They rounded a corner, and the church property was spread out before them on a small hill, taking up a full city block. At the forefront was the historic church, built sometime in eighteen-whatever. A steep staircase led up to the main entrance of the stone building, a large rosette-stained glass window placed above. It was an impressive structure; stone blocks for the walls interspersed with magnificent stained-glass windows fed onto a sharp peak. From the front corner of the peak was a graceful steeple that went up another three or four stories with a gold orb and cross situated on the apex. As they grew closer, Ryan couldn't help but wonder how many thousands of christenings, weddings and funerals had taken place here over the centuries. Entire lifespans, from birth to death were marked within those walls. Laughter and tears, in an atmosphere of prayer and worship had gone on for lifetimes...

Lifetimes.

They passed the front steps of the church and continued down the street, a wrought iron fence marking the boundary of the property until they came to the end. There, two imposing pillars, of the same grey limestone as the church guarded the small roadway, wide enough for just a single vehicle that led into the cemetery.

Betty stopped and turned to Ryan. "Over the course of years and years, stories are told before being written down. In your tour book, you tell the tale of an old woman who got hold of a magic potion that gave her eternal youth, but at the cost of her children's lives, right?"

Ryan nodded. "Yeah, I told you guys that story...but it was from the property line." He gestured at the pathway before them leading inside. "You want us to go *into* a cemetery. At night." He looked upwards. "Under a full moon." He huffed another sigh. "Oh boy."

Betty's arms were folded in front of her. "You told us a legend. We're going to learn the truth." She turned.

No chain nor gate barred their way, and in silent procession they ascended the gravel drive, their way illuminated by moonlight. Its rays speckled through the now almost barren tree branches, their feet crunching on dead leaves strewn from the autumn breezes.

But no breeze blew now. But for the sounds of their feet along the driveway, crunching on leaves and gravel, there was no sound in the night at all.

When the ground leveled off, the community of the faithful departed stretched before them. Headstones, row upon row, interspersed with occasional mausoleums and assorted monuments followed the rolling landscape, the size of a couple of football fields. Some of the mausoleums were small, tiny cabins of stone the size of a small camper. Others were grander, belying the past wealth and status of the family members interred. Other monuments were simple obelisks reaching toward heaven, while others were statues of weeping angels.

In all four years he had spent attending college in Villmore, Ryan had never been curious to explore this place. He passed it often enough, heading from his apartment or the campus nearby to the downtown core on Friday or Saturday nights. Through autumns, winters and springs over four years he walked past this driveway never giving a thought to the lives once lived, now honored by carved stone, their remains entombed within. Such is the nature of youth.

Now, seeing this burial ground for the first time, a sense of loss and grief touched his heart. He blinked a few times. He couldn't recall a single thing about the cemetery where his own parents were now laid. That whole week from the moment he learned of their death, through the entire funeral process was a smear of memory; not a single detail stood out to him other than Melanie's weeping. Some minister or whatever gave a sermon, some friends of his parents gave testimonials to their goodness, but really, he remembered almost nothing other than a suffocating sense of 'it's over'.

As he looked across the necropolis before him, he felt a strange sense of comfort. Each of the headstones and monuments stretched out were markers of other people just like him who had gone through the same kind of thing. And one day, there would be people who would weep for his own passing.

Somehow, that gave him a sense of peace; the universe will unfold as it should.

He snorted.

"What's the joke?" Doris asked him from over his shoulder.

"Me," he said, shaking his head slowly. "I'm the joke." He waved his hand at the graveyard. "For some stupid reason, seeing these lives once lived, now silent, makes me feel...I don't know...peaceful or something."

"Not all scaredy cat'ed, huh?"

"No... and the fact that I'm not is kinda funny." His mouth quirked in a short and sweet smile. "And that's the weird thing. I'm in a graveyard at night, under a full moon and I'm perfectly comfortable."

Her hand cupping her chin, Doris' eyes went to the top of her head. "Yup."

"Yup what?"

"You're unusual."

Ryan rolled his eyes back at her. "Look who's talking." When she just batted her eyes at him, he asked, "So why are we here?"

"We're going to meet someone."

"Like that guy from the jail? Ronald?"

"Well, yes and no. Yes, in that it's someone who's been...well, 'stuck' maybe? But unlike Mr. Grafer, Emily is far, far from innocent."

"What do you mean?"

They were still walking in a group. Doris turned her head to her husband. "I'm just going to talk to Rynie for a bit, hon."

John nodded. "G'head, doll. I'll stick with the others."

Doris took Ryan's hand and guided him to the side of the drive. She let the group proceed a bit before turning to him. "Well, Rynie..."

He felt his annoyance flair again. "Wait a minute. Hold it right there!"

Doris was taken aback by his outburst; her eyes wide in surprise.

He jabbed a finger at her. "What's with this 'Rynie' stuff, huh? Where'd you hear that name?"

"What do you mean?" she asked innocently.

"I mean 'Rynie'. Where'd you find out about that?"

"But that's your nickname."

"Not since I was five! My mom called me that until I went to kindergarten!" The memory of him being taken to his first day of 'real school' came back to him all at once. Mom had him by the hand as they walked the two or three blocks to the school. He was just a little kid, but he knew it was a big deal. He had his first 'real school' backpack, new clothes and was so excited to finally, finally be a 'big kid'. He knew his real name was Ryan, but his mommy and big sis Melanie always called him 'Rynie'. That morning, as they walked together, he told his mother that he was a big kid now and that he didn't want to be called 'Rynie' anymore. He recalled the funny look on his mother's face as she listened to him and nodded, her eyes shiny. And now Doris was looking at him the same way. "How do you know about that?"

"Hold on cowboy! I just..." Doris' eyes darted from side to side. "I just..." She waved her hands sharply. "I'll explain later, alright? I wanted to let you know who we're going to see, not to get the third degree!" She stuck her chin up at him. "You *do* want to find out what we're doing here, don'tcha'?"

He stuck his chin out the same way. "I'm gonna want some straight answers!"

She held her hands up in mock surrender. "Deal." Dropping them, she said, "So, about our foray here..."

Ryan pursed his lips. "Go ahead."

"Okay then. I'm going to tell you about Emily Donahue. So listen, will ya?"

"I'm all ears."

Doris crossed her arms in front of her. The moonlight was kind to her. Two nights ago, in the streetlights, Doris was an old woman playing dress up in her bobby-soxer getup. The white blouse, pleated skirt and saddle shoes had looked kind of ridiculous on her. But here, in the night dappled with moonlight, he could see how she must have looked back in the day. Her lustrous hair, obviously a dye job (right?), fell over her shoulders in flowing waves, the lines and wrinkles on her face were softer in the light, and her eyes were sharp and intense on him. "Okay. I'll keep it short as I can, I don't want to keep the others waiting too long."

Ryan just nodded.

"Way back in the olden days, back when this church and cemetery were practically new—"

"You're talking the 1800s?"

"Yeah, around that time. Back in those days, women didn't have many rights. In fact, once a girl married, she was pretty much her husband's property. And Emily Kelly was one such girl. Her father married her off to a local man, one Daniel Donahue when she was but eighteen years old."

"That sounds sort of like the story of Claudia Wheeler."

Doris shook her head. "Not at all. Emily wasn't trying to save her family; it was just the way things were. He would take care of her, and the children they had, and that was how it was."

"Sounds like no big deal then, right?"

"Well, she had her first child within a year of getting married. And less than a year later, she had her second child."

"Whoa...Irish twins, huh?"

Doris shook her head. "More like 'Irish Quintuplets. Within five years, Emily had five children."

"Holy shit!"

"It wasn't uncommon at the time, to be honest. Many families were large back then. Women bore children a lot more back in those days…" Doris' eyes got a far away look. "And many of those children never survived. Emily's children all did." She looked down at the ground. "But it was a hard burden for a girl so young to bear. She didn't have any help at home, and looking after five children, all practically babies was a terrible weight. Emily was overwhelmed by it all."

"You kidding? I would have lost my mind!"

"I'm glad to hear you say that. You mean that, right?" When Ryan nodded, she continued. "In five years, Emily transformed from a lithe teenage girl into what she called herself, 'a breeding sow'." Doris blinked. "In five years she went from a 'comely lass' to a 'matron'. Thick waisted, thick ankles, and her hair began to turn gray." She looked up at Ryan. "She was 23 and looked like she was in her fifties or sixties."

"That's pretty harsh."

"Oh, there's no doubt she was hard on herself. No doubt about that. Still…I don't know how she did it…"

"Did what?"

Doris got a far away look in her eyes. "Maybe she met a travelling s orceress…back in those days, there were people who wandered the land mixing potions, or casting 'spells' or what have you…most of them were charlatans and fakes, but occasionally there were genuine mystics also." Doris shrugged. "Or maybe Emily made a deal with the devil…those aspects are lost in time."

"Aspects of what?"

Doris was now talking as much to herself as to Ryan. "I only had one child…" she said, gesturing at the group further down the laneway. "That scamp! He started calling himself 'Moon Dog' right around the time the Beatles played on Ed Sullivan!" she said with a small laugh. Then she sighed. "I always wished I had more…but that wasn't meant to be."

"Why not?"

Doris' shoulders shrugged. "Because…" she looked at Ryan with an uncertain expression. "… let's just say for now that my dear husband John wasn't around enough and leave it at that for now, okay?" Her expression brightened. "John Junior—I called him 'JJ' when he was a boy—was the light of my life for many, many years." She held up a hand. "But I digress. I only had the one kid, and JJ was a handful, let me tell you. I can't begin to imagine having five kiddies in tow!" She glanced upwards. "So, yes, Emily was overwhelmed, wouldn't you think?"

"Sure…"

"She *did* something. Exactly what, I don't know. What I do know is that whatever it was, she got a new lease on life. She got her energy back, and in a very short time she lost all the baby weight she had put on, and transformed herself from a 'breeding sow' as she called herself, back into a young attractive woman."

Ryan shrugged. "Maybe she dieted or started working out."

Doris barked a laugh. "This was in the 1800s kiddo! You think there was a Jack LaLanne on every corner? Weight Watchers meetings?" Her face became solemn. "No, Rynie…it was something else. Something darker." She sighed. "As Emily's appearance improved…as she began to regain her vitality…her children…" Her voice faded and she looked away.

"What about her kids?"

Doris blew out a huff of air. "Her children started to…well…waste away. It started slowly; nobody in town really noticed at first. It began with her eldest, a girl named Angela having trouble catching her breath from just simple walks. At the same time, Emily's hair regained its luster and sheen." Doris slowly closed her eyes and re-opened them. "Within a few months the child could no longer walk. Then the same affliction took hold of the next child, her first born son, Thomas. It started with shortness of breath, and then he too lost the ability to move his own limbs."

"Could it have been something in the water? Back in those days sanitation wasn't a priority."

Doris shook her head. "No. By the time her youngest, a mere babe named Gwendolyn took ill, Emily had not only regained her original youthful appearance, she became even *more* beautiful! Walking around the downtown on Saturday afternoons, people would stop in their tracks, absolutely besotted at her beauty! A poor farmer's wife, simply going to the dry goods store, or visiting the other businesses in town...Emily Donahue coming to Villmore caused a stir among all the population." She looked up at Ryan. "But yet, people were afraid of her. Not a single townswoman would approach her to ask her secret for recovering her uncanny beauty. Nobody was brave enough to engage her in conversation. Even those simple townsfolk, poorly educated, barely literate, most of them—even those people sensed that there was something unnatural about Emily's rejuvenation. They would admire her dazzling beauty, but only from afar."

"So, what happened?"

"Rumors began to flow that Emily was some kind of witch. Nobody knew just how she managed to do it, but the town came to the common belief that there was a link between Emily's enchanting allure and the decline of her children's health. There was talk of her taking them to the town doctor, and not being very interested in his puzzlement. They increased in venom as her children began to pass away. Within five years of her eldest daughter becoming short of breath...all of her children were dead."

Doris scoffed. "That story in your tour guidebook is the result of two hundred years of gossip being passed down generation to generation. The seed is true—a woman's children died as she became more youthful—but she never did anything with potions. *How* it all came about is lost in time."

"What happened to Emily?"

Doris dropped her head. "She hung herself the day her youngest was buried." Doris pointed down the laneway. "All of them are buried here, mourned by the ghost of their mother."

"Oh wow."

"Yes." Doris reached out and took Ryan by the arm. "Now let's get to the bottom of this mystery, shall we?"

Chapter Thirty-Three

Consecrated Ground

Doris took Ryan by the hand and they caught up with the group, still led by Betty and Bill. They stepped off the drive onto the grass meadow.

"Now watch yourself," Doris said in a low voice. "Make sure you walk between the graves and not on top of them."

"Why? Is it bad luck or something?"

She swatted him. "No, it's disrespectful, you fool! It's alright for children to do, but you should know better!"

Well, that made some sort of sense. Who would want people tromping over their final resting place? He nodded. "Where are we heading?" The group was picking its way down to the far end of the cemetery.

"We're going to the 'workman's section' of this cemetery. These plots are for the poorest members of the congregation. The simplest and plainest resting places, squished as closely as possible."

They arrived at the farthest reaches of the graveyard, set up against a row of evergreen trees marking the boundary of the church property. Each row of headstones had an overgrown gravel path marking the rows. They headed down the furthest most pathway and stopped.

Ryan pointed. "And with the simplest of headstones, huh?" The grave markers were small slabs of stone, rising above the ground no more than a foot or so. They bore a name and dates of birth and death and that was all. No flowery phrases of loss and grief, no last testimonials to the living. He looked up and down the simple rows. This area was more of a filing cabinet than any sort of memorial garden. The poor—ignored in life and quickly forgotten in death.

Betty and John stopped. "We're here," she called out.

The rest of them gathered on the narrow path that separated the rows. Ryan looked down to see five even smaller headstones lined up one next to each other, gathered even closer than the other graves.

Angela Donahue.

Thomas Donahue.

Peter Donahue.

David Donahue.

Gwendolyn Donahue.

He looked up and down the markers. "Where're their parents?" he asked.

Betty shook her head, still staring down at the small group of markers. "They refused to bury Emily here."

"Why?"

"Because she killed herself. That's considered a mortal sin. And so she could not be buried on 'consecrated ground' back in those days."

"Man, that's cruel."

Betty nodded. "And their father lit out when Emily's body was discovered." She gestured at the smallest headstone on the end. "Gwendolyn was just five years old, and by the time she passed on, the town pretty much shunned the Donahue's, despite Emily's great beauty. Not many people attended the funeral, nor the service at the gravesite…" She turned and looked back at the church. "When they gathered around the grave after the service in the church, Emily slipped away…" She pointed to a copse of trees set back along the edge of the church property. "They found her hanging over there." She dropped her head again. "Emily's husband was never seen again. He left everything; the farm, all his belongings, he didn't even claim Emily's body for burial. They finished the service for poor Gwendolyn here, and realized that Emily wasn't among them. They found her shortly after…and her husband just shook his head and walked away." A tear rolled down Betty's cheek. "Such a tragic family."

Ryan couldn't help himself. "Don't blame the guy at all. What kind of woman condemns her children to death for her own vanity?"

'I did no such thing!'

Chapter Thirty-Four

Abide

F rom the nearby stand of evergreens a woman dressed all in black, with a veil of black netting covering her face strode over to them.

"I never raised a finger against any of my children! It's all lies I tell you! Lies!" She shook her gloved fist at Ryan as she walked over to the group of headstones. She put her hands on her waist and leaned forward. "I never did a single thing against my children!"

She pulled back her veil, and Ryan's jaw dropped. Doris was absolutely right. Emily Donahue was the most beautiful woman he had ever seen.

She caught his low gasp and strode over to him. "Oh-ho! Another man smitten, eh?" she said. "Tell me, boy! What color are my eyes?"

They were the loveliest olive eyes Ryan had ever seen. Green and brown danced in them; she had the eyes of a pedigreed cat. "Olive," he said.

"Oh really?" She marched over to Betty's husband. "Ahoy sailor man! What color are they?"

Bill didn't waste a moment. "I don't know what's the matter with you, Ryan. These are the prettiest baby-blues I ever laid eyes on," he said, his voice low. "I mean…next to yours of course, Betty."

"You're nuts Bill," Betty responded, looking at the woman's eyes. "They're grey! Almost like ice, they're so pale!"

"Bah!" the woman waved a hand sharply. "Yes, you all think I'm the most beautiful woman who ever lived! Yet when I look in the mirror, I still see that breeding sow I've become!" She turned, looking each of them in the eye. "I'm cursed, can't you see that? Cursed!"

"By who?" Ryan asked.

Shaking her head, Emily said, "I have no idea." Her voice broke. "To watch my children waste away, one after another after bearing and raising them…" Her voice broke. "That's a curse if ever there was one," she finally said, her voice soft." Her eyes fired again. "Oh, I know what you're all thinking, how could this woman say such a thing, when she saw her children, one after another take ill and die… For five years, I bore them, and then for the next five years I watched each of them fade away and die."

She slipped to the ground that covered the coffins of her children. "Albert and I were happy, you know! Yes, I was saddened about losing my maid's figure!" She shot a look at each of the women present. "Look at all of you! Were you proud looking at your reflection in the mirror after leaving the birthing bed?" When there was no reply, she shouted, "I was as good a mother to them as any of you! The gossip began when my second began to take ill, and when my third…poor, poor Peter…when he took sick…the entire town turned against me!" Her eyes filmed. "Even my own husband…he believed all the tales told; he wouldn't look me in the eye. And when little Gwendolyn fell ill…he slept in the barn, leaving me all alone to tend her."

Ronald Grafer elbowed his way to the front of the group. "You're Emily Donahue."

She nodded.

"I heard about you as a lad growing up. When we were being bad, our mothers would threaten us to behave or we'd be sent to Emily Donahue's home to waste away while she grew fair!" His face turned into a mask of confusion. "But you were long dead and gone when I was a lad! Are you a ghost?"

Emily patted her chest with a resounding thud. "I don't know what you mean. I buried my dear Gwendolyn just..." her face now mirrored Grafer's look of bewilderment. "It was just the other day...I think..." Her face went slack with fear. "What's happening here?" She turned to look at each person before her wide-eyed. "I miss my children so much!"

Ronald crossed over to her and sat beside her. "Aye, as do I, ma'am. And me poor dead wife."

Emily looked down at the ground. "My Albert grew to hate me, sir."

Ronald put his arm around her shoulders. "Well, for what it's worth, I believe you speak truly."

Emily sat back. "Tell me sir, what do you think of my appearance?" Her voice was timorous as she lifted a hand to the side of her face. "What color are my eyes?"

He blinked at her in puzzlement. "Why brown of course."

Ryan disagreed; she had olive eyes. Well, some of the others would disagree; Bill thought them blue, and Betty saw them as pale gray. What the hell?

She stood. "Do you find my figure appealing?" she asked Ronald, doing a little spin.

"You're a healthy gal ma'am," he replied. "No disrespect, but it seems you've been tasting the butter churner a fair bit whilst doing your chores perhaps?"

Ryan saw a young girl who could walk a runway at Fashion Week, no problem. She could be on the cover of Vanity Fair with hardly any touch-ups; she had curves that wouldn't quit! What's up with butter churning? She looked like a model! A well stacked model at that!

"You see me!" she cried out to Ronald. She tore off her hat.

Ryan saw the most electrifying cascade of red curls pour from down her shoulders. It was breathtaking.

"What color hair do I have? What is its appearance to you?" Emily asked in a quiet voice to Ronald.

He got to his feet and bent to her. "It's nice enough I s'pose...sort of mousy to tell the truth. Musta' been having all those babes so close together...a sort of dull brownish color. Could do with a brushing maybe?" Ronald shrugged. "I've never been a ladies' man, missus; I don't know what you want me to say!"

Doris hooted. "Are you outta your cotton-picking mind Ronald? She's one swell blonde! She looks like Veronica Lake for Pete's sake!" She pointed at Emily. "Look at how it runs off her shoulders like a river of gold!"

Ryan's jaw dropped. Blonde? What the—

"Blonde? You need your eyes checked, Ma." Moon Dog called from the back. "She's got the cutest page boy hair style I've ever seen! Like that chick from that movie 'Breakfast At Tiffany's'! And she's as sleek as Audrey Hepburn!"

"*Enough!*" Emily shouted.

They all stopped and stared at her.

"Why are you here? Why do you see me at all?" She looked over her shoulder to the copse of evergreen trees that formed the back border of the church grounds. "And what happened to the oak trees that were there?" Her head dropped. "I can remember going to an oak tree...so tired of it all...so weary of grief..."

She held her hands up in front of her. "I had taken a length of rope from the gravedigger's barrow that had been beside poor Gwendolyn's grave..." Her voice was barely above a whisper. "I was afraid to do it... but that fear was less than the years of agony before me…" She rose her eyes back to the tree line. "It would be painful for but a moment, I thought…much shorter than the birthing bed's agony…and…it would release me from the years of torment before me. I said to myself 'If I find a limb that would suit my needs, I'll do it'. I remember thinking that. If God wanted me to do it, there would be a proper tree waiting." She turned and looked at the group. "And it was there, like an outstretched arm beckoning me…beckoning me to peace."

She crumpled back down to the ground. "And…and now I'm here. No more whispers behind my back. No more glares of disgust from my neighbors…" she covered her face with her hands, "… nor my husband!" Her shoulders heaved from her sobs until she stopped and looked back up.

"At first, when Angela took ill, he was as supportive and loving as one could be. When my second one Thomas began to ail, he told me that the Lord was testing our faith! But then…" She looked at each member of the group, "… then rumors began to make rounds. 'What sort of home did Emily keep for two of her children to get so ill? What sort of mother lets this happen?' they asked each other. Instead of coming to my aid, instead of being 'Christian', they forbade their own children to be among mine."

Her voice took on a grittiness like two bricks grinding together. "And the last time we came to church as a family, the rest of the congregation filed out the door! Not one person, neither the pastor nor his wife, not a single person spoke up for me and mine!" She shook her head slowly. "No wonder Albert's heart left me."

Emily rose to her feet, watching the group. "And now you're here." She gasped. "Oh! The oak tree! I remember now!" She held her hands before her. "I'm dead, aren't I?"

Ronald Grafer stepped from the group and took her hands. "No more than I am, darlin'," he said in a gentle voice as he took her hands.

Like a sheer curtain parting, Ryan saw Emily's appearance shift before him. In an instant her hair's red flowing ringlets vanished, replaced by thin, dull brown locks. Gone in a blink was her perfectly formed face with that cute as a button nose and flawless complexion; replaced instead by a lined, worn visage of a woman whose time on earth was marred by unbearable grief and sadness.

The rest of them all gasped at the same moment Ryan did, all of them seeing the image disappear and Emily's true form show itself.

Emily's fingers tightened on Ronald's. "I think you're dead as well, sir."

He swallowed and nodded. "Mayhap. But I'm to go with these people and see my wee ones. It's been a long time, I think." He looked over to the rest of them. "Hasn't it?"

Doris replied, "Yes. Too long for you both. Come with us now. It's time."

Ronald nodded. "Aye," and started towards the group, guiding Emily.

"No!" she said, stopping abruptly.

"It's alright, dear," Doris said, beckoning her. "We'll look after you."

"No! I'll not go with you! Did you not hear a word I said? I killed my children!"

"No Emily, you didn't."

"The entire town said I did! The pastor wouldn't even bury me with them! Of course, I must have!"

"Sweetheart, no. Those were just lies and rumors."

"Lies said over and over and over become the truth!" she spat back. "I go with you, and you'll send me to damnation!" She shook herself from Ronald's hands and backed up. "Stay away from me! Stay back!"

Ryan watched dumbfounded as the woman backed up from them, past the grave markers, again at the tree line.

"No, Emily!" Doris called out to her. "There won't be any pain for you! We'll bring you to your children!"

"Liar! Just like the townsfolk! You lie!" She went behind the trees. They could only now hear her voice. "I'll abide here by their graves. Let that be my penance. There could be nothing worse."

Ryan called out. "Emily! Your kids probably suffered from Muscular Dystrophy! Someone cast a spell on you or something to make you appear younger! But you're not at fault for your children! They just got a disease!"

"Stop it with those magical words! Musical-whatever! I'll not listen to you! Be gone villains! Leave me be!" Emily's voice shrieked in the night. "Get thee hence!"

Doris nudged Betty. "I don't think she'll come with us."

Emily continued to scream from behind the trees. "Leave me be! Leave me alooooonnnnne!"

Betty looked over to her husband. "We tried, Bill. We really, really tried you know."

He dropped his head in resignation. "I think we should move on now." He called out to the tree line. "Another time perhaps, Emily! We're just trying to help!"

"Then leave!" She shouted back, her voice high enough to break glass.

"So be it." Bill turned to the others. "Let's head back,"

"Wait a minute!" Ryan said. "We're just gonna leave her?"

Bill nodded. "The universe is filled with tragedies that happen every day, son. Many of them are of our own making, and others are what befall us. And others, like Emily's are a result of how we cope with unexpected and undeserved suffering. Emily is coping as best she knows how, Ryan. She...like all of us...will find her own way. This is not her time yet. Yet." Bill gestured down the pathway. "We've done what we could, and she's not ready. Yet."

He drew a deep breath and let it out. "Emily will abide."

Chapter Thirty-Five

I'll Fill You In

Ryan felt a sense of loss as they headed down the driveway to the street. He was also baffled by what had happened this evening. Last night he'd hung out with a ghost until he fell asleep, and now tonight he met not one, but *two* ghosts! And not some actors acting parts either. What happened with Emily just now, her appearance changing so utterly completely... that was no special effects, that was the real deal.

He's seeing *ghosts*!

Real live rootin' tootin' ghosts!

Well... as live as a ghost could be anyway.

He snorted at the absurdity.

"What's so funny, bub?" John asked from beside him. Doris' arm was looped through his.

He looked over at John. Oh maaan...here we go again.

Two nights ago, John looked like some old geezer playing GI Joes or something for Halloween. He was still dressed in the same getup. An olive-green outfit; mid-length jacket and some kind of cargo pants tucked into high leather boots. But three days ago, his clothes hung off him as if he was a scarecrow. But tonight, he filled his clothes out like a much younger man. John's eyes were clear, and in the darkness, as the moon was now playing hide and seek with clouds, Ryan could see the handsome young man he once was.

This was getting weird.

"Well?" John asked. "On a night like this, we could all use a laugh. What's the joke, bud?" Except John's eyes weren't laughing.

"Take it easy, hon," Doris murmured. "He's just a kid."

"Ha! No older than I was when—"

Doris slapped John's arm. "Can it already!"

"It's okay, Doris," Ryan said. "I was snickering because...well, this is one hell of a night, huh?" He jerked a thumb behind them. "Emily... she's a ghost, right?" When they both nodded silently, he added. "You mean that? You telling me the truth?"

"Yeah," John said.

"Cross your hearts?"

"Hell, bud, I'll swear on my kid if that makes you feel any better, how's that?"

Ryan let out a sigh. "Like I said... this is one weird night."

Now it was John's turn to snort. "You tellin' me. This has been one hell of a couple of nights, kiddo."

Doris snuggled into John's arm. "Awww c'mon, honey! It's been some time since we had a chance to get out and around, right? It's not so bad, is it?"

John wrapped his arm around her. "We oughta go dancing."

Doris giggled. "Yeah, like there'd be a USO club open with a swing band playing!"

"Yee-haw! Tommy Dorsey's 'Boogie Woogie!'" John replied with a laugh. He looked over to Ryan. "That's how we met, y'know. I was laying over in

New York city, getting ready to ship out to England. We got a two-day pass and me and a bunch of buddies went to the USO club in Manhattan to see if we could find some tomatoes and get some dancing in!"

"And there I was!" Doris replied with a laugh.

John snorted. "Yuppers! There you were! Fell for ya like a ton of bricks."

"Feeling was mutual."

"So, what happened?" Ryan asked. "You waited for him to get back and got married?"

"Heck no!" John said. "I went AWOL for six more days! We hopped a train to Atlantic City, got hitched and spent our honeymoon down by the boardwalk!" He nudged Doris. "Spent the whole trip to England locked up in the brig!"

"Like I don't know! You sent me letters every day!"

"Yeah! And wrote you everyday till we headed out on D-Day in '44." His voice got soft. "I mean, I fell for you in New York, Doris... but I fell in love with you that year in England getting ready for D-Day."

She shook her head. "My parents almost killed me when they found out I got married! They thought I was kidnapped or something! Eighteen-years-old and a war bride!"

"Yup." John gave Ryan a sly look. "And a mom to boot!"

Doris nodded.

"What do you mean?" Ryan asked, his eyes wide. "You got pregnant? At eighteen?"

Doris nodded and held up her left hand, flashing him a gold wedding band. "But it was all proper. This isn't just a wedding ring; it's a life-saver. My parents would have really killed me if I wasn't married when I realized I was pregnant." She tilted her head behind her. "That's our only kid, John Junior. I called him 'JJ' growing up, but he started calling himself 'Moon Dog' when we moved out to Los Angeles in the sixties."

"Wish I'd seen him grow up," John said, sadly. "I mean, I kinda *did*, but y'know..."

"Oh...you guys broke up after the war?"

Doris looked at Ryan with sadness. "Nahh...we pretty much broke up *during* the war..."

"Can it, baby. Now's not the time." John said, giving her a nudge. He looked back at Moon Dog and Star pushing their child in the stroller. "Kid turned out great, though, didn't he?" he said to Ryan.

"I don't know him; we haven't had too much of a chance to talk."

"Wanna bet?" Doris said, with a sly smile.

"What's that supposed to mean?"

John reached over and gave Ryan a playful slap on the shoulder. "Don't sweat it; I'll fill you in."

They all came to a stop at the driveway entrance and before Ryan could ask anything else, Betty addressed the group. "Hey gang! I think it's time to call it a night, what do you say?" She pointed to Ryan. "Could you lead us all back to the place where we started, hon?"

Ryan shrugged. "I guess so, but you guys know the way, don't you? I want to talk to John and Doris some more."

John put his hand on the small of Ryan's back. "Don't worry, trooper. I'll fill you in on all the scuttlebutt, promise."

"Soon as we get back to where we started, hon," Doris chimed in.

Ryan rolled his eyes. "Okay. I'm going to hold you to it." He adjusted his top hat and gave his cape a theatrical swirl and went to the head of the group.

Turning he faced everyone. "I think this is our last night together," he said. "Welcome, Ronald Grafer. We're glad for you to join us, I think..." He looked out at the rest of the group. In the last couple of nights he had grown fond of them all in a weird way. He pulled the tour guide manual from his back pocket and thumbed through the pages until he found the page that had 'Final Words' printed at the top and began to read. *"I hope you enjoyed your walking tour of the mysteries and oddities of this small part of our fair city Villmore. The universe has many, many mysteries, the stars above look down on us as we live our lives, each one of us living out a story for their amusement and hopefully education. Lives lived and ghosts visited..."* He looked up at Ronald Grafer, and for some reason didn't feel even a hint of fear. Which was weird as hell.

Looking back down to his manual, he ended with *"and I hope these tales of woe and sorrow and mystery leave you with a deeper appreciation of the life you have before you. And now let us return to our everyday life that awaits us upon our return."*

He doffed his hat, took a deep bow to a smattering of applause and led the group back to where they started from.

Chapter Thirty-Six

It'll Be Okay...

It wasn't a very long walk back to the rally point at the podium that stood before the St. Regis Hotel where they first assembled. Once again, the streets were deserted, and the bar inside, although fully lit up, was empty. Not just of patrons, but when Ryan looked through the window, he didn't see anyone behind the bar.

In all his time living at Villmore as a student, he'd been in that antique bar a bunch of times. It was always busy—even on 'quiet' nights there were still people drinking at the bar and at the very least a bartender and server inside. And this was a Saturday night; the place should be jammed.

Tonight? It was like the place had cleared out for a fire drill or something.

On top of that, there wasn't anyone on the street besides him and his group.

He addressed them all one last time.

"I hope you enjoyed yourselves. I think this is my last night doing this."

"Why, hon?" Helen asked. She was standing over by the two tykes in their strollers; pretty much what any doing grandma would do, right? And just like John and Doris, the years had fallen from her as well. When he first met her, she was a heavyset elderly woman in that polka-dot house dress. The dress was still the same, yeah; but now she looked more like a 50's pin-up fantasy of a city housewife—a flat stomach, her thick ankles now slender and attractive, and the rest of her figure had gone from flaccid to voluptuous. He snorted. A brunette knockout in a house dress, every FedEx driver's fantasy.

Beside her was her husband Dick, and also the ghost of Ronald Grafer; who didn't look like a ghost at all. He looked like a shabby man and was smitten with the children in the strollers, squatting down and playing peek-a-boo with them.

Ryan took a breath. "My sister just told me that I won't need to do this job anymore. And my big dream is to go to New York city and take my chances breaking into an acting career in The Big Apple."

Doris piped up from the back of the group. "The Great White Way is waitin' for you hon! Is that it?"

Ryan grinned and nodded.

Before he could reply, Betty spoke up. She and her husband were closest to him. "Maybe we have a better idea, Ryan."

She moved through the group, holding the hand of her husband until they were both in front of him. Again, the years had fallen off of them. Both she and Bill, in their Navy whites practically glowed. "Maybe you come along with us, okay?"

"Come with you guys? Where?"

She made a small shrug. "To a better place, hon." She glanced over her shoulder to where Ronald Grafer was still playing with the young ones. "We'll settle Ronald in, and we'll have plenty of time for you too!"

She smiled brightly at him. It was a friendly smile, no doubt. He glanced over to Bill, whose head was tilted off to one side, watching him with a gentle and friendly smile. When their eyes met, Bill said, "That's a good idea, honey."

"What? You want me to go off to your hotel with a ghost?"

Betty's head went from side to side. "Well...not exactly, but kinda..."

Fear, then terror shot through Ryan like an electric shock starting at the back of his skull. "But he's *dead*! What the hell does that have to do with me?" He took a step backwards.

"Take it easy, honey," Betty said, holding her hands up. "You just don't understand. We came here... we *all* came here because it's *you* who needs us, sweetie."

"I'm just trying to do an acting gig, Betty! What are you talking about?"

"Ryan, Ryan..." Betty took a few steps toward him, and he leapt back. "Please, baby, just listen."

"To what!" Ryan backpedaled even more steps. He watched the rest of the group. They had all grown silent watching him and Betty. "What the hell's going on?"

Betty kept advancing. The rest of the group, in silence, took a few steps towards him. "Ryan, you need to understand this is all for the best..."

"Best for what!" He put up his hands, palms out. "Just stay back, okay? Go on and do whatever the hell else you guys are up to, just leave me out of this!"

"Baby, baby...shhhh...it'll be okay..."

He was backing up the sidewalk, and Betty was still coming. Now the rest of the group was following. None of the others said a word, just following Betty's lead. All of them were looking at him with expressions that under any other circumstances would have felt pretty damn nice. Mildred had the expression he used to see on the face of the dental assistant when he would be getting a filling; her eyes filled with compassion and comfort. Her husband Bob was nodding at him like a Little League coach when he would step into the batter's box, knees shaking.

None of them looked threatening in any way. And that, more than anything scared the hell out of him.

Ryan stopped for a moment, and yelled out to them. "You guys go do whatever you want to do! I'm outta here!"

He turned and fled up the street as fast as he could and didn't look back.

37 'I'm Claudia Wheeler'

When Ryan turned onto his street, he saw her figure waiting again on the front steps. Just like last night, Claudia was wearing a white nightgown with a burning candle beside her. But unlike last night, she had let her hair down; it cascaded down well past her shoulders in dark waves.

Buster the kitten was nestled in her arms when she looked up to see him approaching.

"Oh Ryan! I'm so glad you returned!" she said with a large smile.

Ryan stood looking at her for a moment before sitting beside her on the steps.

"What's wrong, dear?" she asked.

He shook his head. "This is one hell of a crazy-ass night, let me tell you."

"Oh? How so?"

Ryan looked at her. Her face was the picture of curious concern. The hell with it, he'd just dive right in and pick up the pieces afterwards. "Claudia..." he reached over and took her hands. "I don't know how to tell you this..."

Her eyes widened. "Tell me what? What's the matter?"

He took a deep breath and let it all out and said, "Claudia, you're a ghost." There.

She blinked a couple of times as she held his gaze. "A ghost." When he silently nodded, her face lit up in a smile. "Of course I am, you silly goose!"

What the hell? "You know?"

She nodded. "Yes."

"How long have you known?"

She gave her head a small shake. "I really don't know the answer to tha t..." Her voice faded and she looked up at the full moon hanging overhead. "Sometimes it seems that I've just come to realize it, and yet, other times it seems like I've known it for years and years..." She looked over to him. "It's a very strange thing... to be dead, but to not be gone." She blinked a couple of times. "Every time I stir...it's all new to me again, but at the same time it feels like an old memory." She put Buster beside her on the steps and covered her face with her hands. Her voice a moan, she said, "Oh Ryan, what am I to doooo?"

He reached over and put his arm around her. "I think I might be able to help."

"How?"

"I think you need to go over to the other side, Claudia."

"But I caaan't! If I was meant to, why haven't I already?"

"Beats me. I don't know a damn thing about ghosts or 'going over' or any of that stuff. But I *do* know something."

"What?"

"There's a whole bunch of people just a couple of blocks away who are up on all that shit." His mouth quirked. "My sister Melanie also knows a bunch of stuff about this kind of thing."

"Really?"

"Yeah." Damn. If he had his damn phone, he'd be able to call her to come and give him a hand with this crazy situation! "She's seen ghosts herself." He shook his head slowly. "Actually, remember last night when I said to you that I thought I was supposed to ask you in? Melanie told me that; that's how I knew to ask you in."

"So what am I to do?"

Ryan got to his feet and held out his hand. "You'll come with me, and I'll introduce you. They seem to know about helping people cross over. They've rescued a man—well a ghost like you, to be honest—and they're going to help him cross over. I'll bring you to them and we'll see if they'll take you under your wing."

"Where is he crossing over *to*?"

Ryan's eyes widened. "Geez, I never thought of that exactly. Uhh... 'Heaven' I guess."

"Why do you say that?" Her eyes narrowed suspiciously. "Maybe it's..*the other place*."

"Nope. No way. He was an innocent man who was hanged. If there's one place he deserves to go it's the better place. And the group I was with? The ones that want to help him? They're definitely not from..." He pointed a finger to the sidewalk. "Down there, if you know what I mean. In fact, they told him that he'd be able to reunite with his children and his dead wife. When they told him that, he was really happy."

Claudia let out a sigh of relief and nodded. "Well, that sounds promising then. I'd like to move on to a *better* place, certainly." She flashed a smile. "And going along with such a person would be...a comfort." She looked at him with hopeful eyes. "Will you come too?"

"Well, not to the other side or anything, but sure, I'll bring you to meet them." He snorted a chuckle. "Doris will be tickled pink to meet you! She's the one that knows a lot about you. And John—that's her husband—he's the guy who was yelling to you the other night from the street." He rolled his eyes. "This is gonna blow their minds!"

Claudia leapt to her feet. "Then let's do this, by God!" She was jittery with excitement. "Are you sure they'll accept me?"

"Yeah, I think so. I think they wanted to bring you along all the time, to be honest. They've been interested in you all along."

"And you'll vouch for me?" Her eyes were begging him.

"Vouch for you? I can't wait to introduce them to Claudia Wheeler!"

"Yes! I'll come up to them and curtsey! And I'll say to them 'How do you do?' just like a cultured person! And then I'll say 'I'm Claudia Wheeler'!" She clapped her hands.

"Except you're not!" cried a voice from the top of the steps.

Chapter Thirty-Seven

Let Me Prove It

Melanie was standing at the top of the steps to the house, her arms akimbo on her waist. She slowly came down the steps, her eyes holding Claudia in a steely gaze. "I don't know who the hell you are, lady, but I know for certain you're not Claudia Wheeler."

The woman's eyes narrowed. "I certainly am! And who pray tell would you be?"

With a hiss, Buster squirmed out of Claudia's grasp. He hit the ground and took off down the street before anyone could do anything.

"Who is this woman, Ryan dear?" Claudia said.

"That's my sister Melanie," Ryan said. He was staring wide-eyed at his sister, his mouth hanging open.

"Step away from her, Ryan. This spirit is up to no damn good."

"But Mel!"

"Step away, bro. I know evil when I see it, and I'm looking at it right now."

Claudia's eyes turned into a glare. "How *dare you*!"

Mel was on the sidewalk and shoved herself between Ryan and the ghost. "I sure do dare. Okay then...*Claudia*...where were you born?"

The ghost's mouth hung open, her face slack. "I...I can't recall...some where in the countryside of course, the town of Oswego I believe."

"Oswego's a county, lady. What village?" Mel's eyes were viscous.

"I... don't recall!"

"I'll bet! What brought you to Villmore?"

She brightened. "I'm to marry Mr. Mayhan!"

"You can remember William Mayhan? What did he look like?"

"Oh, he was the most handsome of men! Sturdy of build with the finest of face! He—"

Melanie cut her off. "Okay then, here's an easy one. How many brothers and sisters do you have?"

"I...I cannot recall..." she clutched her hands together at her breast. "But I truly loved them so!"

"You're full of it."

Again, Claudia's eyes flared. "Why you insolent—"

Again, Melanie waved her off. Turning to Ryan, she said, "This bitch can recall William Mayhan, a man Claudia never met, but can't remember the names of the brothers and sisters she grew up with."

"Yeah sis, but maybe all the time and...y'know, ghosty stuff?"

Melanie shook her head. "Nope. She's lying through her teeth." She turned back to Claudia. "I don't know who the hell you are, but I know for a fact you're not Claudia Wheeler."

"No! Ryan! Tell her so!" She reached out and clutched Ryan's chest.

"Get your hands off of him!" Melanie grabbed at Claudia's hands, but only held air. Her grasp passed right through the other woman like she was a hologram. There, but not really. "Ryan! Pull her hands off of you! I don't know what her game is, but she's not who she says she is!"

Ryan was shocked watching his sister flail at Claudia. She was solid to him, tugging at his shirt, but Mel wasn't able to grab her at all. "Hey..." he said to Claudia, "leggo of me, k?" When she didn't, he threw his arm across his chest, breaking her grip. He backed away a couple of steps, bumping into his sister. "You sure, Mel?" he asked.

"Ryaaan! Pleeeease believe me!" Claudia shrieked, her voice high. She held her hands out to him in supplication. "You're the only one who can help me go over!"

Melanie was holding a few pages in her hand. She waved them at Claudia. "You're not Claudia!" She turned to her brother. "After you left for work tonight, I went to my hotel and looked online for the true story of Claudia Wheeler. This is what I found." She held up the pages. "I had them printed out. This..." she held up a sheet, "is the article from the local paper from when Claudia died." She shot a withering look at the ghost. "And judging from what's going on here, I think she was murdered."

"I don't remember..." Claudia said weakly.

"That's because you're *not* Claudia!" Melanie held up the newspaper article print out, and then a second sheet. "*This* is Claudia! This picture was taken just a week or so before she was killed! She was supposed to do something with William Mayhan...the newspaper article says something about being invited to Villmore for an interview or something, but she wasn't found suitable." She turned to the ghost. "And then the paper goes on saying that witnesses say she killed herself. Some guy named Hester Grolsch said he saw her jump. I think he pushed her."

The ghost stayed silent as Melanie handed the blown-up photo of Claudia Wheeler to Ryan. "As you can see bro, Claudia was a beautiful blonde, and that's just for starters." She handed another picture to Ryan. "And that's her with her family." She turned to the ghost. "And you're *not* Claudia. Not with that brown hair."

The ghost closed her eyes, clenching her hands in frustration.

"Who are you?"

She opened them. "Does it matter? I'm simply someone trying to cross over to the other side."

"You don't look trapped to me," Melanie said. "You can go over any time you want, can't you?"

"It's not quite that simple...when I was on my deathbed, *they* came for me. I saw them all waiting for me...but they weren't kind like Ryan. They were...*malevolent*. I declined their summons. While they awaited my demise to take me away, with my last breaths of life, I rose from my bed and opened the windows to my chambers. And when I breathed my last, as my body fell to the floor, I escaped out the window from them!" She made a small laugh. "It would seem that the denizens of Hell itself have limitations on their abilities. They weren't able to pursue me. Ever since, I have wandered these streets at night, hardly ever seeing another person. The only others I ever met were other lost souls until I saw your group at Claudia's window." She let out a sigh. "I could tell that the group you were with were far, far from malevolent. I also know that Claudia can never leave her chambers at the St. Regis. She died in those chambers, not on the street below." She tilted her head from side to side.

"How do you know she died in those chambers?"

"Her murderer told me, dear." She grinned now. With a grin of pure malice. "Shortly before he too, passed on. A dying confession, perhaps?" she added, batting her eyes. "I went on to live a long life with my brother and his family. I grew old and frail, and like all people, my last days came upon me." She cut the air with the side of her hand. "But I absolutely refused to accompany those who came for me!" She looked up at them with sly eyes. "Dear Hester was among the group, and I know he was no innocent angel sent to fetch me to Heaven, I can assure you that!" She put her hand to the side of her face. "So, when I saw you wandering the street with that particular group of people, looking to bring Claudia with you, I surmised that they were from a kinder place..."

Melanie nodded sharply. "You're damn right about that."

Ryan shot his sister a look. "What do you mean by that? How would you know?"

Melanie waved him off. "I'll explain later. Once we get rid of this bitch."

The ghost reared up. "How *dare* you!" In that moment, she transformed from the comely young woman into a wizened hag. She pointed a now brittle looking finger at Melanie. "How dare you!"

"How dare you! You sneaking bitch! I don't know what you did, but I know that you're evil!" Melanie turned to Ryan as she reached into her purse. "Let me prove it too you, bro. I carry Holy Water with me at all times since my adventure in the Catskills with my girls from college."

The woman stepped towards Melanie. "I know you love your younger brother, very, very much. I too have a younger brother..." She reached out to Melanie.

Melanie backed up a few steps out of reach. She pulled out a plastic flask the size of a bottle of Visine eye drops and unscrewed the cap. "Begone, evil one!" she cried out. She splashed it at the ghost, who recoiled screaming. Melanie pursued her, splashing the water at her over and over. "Begone from here! Go back to your lair! Leave us be!"

The ghost skittered backwards on her feet, her arms flailing trying to avoid the droplets of blessed water. When they landed on her, small puffs of steam bloomed. She screamed again.

"Go to hell!" Melanie roared.

"I'm already therrrre..." the spirit wailed. The old woman turned and began trotting down the street, her shoes making a tock-tock-tock sound on the pavement. "I'm already therrrreeee!" she cried again as she faded into nothingness.

"Holy shit!" Ryan said.

"Nope. Holy *Water*."

Chapter Thirty-Eight

Trust Me

"Mel, how the hell did you know that she wasn't Claudia Wheeler?" Ryan asked.

Melanie was still staring at the spot where the fake ghost disappeared. "Because Claudia's *trapped* in the St. Regis Hotel."

"She's trapped there?"

"Yeah, I think so. She died in that room unexpectedly. That hag, disguised as a young woman, told us that she was murdered. Maybe she didn't even see it coming, you know?"

"Maybe we need to get her out of there?"

Melanie nodded. "Yes. I think that's the whole reason this whole thing's been going on." She turned to Ryan. "I think it's up to you to get her out of those rooms."

"Me?" When Melanie nodded with sad eyes, he added, "Why me?"

"Let's just try this my way for now, okay? You trust me, right?"

"Course!"

She looped her arm through his and they headed back to the St. Regis. "Good. Let's go."

⋙⋙ ⋘⋘

It was a short walk, and it was made in silence. Just like the first night, they came up to the tree where Ryan had rescued Buster. And sure as anything, he was sitting beside the tree. He was sitting, attentively watching them approach.

"Buster!" Ryan said with a smile as he scooped the kitten up in his hand. "You wanna come on an adventure?"

"Mew."

Melanie just shook her head at him. He was still wearing his top-hat and cape, and there was an inner pocket that he carefully snugged the kitten in. "You're not allergic to the kitty, are you?"

Ryan's eyes widened. "Yeah, you're right, I'm not. Isn't that great? I can *finally* have a pet of my own!" He snuggled Buster. "I could never have one 'cuz of my allergies; but ol' Buster doesn't make me so much as sniffle, let alone sneeze."

"Yeah... I can see that."

They rounded the last corner, and again Melanie could see the crowd of tourists that Ryan had been guiding for the last three nights. She saw that there was a new member; a man dressed in shabby, threadbare clothes. They all remained silent as she and her brother approached.

The two toddlers were again at the front of the crowd, still in strollers. When they saw Melanie and Ryan appear they began hopping in their seats, burbling and squealing in excitement as they drew up to them.

Star was behind the stroller of the little girl. She also let out a squeal of delight at the sight of them and raced out into the street and embraced Melanie.

"Oh Melanie! Melanie!" she said over and over. "It's so wonderful to see you!"

Melanie hugged her back. "I'd recognize you anywhere N—"

"Call me 'Star' for now, okay?" She looked askance at Ryan. "It's not yet time, is it?"

"Not yet. But soon."

"How the hell do you two know each other?" Ryan asked, baffled.

Star had her arm around Melanie's shoulder. "Me and your sister go way back, hon. Way, waaay back!"

Before Ryan could say anything else, Melanie spoke up. "I think that he's got a big job to do first, 'Star'."

"Claudia?"

Melanie nodded. "He's the only one here who can do it. Am I right about that?"

She nodded slowly. "I think so. So much of this is still a mystery to me, believe it or not."

Melanie gave her another hug. "I totally get it. More often than not, I'm flying by the seat of my pants when I get mixed up in stuff like this."

"But if your heart is true…you're able to cope, right?"

"Damn right."

"Language, young lady!" Star said, stifling a laugh. They hugged again.

Melanie jumped a little and looked down the street. "Look, let's get this off the street, okay?" she asked in a low voice. "I don't want to get run over, okay?"

"Hey…what the hell's going on here, guys." Ryan's voice was firm. "There's not a car in sight, Mel." He looked around the street. "In fact, aside from us, there's nobody else around."

"Well…you're kind of right, Ryan," his sister replied. "But now you have to get up to the fourth floor and have Claudia come down to us, okay?"

"Why me? I mean, sure, I'll be happy to; but how come none of you other guys went after her?"

Melanie still had her arm around Star's waist. "Because, out of all of us here, Ryan, you're the special one. Only you can do it." She looked over to Star. "I'm right, aren't I?"

Star nodded. "She is." She pointed at the entrance to the hotel's bar that faced the sidewalk. "Just go through the bar to the main lobby area. It's different now, but you'll find stairs that will take you up to the third floor. Then you need to hunt around and find the staircase to the fourth floor. It's been sealed off, but you should be able to find it. Then go up and fetch Claudia, dear."

"Okay. I guess so. But why the hell do you guys want to meet another ghost? Hasn't meeting that guy—" he pointed at Ronald Grafer standing off to one side, "been enough for you already?"

Melanie spoke up. "Please Ryan. Just go get her. It will all make sense when you bring her down to us, okay? Just trust me for a little bit more." She held out her hands. "I'll look after your kitten 'till you get back, okay?"

He passed Buster to her before shaking his head and turning to the entranceway to the pub. "I feel like I'm being led around by my nose, y'know."

Chapter Thirty-Nine

I'll Abide

R yan went through the entrance of the bar and immediately felt
afraid.

It was well lit, not one of those dark hole-in-the-wall joints. Golden light
shone from the fixtures over the bar illuminating his way, glistening off the
mahogany wood and terrazzo floor. The building had been converted to
luxury loft apartments a few years ago, but the owners kept the bar. Instead
of ripping it out, they restored it to how it must have appeared the day the
hotel opened back in the 19th century.

But what made Ryan uneasy was that despite it being fully lit and open,
the place was deserted. Except for the mirrors. He looked at the mirror
behind the bar and saw what he could only describe as flitting shadows
moving in it. He saw dark shapes in the mirrors, some of them were still,
others were moving in the background. It was strange as hell and gave him
a sense of foreboding.

He got out of the bar as quickly as he could, pulling open the glass door
at the opposite end that led into a lobby. On the far side was a grand staircase

that went up, and to his left there was an elevator. He felt fine, so headed for the stairs. Besides that, he figured that the stairs were in the original location from when the place was first built. Maybe that would give him a clue on how to get to the fourth floor.

As he came to the landing of each floor, he could hear the sound of music or a TV coming from the closed doors to an apartment. He continued further up. The only noise he could hear was either TV sets or stereo systems from behind the closed doors letting out muffled sounds. He didn't hear nor see a single other person as he made his way.

At the landing of the third floor, he looked around. Just like the floors below, he was in a wide hallway with closed apartment doors on either side. What the hell was he supposed to do now? He went to one end of the hallway, there was a window at the end of it, looking out over an alleyway.

He went to the other end, but only found a blank wall.

He went up and down the corridor again, hoping to see a service closet or something, but no luck. All the doors were marked with apartment numbers. Damn it! How the hell was he supposed to get up to the fourth floor?

He looked up at the ceiling, ten feet above him. "Claudia!" he called out. "Hey Claudia! If you're there, I could use a little help here!"

Nothing from above, and nobody stuck their head out their doors to see what maniac was shouting in the building. He let out a snort. They were probably on the phone to the cops instead.

The corridor was nice and wide, not like most of the apartment buildings he had been in during his time in college. A decorative table was also set out by the elevator, along with a couple of chairs. Sure, it looked snazzy and elegant, but he'd bet ten bucks that those chairs had never been sat in. He shook his head and walked down towards the window again, calling out at the top of his lungs to Claudia, his face turned up.

Waitaminnit.

His eye caught something in the ceiling down by the window. Nestled up at the top of the wall, in the corner where it met the ceiling, painted the same color, was a lever. If he wasn't staring up at the ceiling, he would have missed it. It was just a slender shaft of metal, over a foot long and just an inch in diameter. At one end was some sort of metal box about six inches square. Like a gearbox or something.

"Gotcha!" he said aloud. He jumped up as high as he could, but didn't get close.

Nooo problem.

He ran down to the elevators. The hall table that was opposite the elevators looked promising. He hopped on top of it, and oh yeah, he was able to touch the ceiling with no problem. He dragged the table back down the hall, under the lever and jumped on.

"Here goes nothing," he said, and yanked on the lever. It dropped easily. And nothing happened.

What the hell? He expected something to happen! He stared down the hallway to see if maybe something was going on down there. Nope. Damn it.

"Awww come on!" he said aloud, and shoved the handle back up.

"Holy shit!"

With a hiss of hydraulics, a six-foot-long section of the ceiling separated and slowly lowered. At the same time, a set of stairs unfolded. The whole assembly looked like some kind of insect waking up.

He hopped off the table and ran to the foot of the attic stairs. That's what they reminded him of, the attic stairs in the bungalow house he grew up in. Every Christmas season, Dad would pull down on a fingerhole in the ceiling at the end of the hallway, and a set of stairs would unfold so he could go up and get the Christmas lights, just like ol' Clark Griswold in that Chevy Chase movie.

"Boy, when you guys seal off a floor you didn't kid around, did ya?" he said aloud, looking up into the dark hole above him.

He was staring up into utter blackness. He'd always been frightened by the dark as long as he could remember. He looked at the line of steps ascending hoping that there was some sort of light switch or something, but no luck. Damn it.

Taking a deep breath, he kept going up the stairs. They were sturdy, firm under his feet which was good. If he had to bail fast, he wouldn't break his neck running down.

He really hoped he didn't run into anything that would make him want to run...

Damn it—if he only had his phone, he'd be able to use the flashlight app!

At the top, he closed his eyes in the hope that he'd get some night vision. After a moment or two, he opened them. Nuh-uh, it was just as dark. How the hell was he supposed to pull the rest of this off?

"Just do it, Ryan, okay?" he said aloud. The sound of his own voice gave him just enough courage to get off the stairs.

He knew he was at one end of the building. He also knew that the window where they'd seen Claudia in was also at the end of the building. The problem was that he didn't know if he was at her end, or was she all the way in that ink black at the farther end.

Who the hell was he kidding? The way this night was going, she was going to be alllll the way down there!

Dammit.

He began to carefully slide one foot in front of the other. He hoped that they kept the flooring in when they renovated. Otherwise, he'd fall through the ceiling below.

After going about four or five steps, he looked over behind him to make sure that the stairwell was still open. Sure was, but it felt like it was a hundred feet away.

He kept one hand on the wall and continued down the hall.

His hand stopped when he felt a door jamb on the wall.

He started banging on it. "Claudia! Please let me in! It's Ryan! You saw me on the street tonight! I'm here to get you out!"

Nothing.

Should he kick the door open? Like in the movies? He stepped back and raised his foot.

No. Melanie said something about being asked to come in, right? Shit! What the hell, he'd try it her way first. He passed by the closed doorway continuing down the hallway. He found a second doorway, and tried again with no joy.

Double damn.

He kept feeling his way down the hallway until he bumped into a wall at the end. He traced the wall over to the opposite side of the corridor and began working his way back.

Again, he found a closed doorway, and knocked and called out, and again nothing.

When he got to another doorway, he called out again. "Hey Claudia, I'm trying to be polite here! Please let me in! You'll thank me for it!" Once again, zip.

He was back to where the stairway was. Its opening was in the center of the corridor, so he went to one side. The light coming up enabled him to see that there were just two doors left. The one on his side, and one on the opposite side. He banged as loud as he could on the doorway closest. "Claudia Wheeler! This is Ryan Walker! I'm here to take you to your family! Please let me in!"

"Do you speak truly?"

He let out a scream, jumped about a foot in the air and spun around.

The voice came through the door on the opposite side of the hallway. "Claudia? Claudia Wheeler?" he called out as he made his way over to the doorway.

"Who are you?" came the voice. "Where is Mr. Hester? Is Mrs. Pynchon there?"

Ryan let out a sigh. Who the hell was she talking about? "Uhhh, no. I'm all alone out here. Please open the door."

"No! Mrs. Pynchon would be furious if I allowed a gentleman in my chambers without an escort! She was very, very clear! 'The St. Regis Hotel is not a bawdy house', she said. Although...I'm not sure what a bawdy house is."

"Uhhh...I think it's a house of ill repute."

"You're speaking in riddles, sir; I don't know what that means either." The voice on the other side of the door was sounding impatient. "Where did Mrs. Pynchon go? And what happened to Mr. Hester?"

Ryan didn't know what she was talking about. He laid one hand against the door and leaned in. "I'm sure this is pretty strange for you, Claudia—"

"How do you know my name? Did Mr. Mayhan send you? When is he coming?"

Mayhan. There's that name again. She was supposed to get a job with him or something. And well over a hundred years later, she was still waiting? This was beyond cruel. Ryan looked up towards the ceiling. Great job there, God. She's been stuck here all this damn time. His nostrils flared. O.K. then, God—I got this, I guess. He closed his eyes to think for a second before saying, "I don't think he's going to be coming."

"Oh dear! What's to become of me then! And what about my family! He was to propose marriage!"

"You were supposed to marry this guy?"

"Yes! And he'd look after my family! If I don't marry him, my father will be sent to prison and my family to the workhouse!" Her voice was high pitched and coming out in gasps. "Wha- what is to become of us then!"

Ryan dropped his head. All the things she was so anguished about had already been resolved one way or another, for good or for ill generations ago. But how the hell was he supposed to tell her that? Especially through a closed door!

"I think I can explain it all to you. Please open the door."

"No."

Dammit! Ryan gritted his teeth. "Then...I don't know how I can help you, Claudia." There was no response.

Who the hell could blame her? These last three nights have been as weird as a carnival funhouse for him. What the hell could being in that room for more than a hundred years, be like for her? He looked over to the entrance ladder descending from the floor. He sure as hell wasn't going back empty handed.

Ryan sank down to the floor and rested his back against the door. "Very well, Claudia, then I'll wait here. For as long as it takes for you to trust me and open the door, I'll abide."

It was silent for a few moments before she spoke. "Do you speak true? You could easily force your way in; these doors are quite flimsy."

"Yeah, I know." He bumped his head against the door lightly. "I could probably put my fist through it, let alone kick it open, but..."

"But what, sir?"

"But I'm trying to be the good guy here, dammit!" he spat out. "What kind of good guy would I be if I had to kick open the damn door? You're not in any danger...you're just...confused, I'll bet. I wouldn't be helping you out by breaking in, would I?"

He heard a rustle from the other side. When she spoke, her voice was at the same level as his head was, sitting on the floor. "How do you know that?" she asked, her voice small. "How do you know that I'm confused?"

"You are, aren't you? Things aren't fitting together for you the way they used to, are they?" He heard a small gasp from the other side and pressed on. "Like the world is somehow off kilter? Like being in a room and all the pictures are askew? Or like being caught in a rainstorm, but not getting wet?"

"Yes... I keep having dreams...and my memory is clouded. I remember Mrs. Pynchon and Mr. Hester, but I can hardly recall my family..." Her voice began to shake. "And... and when I look out the window of my room it's always night time... but the streets below look different now. There are no wagons nor workmen, just carriages without horses travelling up and down the streets... and the people... their clothes are different... it's all very strange. I sit back in my chair and close my eyes... and I *think* I sleep, but then when I open my eyes it's still night time, but the streets below are changed again."

"Pretty odd, right?"

"Yes." Her voice quivered. "What's happening to me?"

Ryan let out a sad sigh. "And then you sleep again, right?"

Softly, she replied almost a whisper, "Yes." After a moment of silence, she asked, "Are you truly a man of honor?"

"I *think* I am. I mean, I try to do the right thing."

"What is your name, sir?"

"Ryan. Ryan Walker." He started when he heard the doorknob above his head begin to turn and got to his feet as it opened.

"How do you do, Mr. Walker. Please come in."

Chapter Forty

Shall We?

S he was half hidden by the door, her head leaning over. "I have your word as a gentleman that you won't do anything untoward?"

Ryan nodded. She looked like she was still in high school. Her face still had remnants of childhood; her cheeks still plump with early years, not yet firmed into the countenance of an adult. Her eyes were wide and hopeful, lacking the learned suspicion that's one of the hallmarks of a child becoming an adult.

She was *pretty*. Not gorgeous like that poor woman Emily Donahue had been, nor alluring the way the Fake Claudia's ghost was; no—Claudia Wheeler was the girl next door, still unmarked by life's tragedies. Too old to play with dolls, but still young enough to wish upon a star.

Her brow knitted for a moment, watching him gaze at her. Then with a quick nod, she held the door open the rest of the way and bade him enter.

It was like stepping through a time machine. Her room was immaculately clean, all the furnishings in place. Near the window that he would see her at from the street was a wingback chair. Unlike the vinyl covered ones by the elevator, this was upholstered in sturdy fabrics. The only light in the room was the candle in the brass holder on the small table beside the chair.

"I would like to leave the door ajar, Mr. Walker. Should Mrs. Pynchon return, I do not wish to incur her wrath." She flashed a quick smile. "Although I'm sure she'll be quite upset for a man to be in my chambers without escort anyway."

Ryan nodded, but said, "If it makes you more comfortable, then by all means leave it. But Mrs. Pynchon won't be by, Miss Wheeler."

"Oh? Is she seeing Mr. Hester off?" She stepped to the doorway and looked out. "Oh my! What has happened!" She spun around to Ryan. "What has happened outside? Why is it all so dank and dusty out there?" Her eyes had widened in fear.

Ryan held his hands up in an attempt to comfort without approaching her. "Yeah, it's pretty wild, isn't it?" He looked around the room, a perfect example of Victorian Era decor. "I can understand your surprise." He was just as freaked out as she was. She was taken aback by what she saw outside in the hall, and he was amazed by what was in this room.

She was wearing a cotton robe over a nightdress that went down almost to the floor. She clutched the folds of her robe close to her throat as she stared at him. "Are you some sort of witch or something sir? Are you a demon?"

"No."

She looked back out at the hallway. "But the light is coming up through the floor!" She turned back to him. "Why is that?"

"That's a ladder sort of thing that leads to the floors below. The staircase is..." he hesitated. No point in freaking her out completely. "The stairs are not usable. That's how I was able to get up here to you."

He stepped over to the window. It was closed, but the drapes were open. His eyes widened in surprise when he looked down. The side street below was as busy as any Saturday night in Villmore. Cars were rolling past, and he could see people, some alone, others in small groups walking on the sidewalks. Most of the people he saw were young people, students as he had been, heading out for a Saturday night. It was the first time all night he'd seen other people.

Claudia came up beside him. "Why do those carriages have no horses?" she asked.

"They're cars. They don't need horses."

"Car? Like a rail car? Don't be silly. They would need an engine to pull them."

Shit. He wasn't going to get caught up in explaining automobile technology to her. Who was he kidding? Outside of putting in the key and making sure there's enough gas, his knowledge of cars was pretty thin anyway. "Well...they have a thing inside them that makes the wheel turn. And like a train, that thing is also called an engine. It's a lot smaller, but those...*cars* are much smaller than a railroad car, are they not?"

Claudia was off onto another subject. "And why are they dressed so oddly? None of the men are wearing hats, and the ladies...my goodness!"

Oh yeah...Saturday night clubwear was scandalous for someone from her era. Ryan suppressed a joke about hormones. Instead, he said, "Yes, you're right." He turned to face her. "It is strange, isn't it?"

She nodded.

Okay, time to let her know what was really going on. Ryan took a deep breath. "Remember when I asked you if you felt the world was out of sorts?"

"Yes."

He pointed to the street below. "You're seeing things that just don't make any sense to you, aren't you?"

"Yes."

"Things in the world have changed massively since you checked in to the St. Regis, Claudia. A lot...and I mean a *lot* has gone on."

"What are you trying to say, Mr. Walker?" Well, she didn't look fearful, more curious.

He gestured out the window. "That's how the world is now, Claudia. But you're not part of it."

"What do you mean?"

Well, here goes. "You're now part of another world."

Claudia went very still, frozen in place. The only part of her that moved were her eyes as she searched Ryan's face. Slowly they widened, her brows arching up. She opened her mouth and closed it. She blinked a few times, then said, "Mr. Walker, are you telling me I'm dead?"

She was a hell of a lot smarter than he'd given her credit for. Ryan nodded silently.

Claudia let out a huff of air and nodded in return. "I see." She looked back out the window. "How long have I been dead, sir?"

"More than a hundred years."

Claudia dropped her head and put a hand on Ryan's shoulder. "Then...then all my family is dead as well...even little George died an old man many years ago?" her voice barely above a whisper.

"Yes."

She lifted her head. "Then where are their spirits? You tell me I'm dead, and so I must be a spirit now, yes? A ghost?" She held her hand up. "But how can that be? I look like a normal person. I would have expected me to be wispy...like a fog...but I'm not." She tilted her head to him. "Are you an angel? Are you here to take me to Heaven?"

Ryan laughed. "I'm no angel, Claudia, believe me!"

"Then why are you here?"

"I..." pieces started fitting together for him. "I think I'm *meant* to be here. I think that you're supposed to come with me so you can see your family once again."

"Truly?"

He nodded.

"Then let's go!" She stepped towards the door and stopped. "I'm not dressed properly! I should change!" She turned her head, looking around the room. "I have clothing...where are they? I can't recall..."

"You're fine, believe me. Nobody will make anything of it."

"Are you certain?" When Ryan nodded, she said, "Then let's be off!" Her face was illuminated with joy. "Time feels strange to me. You say it's been a hundred years, but for me...I feel like I've just been sitting in that chair for a short while. How odd." She pointed at the window. "Mr. Hester had just opened it...and..." she shook her head. "That's the last I remember of him."

Ryan's eyes flitted to the back of the chair. He went to it and leaned over. He wasn't positive, but he thought he saw a faint stain on the headrest. The only remnant of Claudia from when she was alive. "Turn around for a moment, would you?" Claudia complied and did a slow turn. Yeah, the back of her head was as gruesome as that of the kid he saw on the street the other night. That poor kid must have fallen down or something. That kid he saw was as much a ghost as Claudia. He didn't notice it before, but yes, someone had crushed the back of her head. That was how she died. And that 'Fake Claudia' from earlier had a hand to play in it; he knew that in his gut.

But Claudia was unaware of the brutality that had been done to her. It must have been quick as hell.

But Fake Claudia said she had died an old woman. Yet she appeared as a much younger lady. Until she didn't; she morphed into a crone when Mel started with the holy water.

"Hey, before we go, let's try something, alright?" he asked.

"What?"

"I think...that if you put your mind to it, you can appear just as you would like."

"Really?"

"Yeah. Do you have any memories of your time when you stayed here?"

"Oh yes! Mrs. Pynchon took me on a shopping trip! And we went to a hair dresser! It was quite grand! All of the fine dresses! I purchased two and charged them to Mr. Mayhan. Mrs. Pynchon said that was permissible, and that I would need new clothing for after my wedding! I was able to take one with me!"

"Oh yeah? Tell me what it looked like. Close your eyes and remember."

Claudia closed her eyes. "It was very elegant. It wasn't silk, but a wonderful fabric nonetheless. It was the color of red wine, and had these lovely velvet covered buttons down the front." Her eyes shut tightly as she recalled her outfit. "And lace! There were lace cuffs on the sleeves! Oh my, I felt so..."

"Beautiful?"

"Yes! Quite fashionable!"

As she spoke of her dress, Ryan watched as her clothing began to transform. The white broadcloth of her robe began to darken and fill out. The hem dropped to where it was touching the floor. "Did you also buy new shoes?" he asked. As if there was a doubt. A woman shopping? And not buying shoes? Come on!

"Oh yes! Beautiful black shoes! They had a heel on them that felt odd at first, but I got used to very quickly!" She still had her eyes closed. "And the prettiest black bow on the front!"

Ryan continued watching as her dress finished transforming. The hem rose a little as Claudia's new shoes materialized on her feet. It was like watching a YouTube video of a make-over.

"Open your eyes Claudia."

She did, and looked down at herself in astonishment. "Oh! Did I do that?"

"Kinda. As you thought of them, your clothes rearranged themselves. You look really, really good! Turn around, let's see how you look from the back." She did another slow turn, and yup, her head was just dandy now. Her hair looked like it had been fussed over too; freshly brushed and pinned in a lovely coiffure.

When she came back around, he stepped up to her and held out his arm. "Shall we, Miss Wheeler?"

"Oh let's do, Mr. Walker!" she took his arm and they headed out the door.

Chapter Forty-One

Spinster

Ryan closed the door to her room after they exited, then popped it open again and looked in. Yeah, just as he suspected—the room was now a dusty, aged relic of what it once was. All the furnishings were gone, the chair and side table, along with everything else had disappeared. A layer of dust and grime covered the floor like they had never been there. What had once been walls covered with ornate Victorian-era wall paper were now just faded plaster, cracked in places. Claudia's leaving the room had brought it back to what it was meant to be.

It was a little touch and go getting down the ladder assembly from the fourth floor to the third, but Claudia was a trooper. She had looked at it before going down suspiciously. "That *is* just taking me down to the next floor, right Mr. Walker?" she asked in a small voice before they descended. "You're not tricking me and taking me to Hades, are you?"

Ryan shrugged. "If I was actually trying to do that, I'd tell you that it's fine, wouldn't I? You'd get the same answer whether I'm a good guy or some kind of demon, so I don't know what to say other than trust your instincts that got you this far." He gestured at the floor below. "Let me go first; that way if you trip or something, I can catch you."

Claudia laughed. "Oh! You're worried about a *ghost* injuring herself? How gallant!"

Damn, she was right. Ryan just made a hopeless grin and shrugged.

"Ever the gentleman." With a last snort of amusement, Claudia made her way down. When she reached the bottom, she beckoned Ryan to follow.

"See?" he said when he got down, pointing to the staircase leading to the floors below. "Does that ring a bell for you?"

"Yes. It is somewhat as I remembered it to be, I suppose."

"Yeah, I guess you have a point. But a long time has passed since you last came up those stairs.

She nodded slowly. "I suppose so...but that just feels like a dream to me. I would stir in my chair in my room. Occasionally I would go and look out the window, and then return to my chair." She blinked. "It felt to me somewhat as if I simply dozed off for a while. I'd awaken again, and then doze off again." She looked up at him sharply. "You say more than a hundred years have passed?"

"Yeah," he nodded. "At least."

She shook her head slowly. "It did not feel like that to me at all." She looked to the ceiling and the floor above. "For me it just felt like a long restless night."

He gestured to the staircase. "Let's bounce." When she looked at him quizzically, he said, "Let's leave this place," he laughed, holding his arm out again.

Claudia took it. As they made their way down, she asked, "What is to happen to me? How do I move on? Will I be going to Heaven?"

"Actually, I don't really know." When he felt her stiffen, he added in a rush, "But my sister is waiting for us downstairs! She's up on all things about spirits, okay? She'll be able to tell you what to expect."

"Is...is your sister a spirit too?"

He shook his head. "No, she's just Melanie. She's older than us, she's over thirty."

"Oh? How many children does she have?"

Ryan laughed. The idea of Melanie settling down with a guy and having kids? Yeah, right. "She's not married and doesn't have any children."

"Oh, the poor woman. A spinster then?" At Ryan's reaction, she asked, "Why are you laughing? Being a spinster is a difficult station for a woman. Is she deformed in some way?"

Ryan laughed again. Talk about culture shock. "Times have changed, Claudia."

They had stopped at the top of the staircase. "But to be sooo old...and unmarried..." her voice faded, and then she laughed.

"What's the joke now?"

Claudia just laughed. "If what you told me is true—and I do believe you, Mr. Wheeler—I'm over a hundred years old! And I'm unmarried too!" She patted her chest. "The youngest spinster you'll ever meet!" she added with another laugh.

She sure is taking being dead pretty well. She took his arm again and they descended down to the street level.

When they got to the lobby and through the doors to the pub, Ryan looked around. The place was just as empty. But just a few moments ago he had seen plenty of people on the street. But no, they passed through an empty bar.

Oh shit. A wave of sadness washed over him, and he paused.

"Are you unwell?" Claudia asked.

"Please, can you call me Ryan? I think we can be on a first name basis, what do you say?"

She peered up at him. "Very well. What's the matter, Ryan?"

He took a deep breath. "I just realized something that I need to talk about with my sister." He took her arm and guided her to the entrance. "Let's get out of here and meet her, what do you say?"

He pushed open the door to the street with a heavy heart.

Chapter Forty-Two

That's Enough

R yan stepped through the main entrance to the bar onto the sidewalk. Despite his heavy heart, he started to laugh. "Hey! The band's back together!"

In front of him was his tour group. They were still wearing the clothing they had from the very first night, but now, instead of elderly people, they were all in the flush and bloom of their youth from that era.

Doris stepped out of the group and Ryan smiled. "No wonder John fell for you like a ton of bricks," he said. She could have been on a magazine cover from the old days about teenage life during WWII. She had a lovely figure, like a cheerleader, and the cutest smile.

"Yeah, she coulda' been in pictures, huh?" John said, coming up beside her.

Doris rolled her eyes. "Look who's talking! You're pretty hunky yourself, soldier boy!" Reaching out, she took one of Claudia's hands. "I'm really happy to finally meet you, Claudia. I've heard so, so much about you!"

Any fear that was in the girl's face evaporated at Doris' touch. "You know me?" she asked, "How so?"

Doris chewed on her lower lip for a moment. "I know some people related to you."

Claudia tilted her head and pursed her lips. "I don't know who that would be."

With a slow nod, Doris said, "I understand, hon."

Ryan looked around. Yeah, the rest of his tour group had drunk from the same fountain of youth Doris had. Even Helen, the full-figured matron of the group had lost a bunch of weight, and her varicose veins were gone. Her husband looked like he just stepped off a calendar page of 'Hot Guys In Construction' or something.

Yeah...it sort of made sense now. Scanning the crowd, he saw Melanie. She was wearing the leather jacket like she'd been ever since this thing started. She was in a small group, with Star and Moon Dog on one side, and Angie and Troy on the other. The two toddlers were in their strollers, and they were watching him closely.

Claudia tugged on Ryan's hand. "What am I supposed to do now? Who are these people?" Her voice didn't have any shakiness of fear in it; instead, it was curious, as if she was trying to figure out a crossword puzzle and couldn't get that last clue.

Doris gave her hand a squeeze. "Don't fret, dear." She turned her head. "Oh Helen? I think you're up." She turned back to Claudia. "Of all of us, Helen's the real church-goer. This sort of stuff is right up her alley."

Helen had stepped over and patted Doris' shoulder. "It was always a comfort to me. Some of it was hard to take at times maybe, but c'mon; a loving community can be a comfort in hard times." When Doris shrugged, she added, "Well, you didn't *have* to go to church Doris, I went enough for both of us!"

They shared a laugh as Helen replaced Doris' hand in Claudia's with her own. "Now sweetie, this sort of thing is hard to understand, isn't it?" When Claudia nodded, she continued, "You do realize that you're very, very loved, don't you?"

"How can that be? We've just met, ma'am."

"Well, I kind of like you, and this one here," she tilted her head at Doris, "she's been on your side for quite some time."

Doris gave her head a little shake. "Darn tootin'!"

"We didn't come on your behalf at first," Helen continued. "But when we passed your window on the tour, Doris felt very strongly that we needed to do whatever we could for you. You've been trapped far too long, and it wasn't of your doing." She looked over at Ryan. "You did a great job getting her out, Ryan. We weren't able to."

"Cuz you guys are spirits too, right?"

Helen nodded.

Ryan's heart felt like an anvil. "You didn't come here in the first place to bring her over, did you?"

Helen closed her eyes and slowly shook her head. "No."

Holding Helen's gaze, Ryan called out, "Melanie!"

His sister came over, accompanied by the young parents and the children. Her face was sad. "I'm right here, sweetie," she said in a quiet voice.

Still holding Helen's gaze, Ryan said, "I haven't eaten anything for three days."

"I know."

"You're in a leather jacket because it's chilly out, right?"

"Yeah."

"But Doris here is just wearing a blouse and skirt. And Helen's only in a cotton housecoat."

"I know."

"I don't feel chilly either, Mel."

Her voice cracked. "I know."

"Mel, what happened?"

"It was a horrible accident, Ryan." She gestured at the small office door beside the main entrance to the tavern. It bore a sign, 'The Haunted Walk Of Villmore'. "You had just gotten hired as a tour guide. You were so excited for your first paid acting gig. You came out of that office, and were sending me a text telling me." Her face collapsed in grief. She started hitting him on the chest. "You weren't looking where you were going! You walked right into the damn street!" She turned and pointed. "And some car was barreling down and killed you! You idiot! Texting and walking into a god damned car! And now I'm all aloooone! You bastard!"

She burst into tears and fell into her brother's arms. "Oh Ryan! Do you have any idea what you did to me? Ryan, Ryan, Ryan…" She clung to him with all her might, still crying.

"I'm so sorry, Mel…"

She straightened up, pulled a tissue from her purse and wiped her nose. "On the night of your funeral. I was at your apartment cleaning it out when you came out of the bedroom."

Ryan couldn't resist. "Yeah, 'Gotcha' number one, seventy-three…"

"Yeah, you sure did scare the hell out of me!" She shook her head. "I almost had a heart attack myself. Thank God I have experience with paranormal stuff."

"Yeah, it was my most epic 'Gotcha', I guess, huh?"

"Yeah."

"Why didn't you tell me then that I died?"

She started crying again. "Because if I did… I was worried that you'd just move on right away…and…" she covered her face with her hands. "And I didn't want you to yet!"

"How come I don't remember any of it? I don't remember anything other than coming out so excited. They told me I'd start in a week. I was sending you the text..." he held his hands up. "That's all I remember. Is that why I could never find my phone?" She nodded into his shoulder. "That's why I was never hungry when I woke up." He stroked his poor sister's back. "I'm so sorry for being so stupid, Mel. I'm so sorry."

"Yeah," she said with a sigh. "That's why they're called *'accidents'*, you know? It's really not your fault. It's just that going through the rest of my life...without you being here...is really going to suck." She squeezed him again. "I love you so much it hurts!"

Doris put her arms around the both of them. "I know, honey, I know. It'll get easier, take my word for it."

John had stepped up as well. "You were angry with me for years, kiddo," he said in a low voice.

"Can ya blame me! Getting killed on D-Day? Leaving me saddled with a kid and on my own?" Doris rolled her eyes. "But the older he got, the more Moon Dog—"

"I *hate* that name!" John laughed.

"Okay! The older 'John Junior' got, the more he looked like you! Watching him grow up, I fell in love with you all over again." She rested a hand on her husband's cheek. "Though it sure woulda' been swell growing old with you, ya lug."

Melanie continued talking to Ryan, her words coming out in a rush. "Back in your apartment after I got over my fright, I figured I'd just followed your lead to go to your job." She stifled another sob and pulled her hands away. "And when we got here... and I saw everyone waiting for you...I knew that you'd be okay, but you had to do some things before leaving."

"How the hell did you know that I'd be okay?"

"Because..." she hesitated, then said in a rush, "Because our great-grandparents knew better." Pointing at Robert and Mildred she continued, "I recognized Great-grandfather Robert first because Mom and Dad had pictures of him as an officer when he flew in the Second World War. When they died, I cleaned out the house, remember? I found a box in the attic of family members going back." She pointed to John and Doris. "There was a bunch of photos of Great Grandpa John from before D-Day."

"Yeah, we didn't even get any wedding pictures done when we eloped," Doris said. "We planned to do a whole shin-dig when he got back." She gave Melanie's shoulder a squeeze. "I'm the only one of these jokers who actually met you as a baby. They all passed on before you were born," she added.

"Well, just so you know, Grandpa JJ was my favorite grandfather," Melanie replied.

"Wait! What!" Ryan's head jerked back. "Moon-Dog's our *grandfather*?"

Melanie just nodded. "Grandpa JJ? Maybe you should take the kids out of their strollers?"

"No sweat, Mel-a-dear..." Putting his hands under the little girl's shoulders, he hoisted her up. "C'mon, Twinkle."

Melanie let out a small noise. "Haven't heard that in a while..."

While Moon Dog lifted his daughter out of the stroller, Troy was picking his own son out of his. "*Favorite* grandpa, huh," he said with a grumble.

"Lighten up Troy, you died when Mel-a-dear was just four years old!" Moon Dog said with a big grin.

"Now boys..." Doris said.

Ryan's head was spinning. "But...but...if..." he pointed at Doris. "If you're my great-grandmother...and..." he pointed at Moon-Dog, "and he's my grandfather..."

"Yeah, that's right, man. But you were so little when we were all passed away," Moon Dog said.

Ryan waved his hand sharply in the air cutting him off. "Then...then..." his voice faded as he pointed at the two toddlers.

"You're catching on, Ryan," Troy said.

Claudia let out a wail. "Now stop it! That's enough!"

Chapter Forty-Three

Reunion

C laudia stood apart from everyone else, wringing her hands. "You're all talking in puzzles! What is to become of me?"

Before Melanie moved a muscle, Doris sprung to the side of the young woman. "I'm so sorry, dear! We got so caught up in our own reunion here that we completely ignored you. I'm sorry." She wrapped an arm around the young girl's waist. "Let's look after you first, okay?"

"What do you mean, 'look after' me?"

"We're going to take great care of you. I'm sure you must be in one heck of a tizzy."

Ryan harrumphed. "She ain't the only one!"

Melanie shook her head. "You kidding me? I'm the only living one in this gaggle of ghosts!" She looked around. "Everyone in the world of the living coming through here is looking at me like I'm out of my mind!"

"What are you talking about? There's nobody here beside us," said Ryan.

"Nobody *living* you mean. You can't see them because you're not alive, Ryan. The same reason they can't see *you*."

"What? You're telling me that there's people walking around?"

Melanie nodded.

"It's weird. When I was up in Claudia's room, I saw all the action going on in the street, but when we got down from it, everyone vanished."

Melanie shook her head. "When you were up there, you were in Claudia's..." she shrugged, "... realm or something? At any rate, you were in her environment, looking out. But now that you're in the environment of the living, the two worlds have a hard time co-existing."

"You sure about that?"

She shook her head sharply. "Not at all. I'm figuring it out as I go along." She held up a finger to make a point. "But... I'm pretty sure that the two worlds are meant to be kept apart.

Doris hushed both of them. "Can we take care of Claudia's needs?" She turned to Helen. "Any idea how we do this?"

Helen made a small laugh. "Nope. Just like Melanie, I'm figuring it out as I go along."

"Oh, that's just great!"

Helen's eyes tilted upwards and to the side. "Hold on, Doris," she replied. "There's something I have—more than you—which will help."

"Oh yeah? Like what?"

"Faith."

It was like she flipped a switch. Everybody went silent and still, watching her as she addressed them. "Being on the other side is a wonderful thing. But when each of us passed, we really didn't know how it was going to go. I'm willing to bet any of you that my own passing away was the easiest of us all. That's because I spent my life with faith. I believed in God, and that He loves me."

"Kinda sexist in my opinion," Ryan said.

"Now you hush and have some respect for your elders, young man!" she said, jabbing a finger at him. When Ryan quieted, she continued. "In a lot of ways, going to church on Sunday, receiving sacraments, saying prayers...all those things made me more willing and able to accept the will of God." She smiled gently at Ryan. "Or as other people have said, I was 'at peace with God how I perceive Him to be'."

The rest of them, including Claudia nodded in agreement as Helen continued. "This world, this life has had joyful moments for each of us, hasn't it?" she asked, scanning them. "You, Claudia, what was a joyful time in your life?"

"Oh, Christmas dinners! Every year they were wonderful! We sang together, and we gave each other gifts we each made ourselves!" She clapped her hands. "And in the summer? When the work was done and supper finished, Mumma and Pappa and all of us would sit outside watching the stars! It was beautiful!"

Helen nodded. "Yes, love and being with your loved ones is a beautiful thing. The sorrows of this world are only of *this* world, Claudia." She shot a look at the others. "Aren't I right, Doris? We didn't know what happiness was until we moved on, right?" Doris nodded in reply. "We've found a peace and a joy that passes understanding, right?"

Doris nodded again. "Yep."

"In my life, when I had faith, that's what I *chose* to believe in. It gave me comfort during trials, and gratitude for the blessings that came my way. So for me, passing on was a fulfillment of that faith. But there was something I used to do to keep that faith strong, and I want all of you to do that with me now." She held her hands out from her sides. "Let's make a circle around this girl." She shot a look over to Melanie. "I love you dearly Melanie, but this is not for you to partake in."

"Yeah, I get it," she quipped. "I don't have enough feet in the grave, right?"

Helen rolled her eyes smiling and shook her head. "Saucy girl." The rest of them gathered into a circle.

"Now what?" Ryan asked.

"Now we pray. Each of you, in the best way you can, ask the Creator to bring Claudia home to her family." She closed her eyes and began whispering. One by one, the others each closed their eyes, silently beseeching the powers that be for mercy, for justice, for happiness. Not for themselves, but as all the most potent prayers ever are, for the sake of another.

Ryan felt out of place for a moment. He was definitely *not* the church-going type. But he couldn't avoid the mysteries of life and the Universe. *'There are more things in heaven and Earth, Horatio, than are dreamt of in your...* science?' Well, he could go with that. He took a peek at Claudia standing wide-eyed with fear and hope.

He closed his eyes again, lowered his head and whispered, "Please..."

It happened in an instant.

"Mumma! Pappa!" Claudia cried out.

Standing outside the circle, Melanie was the first to open her eyes.

Claudia had burst through the circle into the middle of the street.

There, bathed in a glow of honey gold was a family. Claudia flung herself into their midst. Melanie could make out the parents, and a gaggle of youngsters, ranging in age from teens down to just a toddler as they gathered around the girl, holding and hugging her as she covered each and every one of them with tearful kisses.

As the family reunited, the golden light washing over them increased in its intensity. Brighter and brighter, it pulsed until Melanie couldn't make out the figures before her. She lifted her hands to shield her eyes, but wouldn't look away. It was as bright as staring into the sun itself, but without any pain, until it quickly faded.

And was gone.

Chapter Forty-Four

One Foot In The Grave

M elanie watched the circle. Even the toddlers had been part of it, stretching their hands up high, between their parents. After the radiant, blazing glow faded to a mere twinkle, then spark before disappearing she felt her heart break in two.

She clutched her stomach from the pain, collapsing to her knees as all the breath left her body in primal sobs.

Saying goodbye to her parents years ago, and to Ryan just this week had been the hardest things she had ever done.

Up until now.

Now saying farewell to them all again... not to caskets adorned with flowers, but to their faces... oh no, that was too much to bear.

She had no memories of her great-grandparents. And her memories of her grandparents; well, the ones she could recall anyway, were so faded and distant from her young childhood... those generations, despite the blood shared, were never a deep part of her life.

But oh... Mom? Dad? *Ryan?*

It mattered not that she had proof right in front of her that she would see them all again. That was meaningless to her. She was of *this* world, dammit! She felt the cold chill of the sidewalk leak up through her jeans and gloves; she felt the night air chill her face as her tears flowed so freely. This was just *unfair*!

If someone had told her a week ago that she'd see the spirits of her mother and father, along with that of her beloved kid brother... After all, she'd seen and interacted with spirits ever since that insane weekend in the Catskill Mountains... had she been told that she'd have the opportunity to see the spirits of her beloved departed, she would have reacted with joyful hope!

But now...now that it was actually happening?

No... it was a sword cleaving her heart into bloody, painful chunks.

"Hey kiddo..." An arm embraced her over the shoulders.

She turned to see Grandpa JJ's face. He had transformed from the hippie-dippy fashion of Moon-Dog to the Grandpa she recalled from childhood. She inhaled through her nose. Yes, the aroma of tobacco and peppermint filled her head. She fell into his arms.

"I can't do it, Grandpa! I can't do it again!" she wailed. He felt as solid in her arms as anyone. Certainly not a spirit, and definitely not a ghost.

"This is so hard for ya, Mel-a-dear," he said, using his pet name for her from bygone days. Hearing his words and remembering that phrase sent another dagger through her.

She wailed again. Since Mom and Dad's horrid accident, even as the years would pass, every once in a while, like a lightning bolt on a clear day the agony of their loss would pass through her, shattering her for a moment. Without warning, she'd be staggered with the pain of their absence. But tonight? Tonight? Seeing Ryan as she had for the last three nights? She knew... somehow, she knew in her heart that she'd never see him again in this lifetime.

It was so, so much harder to let him go this time around.

And she couldn't even bear to think of how it was going to be to let Mom and Dad go again.

From over Grandpa JJ's shoulder, she looked over to the group as they gathered around her.

And began to wail again.

Mom and Dad had transformed to how she last recalled them. No longer two toddlers in a stroller, they stood as the mature adults they had been on the day they died. Mom in one of those flannel shirts Melanie would always tease her about, And Daddy, as always, in those stupid, brightly colored Nike Air Jordan's.

She used to laugh at her parents' idiosyncratic fashion choices, now seeing them again broke her heart.

"I... I can't do it, Grandpa!" she said, her voice hoarse. "I can't bear saying goodbye again!" She held onto him tightly, again a child refusing the truth. She felt his strong hands stroking her back, just like those old days.

"I know, Mel-a-dear, I know dumplin'..." he said over and over. "I don't think I'd be able to either if I was in your shoes..." He stroked her and rocked her back and forth, both of them on their knees on the sidewalk.

Melanie looked up at the group that was her family and it struck her.

Up until just now, she had seen all the living people who were on the street passing by. They'd give her odd looks, and without realizing it, side-step around where any of the other spirits were standing.

But ever since Claudia's family came to take her home, all the other living beings around had disappeared.

She now had one foot in the other side.

"One foot in the grave," she said out loud.

"What's that dumpling?"

"Let's get up, Grandpa." She disentangled herself and they got to their feet.

Chapter Forty-Five

All Ashore...

M elanie wiped her nose on the sleeve of her jacket and rubbed her eyes.

Mom stepped before her. "Baby..."

Melanie hung her head. Staring at the ground, she said, "You're about to die again you know." She heard Mom gasp and looked up at her. "It's true. Three years ago, I had to say my last goodbyes to you. Three *days* ago, I said my final goodbyes to Ryan. And now I have to do it all over again!" She set her lips firmly. This was so past being unfair that she didn't have words to describe it.

Mom reached out, and just like Grandpa JJ, Melanie could feel her hand against her cheek as solid as anything. "But Melanie... if we didn't come, Rynie wouldn't be able to cross over! Is that what you want for him? Would you rather that he haunts this place?" she asked, gesturing to the St. Regis Hotel. "Or his apartment? Would you rather that he have an existence like Claudia had? Or that poor, poor man who had been hanged unjustly?" She went silent, waiting for Melanie to reply.

Hearing Mom call Ryan by his childhood pet name 'Rynie' cut a new wound in her heart. "But why did *I* have to be at the center of all this, dammit! It's killing me!"

Dad came over and stood beside Mom. "Honey-Bunny, we don't *know*."

"But..." Melanie waved her hands at them. "But...you're *ghosts* for heaven's sake! You should know how this works!"

Mom snickered. "Do you know how it *works* when you love someone?" She waved up at the sky. "Do you know how it works when stardust becomes a human being?" When Melanie didn't answer, Mom continued. "These are mysteries, baby. I wish I had all the answers, but I don't." She put her hands on Melanie's shoulders, gripping them firmly. "But I do believe that we're never given more than we can handle. I know this is hard for you —do you think it's easy for your father and me to go back? Do you?"

The bottom of Melanie's chin quivered. "No..."

Mom nodded. "I'm glad to hear that. When we go back, we won't be able to watch your life unfold down here, baby. It doesn't work like that." She gave Melanie's shoulders a shake. "We're going to miss you every single bit as much as you'll be missing us... until it's your time to come to us."

Melanie nodded. "Yeah, I realized that just a second ago. I don't belong with you guys. Yet." She looked around them. "Y'see, I can't *see* any of the living right now."

"Uh-oh!" Ryan said from behind her. "That's not good, sis. It kind of weirded me out these last two days. I haven't seen anyone else on the street during the tours." He patted his chest. "But... I didn't know at the time that I had died." His eyes were wide in concern.

Melanie nodded. "Yeah...that's what I was thinking. I'm spending time with all of you, and I think my grip, or whatever you call it, on the world is beginning to fade." She made a smirk. "Being with you is having one foot in the grave for me."

They all gasped.

"So..." she reached out and clutched her parents as hard as she could, trying to remember this final touch for the rest of her life. They hugged her back just as hard.

She turned to Ryan. "You texting idiot!" she said through her tears, but smiling. "C'mere." They held each other.

"Guess I win the 'Gotcha' contest, huh?" he said, his voice muffled.

"Yeah, I guess so..." She pulled back and looked into his face, again trying to etch a lifelong memory. "I promise, if I ever meet the right guy, he'll take up the challenge, how's that?"

"Fair enough." Ryan tilted his head. "You want to know something?"

"What?"

"I think... I'm not sure... but I *think* that if you didn't come by my place that night... if you didn't show up to clean out my place... I'd be stuck here the way Claudia had been." His face went slack. "Maybe forever..."

Melanie felt something fall into place in her heart. "You might be right. I'll be honest—I was so tempted to just hire a crew to clear your place out and put it into storage. The funeral home has people they recommend doing that." She made a face. "And I was really tempted to." She blinked back more tears. "But... I just *couldn't* hire some guys, y'know?" She embraced her brother again. "It would have been... I don't know... wrong or something? I would box up your stuff remembering you. If I hired others to do that... you'd just be a 'job' for them or something." She let out a weak laugh. "I knew it was gonna be hard as hell to clear your place out, but I had *noooo* idea just how hard!"

"I think you being there, at just that time is what got the ball rolling." He cupped her face and kissed her cheek. "You're pretty damn special, Melanie."

She snorted. "More like cursed sometimes!" She kissed his cheek back. "But yeah, I know what you mean." She put her arm around her brother's waist, and along with her parents, went around to everyone else in the group.

The great-grandparents had remained in their visages of youth. Which was so ironic that it was almost funny—great grandfather and grandmother John and Doris were a couple of teenagers, Doris was only eighteen, and John was just a nineteen-year-old, paratrooper recruit. Embracing them, feeling their own vigor gave Melanie a whole new perspective on how she would look at the elderly from now on. From now on, when she'd see old people, she'd recall this experience—all old people were once young, with lives full of promise.

She embraced Helen and Dick. "You should think about finding a church, hon," Helen said. "I don't care what denomination, or what faith...you belong with people who think about what is to come."

"I'll think about it."

"That's fair," Dick said, rubbing her back and looking at his wife. "You do what you feel you need to do. Nobody's got the market cornered on the truth."

Mildred in her satin dress was on the arm of Robert the Army Air Force Colonel. "I remember your photo," she told him, "but I never saw any pictures of you," she said pointing at Mildred.

"I don't know why," Mildred said. "This guy had tons of pictures of me!"

"Maybe the other kids have them," Robert said.

"Other kids?" Melanie asked. "You mean, I got cousins or something?"

"Oh, yeah!" said Mildred. "I had four myself!" She pointed to the last couple, also in military uniforms. "Betty and Bill had a houseful too!" She snickered. "And don't get me started on the brood Helen and Dick raised!"

Robert grinned. "They're actually your second cousins I think, but yeah."

Melanie chuckled. "I think I'm gonna join Ancestry.com then." She nodded back to her brother and parents. "I'm running low on family on this side of the ol' 'Astral Plane', you know?"

"What's an Ancestry dot com?" asked Betty as she approached them with Bill in tow.

"Ryan will fill you in," Melanie said. She turned to her grandparents. "I know that you guys only had one kid each—Mom and Dad, right?"

Troy and Angie nodded. "Yes," Angie said. "Giving birth to your father almost killed me, to be honest. I had to have a caesarian section, and the doctor suggested that I take care of that at the time."

Dad piped up, "I never knew that! You guys always told me that you just wanted to spoil me rotten!"

"A white lie, dear."

Melanie shook her head. "I've heard of family secrets from beyond the grave, but this is ridiculous!" Everyone laughed.

Grandpa JJ and Nana Star added, "We just used birth control. We weren't all that successful financially when we were younger, and when we finally did make enough to afford more kids...well...it just wasn't in the cards." She had a wistful expression, but just for a moment. "Your mother was plenty for us to be happy though." She hugged Melanie. "You and your brother made it so worthwhile for us!"

Melanie nodded.

A silence descended on all of them.

"Well!" said Melanie, stepping to the sidewalk and waving them into the street. "All ashore that's going ashore!"

"Haven't heard that in some time!" Betty and Bill quipped. Holding hands, they stepped into the middle of the street.

The others joined them, Ryan the last. Again, they formed a circle, holding one another's hands.

Melanie watched as they began to glow with that golden light of eternity. It grew brighter and brighter, pulsing larger and larger until it filled her entire vision. Again, it was meant to be seen; it didn't hurt her eyes at all, despite its brilliance.

And just like that, it winked out.

Chapter Forty-Six

EPILOGUE: The Lord Giveth...

M elanie looked around the now bustling streetscape. Now where the hell did she park her car?

She jumped a foot in the air with the voice near her ear. "And what of me?"

Before her stood that guy who had wandered into the group on Ryan's last tour. She had noticed him standing in the background scuffing his boots on the sidewalk, but with all that had gone on she had never paid him any mind.

"Who... who the hell are you?" she stammered.

"Ronald Grafer." He gestured at the street where everyone had disappeared. "That woman in that group... she told me that she'd bring me to my children." He gulped. "She also said that I'd be meeting me Rose again, too."

What the hell? What the helling hell? Ryan didn't mention this guy to her! Wait, a minute. She fished a copy of the tour manual from her purse and scanned it. She quickly leafed through an entry and looked back up to him. "You're the guy that haunts the old courthouse and jail, right?"

"And the gallows," he grumbled. "Tho' they've been gone some time now." He flexed his hands in front of him into fists and relaxed them. "I was hanged unjustly! I never killed the man!" He looked up to Melanie. "Am I to be trapped here even longer?" His face lined with grief, he said, "I don't know how any of them spirits that wander here can stand it... I tried counting the times I saw the dawn begin to appear before sleeping once. I gave up on that after I counted thousands and thousands!"

He stepped up to Melanie, his eyes flashing. "I did no wrong! Yet I'm trapped here! Why!"

Melanie chewed her bottom lip. "I don't know, Ronald."

He looked up at the sky. "Why, oh Lord! Why?"

Ronald stomped into the middle of the street, his boots thudding each step like he was driving them through the pavement. Still looking sky-wards, he screamed, "What sort of loving God are you! To allow me to be murdered! Murdered by a judge and jury, I was! Me wee ones spread far and wide, their Mama rotting in the ground and their Papa swinging from a hangman's noose! What kind of God is that?" He stretched his arms up beseeching. "I did no man wrong! And you punish me! My wee ones loved Rose! She died before them of disease! Where were you? How *could* you? How could you do this to meeee?" He collapsed onto his knees. "And then leave me here... year in and year out in my pain and loneliness. Why God...why?"

From the curb, Melanie could see cars driving right through the form of Ronald, as if he were a hologram. As much as she wanted to go and comfort the pitiful spirit, she knew she'd be flattened. "Hey!" she called to him. "Ronald! Come here!"

From his kneeling position, Ronald looked over to her. "You're the only one here now," he said.

Melanie almost laughed out loud in reply. Only one? The Saturday night crowd wandering up and down the street would argue that point fer shure! But Ronald sees them about as well as they see him—which was not at all. She waved at him to come to her. "I can't come to you, Ronald! But I want to speak to you!" And he better make it snappy. Sooner or later, someone's going to call the cops about the crazy lady on Main Street!

In a weary manner, Ronald got to his feet and plodded over to the sidewalk, oblivious to the panel van that passed through him. He came up to Melanie. "What would you say to me?" His voice was hollow.

"Where were you when the foundation of the earth was made?" she asked.

His eyebrows knitted. "What?"

She waved her hands at the sky above them. "Where were you when the moon and stars were set in the heavens above?"

His mouth drew into a tight line. "You're speaking in riddles, and I'm in no mood for games, miss." His voice had an edge to it. She better watch herself, was what he was telling her.

Well screw that, and screw him! "I certainly am not telling riddles," she said, her voice even. "Answer the question. Where were you when the earth itself was formed? When the universe came into being?"

"I...I..."

She shook her head slowly, and in a soothing tone said, "You never went to church much, did you?"

"No. That's a woman's job. I work myself to death all week. I'll take my rest at home rather than sit on a bench listening to some parson who's never lifted a shovel in his life tell me how to live."

She nodded. "Yeah, I've heard that lame-o excuse a lot myself."

"I'm not lame; I'm fit and hale."

Melanie sighed. *So much for trying to appear wise and stuff.* "Okay. What I'm trying to do is quote you some stuff from the Bible as best as I can recall. Have you ever heard of the book of job?"

"The book of job?" When she nodded, he snickered. "You mean the Book of *Job*, not job miss." He looked away quickly. "I know it. As in 'The Trials of Job'? Aye..." He sighed. "That's what Rose called that book." His lower chin trembled. "As she lay on her deathbed, she told me to read it." He hung his head. "She was far gone by then.. .died that night... I hadn't the heart to remind her I don't read."

Melanie lay a hand on the burly man's shoulder. Ghost or no, just as Ryan and her family had been, he felt as solid as anyone to her touch. "I understand. I read it for the first time three years ago when my parents were killed." She laughed lightly. "A dear friend of mine, she's a therapist... we had gone to school together..."

"A therapist? I don't understand."

Melanie chuckled. "She's a healer. Kind of like a doctor, but she helps heal broken hearts."

"A sage?"

"Can't wait to call her next time I talk to her! Yeah, a sage."

"Like a parson? Or a priest if you're one of those Catholics? She must be if she was telling you about the Bible."

Melanie burst out laughing. "I'm not even sure if a 'God' actually exists!"

Ronald's jaw dropped. "Now wait; you're telling me of the Bible, and you're not a churchgoer?"

Melanie blinked sweetly at him. *'Welcome to the 21st century,'* she thought to herself. "Let me try it a different way. It's not in the Bible, but it was written by a smart guy. Ready?"

Ronald nodded.

"There are more things in heaven and Earth, Horatio, Than are *dreamt* of in your sciences." When she saw the look of confusion on his face,

Melanie put a hand on his arm. "What I'm trying to tell you is that I don't know why things happen as they do. I *do* know that there's more out there in the world that I can comprehend." She gave him a shake. "Lookit! I'm standing here arguing philosophy on the street with a ghost! If that's not a mystery, what the hell is?" *'Damn, girl,'* she thought to herself. *'Three years ago you were an atheist. Now you're a hard core... agnostic?'*

She took a breath. "We all search for wisdom and understanding as best we can, Ronald." When he didn't reply, she gestured to the street. "Weren't you just praying to God for understanding?"

He glanced upwards. "I think I was admonishing him, to tell the truth," he frowned.

Melanie nodded. "Fair enough." She held up a finger. "But you were admonishing because you couldn't understand, is that right?"

"Aye."

She took both his hands. "That was the point of the book of Job." She blinked back her tears. She had just read it again on the day of Ryan's funeral. "We're only human. We can *never* understand the mind of God." Pointing upwards, she continued. "You didn't place all those stars in the sky, right?" When he nodded, she said, "I don't even know if 'someone' did. But they're up there, right?"

"Do you believe in God?" he asked.

She sighed. "I don't think that matters whether I do or not."

"But why, woman! Why would God do this to me! Why would God do that to my children?" He shook her hands off and grasped Melanie by the shoulders. "What sort of God does that?"

She smiled gently at him as she shook her head. "I don't know."

He shoved her away. "You're no help."

"You don't understand what I'm trying to tell you, Ronald. I don't know the mind of God, okay? I have *no clue* why bad things—terrible things—happen! I'm not going to try to tell you why the world is as it is." Smiling ruefully, she made a resigning gesture. "Good grief, I don't even know my own mind that well! Some days I feel on top of the world, and other days I feel like the biggest loser ever born!" Sweeping her hand upwards she added, "To think that I could understand all that? The stars? The universe? Ha! Not me, Ronald." She tapped his chest. "And not you either."

He folded his arms. "You're not being much comfort, miss."

"I understand. But *you're* not asking the right question. You're asking 'why' instead of '*what*'." When she saw the baffled look on his face, she went on. "Instead of trying to figure out God by asking 'why did this happen', maybe ask instead, '*What* is the lesson here I should learn?'"

"That's pretty weak comfort."

"Believe me, I know. Look, just a week ago, my brother was killed right there," she said, pointing to the street. "Three years ago, my parents were killed in a car wreck. I know what it's like to lose loved ones for no good reason, okay?"

Ronald gasped slightly. "Uh... I'm sorry for your troubles, miss."

She waved at him dismissively. "What happened to me is *nothing* compared to what happened to you. My suffering was caused by a series of accidents. Yours was because you were a victim. But..." she held out her hands. "Both happened under the eyes of God, right?" When he nodded, she added, "When my trials fell on me, my friend Becca—"

"The sage?"

"Yeah. What she said to me was to ask 'What lessons should I be trying to learn' from it." She looked up at Ronald. "And believe me, I sure as hell didn't want to hear that! I was angry!"

"Aye."

"But after a while, when the anger faded, that question remained."

"And what lesson did you learn?"

Melanie slowly shook her head. "I haven't yet." She looked up to him. "But I'm trying. I'm trying, Ronald. And in my trying...just in *trying* to see what's to be learned...the pain lessened. I'm only human."

Ronald bit his lip, and his eyes filled with tears. "The last words Rose said to me on her deathbed was, 'The Lord giveth...'"

"And the Lord taketh away. Blessed be the name of the Lord."

"Aye."

"Sometimes my friend, you just gotta have some faith. Maybe it's in a loving God, or maybe it's just that the Universe is unfolding as it should. In either case, you just gotta have faith."

"In what then, if not God?"

"That this is how it's supposed to be."

Ronald rolled his eyes and looked heavenward. "One day I'd have a bone to pick with him." He raised a fist. "I'd like an explanation, Lord! But..." he dropped his head. "I'm only a man."

Out of nowhere Melanie felt a rush of wind howl through the street, kicking up dust and scattering the litter on the ground. She closed her eyes for a moment and reopened them. Uh oh.

Once again, the streets were empty of traffic and people, leaving just her and Ronald alone.

"Papa!"

They both spun at the sound of a child's voice.

There, once again in a blaze of golden light, stood a group of people in the middle of the street. A woman and a group of children.

"Rose!" shouted Ronald. He broke into a run for three steps then stopped. He spun back to Melanie. "'Tis my family! Rose and the wee ones! Come! You must meet them!"

Melanie shook her head. "No, Ronald. It's your time, not mine. Fare thee well." She felt like she was going to start crying again...

And did.

He ran back to her and lifted her from her feet in a bear hug. "You're wise and good Melanie! Thank you!" He put her back on the ground and looked back to his family. They were waiting for him, waving at him to join them. He raised Melanie's chin and kissed her gently on the forehead. "Go to the cemetery of St. Andrews. All the way at the back and find Emily Donahue's spirit, lass. She needs to speak with you. Promise me you'll do that."

Melanie nodded. "Promise."

"Then blessed be the name of the Lord," he said in a husky whisper. "Thank you."

Spinning on his heel, he ran into the arms of his family like Jimmy Stewart in 'It's A Wonderful Life'. He gathered them all in his arms, planting kisses over and over on them. When he wrapped his arm around the woman, the entire group flared into a golden orb.

And vanished.

In that blink of an eye, the street returned to as it had been. Cars and people scurrying around their business and lives.

Melanie watched with tears streaming down her eyes. She had never felt as grateful to be alive as she had that night.

She was alive and grateful. Maybe that in itself was enough.

"Mew," came from inside her jacket. What the hell? Buster?

She pulled the kitten out and held it up in front of her. "I thought you were a ghost too!"

The little thing looked at her with a tilted head. *Nope.*

She hugged the kitten. "Well, we're in for some fun then, Buster, what do you say?"

"Mew." *Fine with me.*

Tucking her new pet back into her jacket, Melanie tilted her head up to the night sky. The moon would be setting before long. She had to hurry. "Emily Donahue, huh? You got it, Ronald! I'll get her, don't you worry!"

she called out. "If I can help Ronald Grafer, Emily Donahue will be a cinch!"

Ignoring the strange looks sent her way from passer bys, she set off to the graveyard.

THE END

Author's Note

Many cities now give walking tours of haunted places. It was on a Haunted Walk that my own career as a writer began. I was inspired by the tales, but not happy with how they were told, and my debut novel 'The Haunting Of Crawley House' was the result of that experience.

I've been on a batch of 'Haunted Walk' tours, and I strongly recommend them. Especially on nights when there are full moons. Twice I've had the opportunity, and on those particular tours I enjoyed memorable experiences. This book is an ode to those spirits who still linger, and those who tell their tales today.

The tales told in these pages have been inspired by those tours I've been on. As a writer, I'm always looking at things that other people think are mundane, and ask the question 'What if...?'

I ended this story with the tale of Ronald Grafer, because that scene with Melanie chatting with a ghost in the middle of the street happened to me. On a Haunted Walk, as always, I lingered in the back of the group of people, taking in the sights and sounds. A man joined up with us, muttering to me how such and such a tale about a haunted courthouse was all wrong. I asked him what was wrong and he muttered something that sounded like "It wasn't me..."

That was an odd thing to say. Obviously I concluded that this man was mentally ill and scurried up to join the rest of the group.

Later on, after the tour was over, one of the other members of the tour asked me if I was okay. They were worried because they saw me talking to myself for a while at the courthouse stop.

A chill went through me. But I didn't feel afraid; I felt like I was given a gift. And hence this book.

I now wish to leave you all with this final thought:

The opposite of death isn't life—it's BIRTH

Life is eternal, just like Energy. It changes and grows and learns and moves on. Newton's law of entropy only tells half the tale: things move to disorder, only to reorder themselves again in a new way.

I don't understand the how's and why's of that, but I accept it.

Life is eternal. Birth and death are but chapters.

With fondest wishes for you all.

Michelle Dorey

Other Works By Michelle Dorey

Spine chilling tales of normal people encountering wretched evils from the other side.

Each novel is a stand-alone

ALL of Michelle Dorey's work is available exclusively on Amazon

THE HAUNTINGS OF KINGSTON

Eerie tales of ghostly hauntings centered around the enigmatic city of Kingston. Each novel is a stand-alone

The Haunting Of Crawley House

The Victorian era home has a grisly past.

The Haunted Inn

Two scammers are about to find out the hard way that ghosts are real.

The Ghosts Of Centre Street

He's the new gatekeeper to Hell

The Haunting Of Larkspur Farm

This quaint hobby farm has a diabolical secret

The Ghosts Of Hanson House

Four cousins explore an abandoned home where terror has been waiting...

The Last Laugh (based on a true story)
Some secrets should have stayed buried...

Paranormal Suspense

Ordinary people confronting unspeakable evil. Each novel a stand-alone.

The Haunted Hideout
The FBI safehouse is *haunted?*
A Grave Conjuring
The teen girls find an Ouija Board...or did the Ouija Board find them?
Haunted By The Succubus
He was marked as a child. The evil entity returns to claim him...
The Haunted Gathering
Their annual reunion becomes a nightmare when they go to the picturesque resort in the Catskill Mountains.
The Haunted Reckoning
Paige's courtroom victory leads her down a deadly path
Graveyard Shift
Serenity Lodge is haunted. Don't ask the residents suffering dementia if that's true. Ask the nurses.
The Haunted Ghost Tour
This amusing tour is about to become a Death March

Printed in Great Britain
by Amazon

28528168R00148